CASTLE FORKS

CHRIS COCHRANE

To Peter

ISBN 978-1-63784-231-7 (paperback)
ISBN 978-1-63784-401-4 (hardcover)
ISBN 978-1-63784-232-4 (digital)

Hawes & Jenkins Publishing
16427 N Scottsdale Road Suite 410
Scottsdale, AZ 85254
www.hawesjenkins.com

Printed in the United States of America

PROLOGUE

Chris Cochrane glugged the ice-cold water from his glass in an attempt to stay cool in the California heat.

"Want another, Criffer Bob?" his dad asked, holding out his hand.

Chris nodded as sweat trickled down the side of his face. "Yes, please, but drinking as much as Mom said doesn't seem to be helping."

Todd grabbed Chris's empty glass and headed over to the kitchen sink. "Ah, the ice water won't necessarily cool you down, lad. It just helps to keep you hydrated in this heat wave."

"Oh, okay," Chris replied.

Todd loaded the water with ice cubes and handed Chris's glass back to him. Chris had just opened his mouth to thank his dad when his mom rushed into the kitchen, her eyes wide with alarm and her skin as pale as vanilla ice cream.

"What's wrong, love?" Todd asked.

"We...we're in trouble," she quavered and darted back out of the kitchen.

Chris and Todd exchanged glances and followed Cyndee into the living room. Justin, Chris's brother, was perched on the edge of the sofa, gaping at the TV, its screen displaying a video of bright orange flames.

The picture changed to a newsreader in a navy suit with a stern frown on his face. "It's been reported that a wildfire has broken out in western California following heat waves coursing through the state. The blaze seems to be rapidly spreading and has already destroyed ten thousand hectares of woodland. Let's hear more now from Keith Johnson, who's at the scene."

The second reporter appeared on-screen as the blinding wildfire continued to grow in the distance behind him.

"What are we gonna do, Todd?" Cyndee said in a panic, pointing at the screen. "That's not far from here!"

Todd ran a hand through his graying hair, speechless at the sight before him. "Um...I don't know, love. Er...the reporters might give us some information."

Chris's heart pounded with fear, and his limbs trembled. He sat next to Justin on the sofa, his eyes glued to the screen, hoping this nightmare would be over soon.

"So, Keith, what are the fire service advising for people who live in the nearby towns and villages?" the first reporter asked.

"Well, Sarah, based on the previous wildfire that occurred in western California seven years ago, the fire service is strongly instructing residents within a ten-mile radius of the blaze to evacuate as soon as possible."

Justin got up from the sofa and dashed over to the window. "I can see the smoke from here!"

"Right, we need to leave," Todd decided. "We'll listen for updates on the car radio, but for now, we need to pack essentials."

Chris's eyes filled with tears, and Cyndee swooped to his side. She wrapped her arms around him and pulled him close.

"It's all gonna be okay, sweetheart," she said. "We'll keep you safe."

Chris sniffed and nodded against his mom's chest.

"Come on, let's go and pack some things." Cyndee took Chris's hand, and they both got up from the sofa. Chris wiped his face on his sleeve.

"Let's meet back down here in fifteen minutes," Todd said.

*****

Just over fifteen minutes later, the Cochranes headed outside with their luggage. The smell of burning trees filled the air, and in the distance, black smoke drifted into the sky.

Everyone loaded their essentials into the family car, and Todd jumped into the driving seat. Cyndee got in the passenger side, and Chris and Justin leaped into the back.

Justin grabbed Chris's hand and squeezed it tight as Todd turned on the radio. He flicked through a few channels until he found the news.

"…are encouraged to evacuate to one the following evacuation centers: Stonehill High School, St. Michael's College, Oasis Sports Center, Waterfront Recreation Center…"

"Oasis Sports Center, that's our closest," Todd said, starting the engine. "Seat belts on. Let's go."

As the car pulled away from the ranch, Chris's stomach twisted, and he bawled into the car door. Justin pulled his brother away from the window and cradled him in his arms, sobbing himself.

"It'll be all right, boys. Try to stay strong back there," Cyndee said from the front seat, reaching back to hold Justin's hand.

But as Todd sped down the winding roads and swerved around multiple tight corners, the air became thicker and thicker with smoke and ash. Chris covered his nose and mouth with his sleeve. Then he noticed the golden flames at the end of the road.

"Dad!" he exclaimed, pointing at the fire.

"I know, son," Todd replied, his voice now trembling.

He slowed the car to a stop and paused, all four Cochranes staring at the flames ahead as they engulfed the trees on either side of the road.

Todd sighed. "We're gonna *have* to drive through that."

Cyndee stared at him with bulging eyes. "You can't *seriously*—"

"We need to get to safety, Cyndee. We can't go back, so we've no choice but to get to the evacuation center," Todd explained. "Even if I have to break the speed limit getting there."

Justin embraced Chris tighter, and they shook in each other's arms. Chris's heart thumped harder than ever before, and his vision blurred, dizziness overwhelming him.

Todd turned to his sons with fresh tears in his eyes. "We're gonna get to safety soon, boys, I promise. We just need to get past this part first." Cyndee caressed Todd's back. "I suggest that you both close your eyes and open them when me and your mom tell you to."

Chris and Justin nodded and closed their eyes, but as the car rumbled forward, Chris reopened his and watched as they sped down the road. Orange flames enveloped them as the fire burned the surrounding trees and glowing cinders fell all around the car.

"Dad, will the flames get to us?" Chris panicked.

"Don't worry, son, we'll get out of this soon."

Todd continued to drive at speed, but the light breeze had made some of the flames blow into the road farther ahead.

Cyndee exhaled and covered her face with her shaky hands. "This is insane!" she shrieked.

"Oh my god, Dad, are we driving through that?" Justin yelled.

"We have to, Justin…just keep your eyes closed and try to stay as calm as you can."

Chris swallowed hard. His breathing turned to panting. Justin rubbed his back, but Chris could tell his brother was just as scared as him.

Todd pressed his foot on the accelerator, and the engine revved into action. The Cochranes flew past the billowing flames that swished past the windows, but around them, it just got worse.

The orange fog blocked their view of the road, and none of them could see more than a few yards in front of them.

"God, please help us," Cyndee mumbled from the front. "Todd, the car's heating up. It's going to explode!"

"Are we gonna die?" Chris cried.

"No one's gonna die, Criffer Bob," Todd assured, maintaining his speed through the wildfire. "Look, the orange is fading up ahead. If we can just get there and keep going…"

Justin glanced out the window. "Dad, what if a tree falls on us?"

Todd upheld the pace and drove blind through the orange mist, dodging rising flames, golden embers, and falling branches.

Cyndee unbuckled her seat belt and turned around to properly embrace Chris and Justin. "It's all gonna be okay," she said, holding their arms.

"Your mom's right, boys. I think that's the worst of it," Todd replied, slowing the car. "The air looks a lot clearer farther ahead, and I can see a fire crew up there. We're safe."

Cyndee sighed with relief as her eyes swelled with tears. "We're safe, you brave, *brave* boys."

Chris and Justin continued to hold each other as Todd cruised toward the fire truck, rolling down the window. A fireman made eyes with the car and hurried over to the family vehicle.

"Are any of you harmed?" he asked, peering into the car.

"Thankfully not. Just a bit shaken," Todd replied.

The fireman nodded. "I can imagine. The road ahead is clear now. Our crew have put out most of the flames along this stretch, so you should have a safer journey. Where are you headed?"

"We were advised to evacuate to Oasis Sports Center until further notice."

"You'll be safe there. They've got a good team helping evacuees like yourselves," the fireman said. "Stay safe on these roads."

"And you, sir," Todd replied. He hit the gas, propelling the car to safety along the meandering road.

*****

Life soon returned to normal for the Cochranes. Their home on the ranch was spared by the wildfire that swept through the state. Chris relaxed again, but later that fall, leading up to Thanksgiving, torrential rain descended over the nation and flooded the land, destroying many homes beside creeks and rivers and destroying all the crops.

The Cochranes and nearby neighbors believed that events couldn't get any worse, but winter brought the harshest snowstorm the family had ever seen, forcing any remaining wildlife to go into hibernation. It also killed all winter crops.

Chris spent his days and nights praying in his room, desperate for things to get better so he and his family wouldn't starve, but one night, he spotted a strange creature on the grounds of the ranch. It appeared to be a man with pale glowing skin and a lengthy brown mane with giant wings protruding from its back. The creature raised his arms, and new crops instantly sprouted from the soil, as green as ever.

The creature turned and noticed Chris staring out through the window. He paused for a moment, a little startled, but winked at Chris, then disappeared into the darkness.

CHAPTER 1

Chris eyed the suitcases and bags by the front door. A lump formed in his throat.

"Right, I think that's everything," Cyndee said, scanning the hallway with her hands on her hips. "Now do you promise to be a good boy and look after your dad while we're away?" Cyndee walked over to Chris and placed both her hands on his shoulders.

Chris looked up at his mom and nodded, wiping a tear from his face. "I'm gonna miss you," he said.

"I'm gonna miss you too, Criffer Bob," Cyndee replied, pulling him in for a hug.

Chris wrapped his arms around his mom and sniffed into her shirt. She peeled away and stood in front of him, still holding his arms.

"Now a few questions before I go," she said, smiling through the tears. "If your dad falls asleep on the sofa and doesn't wake up by the time you go to bed, what do you do?"

Chris recalled the number of times his mom had asked him health and safety questions like this even if she was just popping to the closest town, but it always made him smile.

"Make sure the doors are locked, the windows are shut, the electrics are off, and my teeth are brushed," Chris replied.

"Good," Cyndee said. "And what do you do if the house gets burgled and your dad isn't around at that moment?"

"Hide and try to call 911, or run out of the house to safety," Chris said, guilty that both his parents had made him promise not to stick around and play the hero.

"Correct," Cyndee approved. "And what grades do you need to get at school?"

Chris smiled. "No pressure, just try my best?"

"Absolutely!" Cyndee replied. "Trying your best is all you can do. So don't let those bullies get to you if you haven't done as well as you wanted."

At that moment, Justin wandered into the hallway from the living room with the last of his things. He ruffled Chris's hair and smiled.

"We'll be back before you know it, buddy," he promised. "Eight months will fly by."

"Yes, and you still have me, don't forget," Todd said with amusement as he strolled down the stairs.

Chris nodded again and peeled away from his mom. She turned to Todd for a final goodbye, and Justin stepped closer to Chris.

"You'll stay in touch from Peru, won't you?" Chris asked.

Justin nodded. "Course. I'll write to you as much as I can and send you photographs of the school we'll be rebuilding. But...with your constant daydreams, I don't expect you to remember to reply."

Both brothers laughed.

"I'll try," Chris said.

"You'd better," Justin said with a smirk. "But if you forget, at least remember what we've talked about over the last few weeks."

Chris racked his brain for a moment. "The witty comebacks to say to the bullies at school if they pick on me again?"

"Yep. Remember those, and you'll be fine," Justin replied.

"But what if they beat me up or something?" Chris said, a little worried that Justin's comebacks wouldn't work.

"*Then* things get legal, and they'll have our family to deal with," Justin said. "Honestly though, if you stick with your friends and teachers at all times, they can't touch you."

Chris nodded and smiled. "Thanks, Justin."

Cyndee kissed Todd for the last time and turned to Justin. "Come on, you. Our taxi's waiting."

Justin embraced Chris and Todd and turned to grab his luggage. Cyndee shouldered a large bag and readied her suitcase.

"Have a safe trip, won't you?" Todd said, his voice breaking. "Let us know when you get to the airport."

"Of course," Cyndee replied, opening the front door. "I love you, both of you."

Chris opened his mouth to speak, but the fresh tears wouldn't allow him to reply. Todd pulled him close and caressed his back.

"We love you too," he said.

Cyndee and Justin stepped out of the house and headed to the taxi parked outside. The driver helped them to load their luggage into the trunk, and they got into the back of the car.

"See ya, buddy!" Justin called out through the window, waving at Chris. "Bye, Dad!"

"Go and make Grandpa Jim proud, son!" Todd hollered back.

"Grandpa Jim?" Chris asked, looking up at his dad.

Todd chuckled. "Don't you remember what your mom said at dinner last night, Criffer Bob? Your Grandpa Jim originally built the school in Peru and taught there for two years, but a disastrous flood destroyed it."

"Oh yeah, I remember now," Chris replied.

Father and son stood on the pavement outside the house and waved as the taxi pulled away. Chris gasped through the tears that blinded his vision. Todd held him tight. Suddenly, Chris drifted away, his mind casting back to the wildfire two years before.

*****

The breeze made the flames blow across the road up ahead. Chris swallowed hard as his breathing turned into panting. "Dad, will the flames get to us?"

"Don't worry, son, we'll get out of this soon." Todd pressed his foot on the accelerator, and the engine revved into action.

Cyndee exhaled and covered her face with her shaky hands. "This is insane!" she shrieked.

"Are we gonna die?" Chris cried.

*****

"Bye!" Todd shouted for the last time, snapping Chris from his flashback and making him flinch. "Sorry, son, I didn't mean to make you jump."

Chris didn't know why his mind had gone back to the wild-fire; it had happened *two years ago*, so surely he should've completely forgotten about it by now? But as his mom and brother completely vanished in the horizon, Chris had a sinking dread that he would never see them again.

He *knew* he was just being silly, and he *knew* his mom and brother would be safe, but the wildfire had made him more aware of how quickly life could be taken away.

"It'll be all right, Criffer Bob. They'll be back before we know it," his dad reassured.

Chris nodded through the heavy sobs and watched the taxi fade from sight at the end of the road. Todd crouched down to his level with tears in his own eyes and took his son's hands.

"We need to be strong while they're away," he began. "So what do you say to going on your first hunting trip this morning? Enough animals should have returned after the wildfire."

Chris dried his eyes and frowned. "I thought you said I had to wait a couple more years?"

Todd smiled. "Ah, well, you've recently turned twelve, and I suppose my father taught me to hunt at your age, so now's the chance to prove you're ready. Plus, it'll take your mind off things."

A wide grin spread across Chris's face, and the pair of them headed back inside to prepare for their hunting trip. Chris followed his dad down into the basement where he kept all his hunting gear.

"Right, here's a list of all the equipment we'll need for the trip," Todd said, handing Chris a crumpled piece of paper. "In fact, that's the very list I wrote for Justin for his first time."

Chris nodded and skimmed the list:

- Rifles plus scopes
- Ammunition plus case
- Hunting knife
- Rope
- Binoculars
- Two-way radios
- Batteries
- Scent attractant
- Towels for sweat
- Sandwiches and water
- Hunting clothes (camouflage jacket, trousers, boots, socks, gloves)

"That's a lot of stuff," Chris said, raising an eyebrow.

Todd nodded. "It is indeed, but don't worry about remembering it all for now. If you go and make some sandwiches and fill up our water bottles, I'll pack the equipment, then we can get you changed into your new hunting clothes."

"Okay, Dad." Chris hurried back upstairs to the kitchen.

Fifteen minutes later, Chris returned to the basement with a large lunch box full of sandwiches and a few extra treats.

"I've made cheese and pickle, cheese and ham, and chocolate spread," Chris said. "And I couldn't leave the chips behind."

"Well done, boy," Todd replied, and he held open the largest backpack. "Put them in here, and we can get you dressed."

Chris did as he was asked, turning to eye the folded clothes on the table. "It looks like army gear," he said.

Todd laughed. "Yes, I suppose it does. It's to help us blend in with the surroundings, making it harder for the prey to spot us."

Chris nodded and unfolded the jacket. "Is this one mine?"

"This entire bundle is yours, Criffer Bob," Todd replied with a smile. "Go on upstairs, and try it all on."

Chris grabbed his new hunting clothes and raced upstairs to his room. He replaced his New York-themed top with the brown T-shirt and camouflage jacket, and he wiggled into his new trousers and tied his black boots tight.

Chris admired himself in the full-length mirror. He felt like a mini-soldier, ready for battle. All he needed was his new equipment. Not waiting any longer, Chris bounded back to the basement.

Todd's face lit up at the sight of his son. "Wow, look at you!" Todd exclaimed. Chris beamed. "You already look like a hunter. Now let's get going."

*****

The berries were almost ripe. A few of them looked ready, so Chris grabbed a handful and quickly inspected them for bugs before popping them into his mouth.

"Stay focused, son," said his father.

"Sorry, Dad," Chris said quickly.

The last thing he wanted was for his dad to think he wasn't focused enough. Chris was a bit of a daydreamer, and he tended to have trouble being "in the moment," as his mom would say. He knew how important it was to stay sharp and observant when hunting.

"Looks like there's plenty sign of deer," Todd said. "It seems like we could go in almost any direction." He rested his rifle on the ground for a moment and paused to think. "What we really want is a buck though. A doe or fawn won't fill the freezer nearly as much. What do you think we should do?"

Chris stroked his chin in thought. "Well, we want to increase our chances of getting a buck, so maybe we should split up? That way, we'll cover more ground?" He suggested it with just a little hesitance.

Todd smiled and nodded. "Good thinking," he said. "You go that way, and I'll come running when I hear you take a shot. That is, if I don't beat you to it." He gave his son a good-natured slap on the shoulder and went the other way.

Chris felt a surge of pride as he walked off. His dad trusted him enough to let him go off on his own. He kept his eyes sharp as he veered down a promising trail that led through a tangle of brush. There was probably a nice clearing on the other side, he guessed, where some game might be resting in the shade. It was worth suffering a few scrapes and scratches to investigate.

Chris wasn't too thrilled with the idea of *killing* an innocent animal, to the point that he'd considered becoming a vegetarian like some of his friends at school, but he wanted to make his father proud. Plus, they needed food for the winter, and where they lived, meat consisted 60 percent of their diet.

Chris tiptoed through the trees and kept his eyes peeled for *anything*. He didn't care if he caught something as small as a hare; he just wanted to impress his dad and show him that he could focus.

As Chris stepped over a tree stump and meandered around a thick trunk, a rustling sound a little farther ahead caught his attention. He peered through the trees and spotted a doe in the near distance. He snuck through the trees and approached the deer. The animal was innocently munching on the grass.

Chris sighed. *I wish we didn't have to kill animals to eat, but if I don't try, Dad and I could starve.*

His entire being filled with guilt, Chris raised his rifle and aimed at the beautiful animal in the gap between two thick trees. He closed his eyes this time and turned away, pulling the trigger a few seconds afterward.

A thunderous *bang* pierced the air, and Chris heard a sorrowful *thump* as the deer flopped to the ground. Chris opened his eyes and looked at his catch. "I'm sorry," he said to the lifeless doe as he approached its corpse.

After trying to recall what his dad had advised about carrying larger animals, Chris stopped for a moment and scanned his surroundings. A loud *snap* caught his attention. He spun toward the sound and spotted a flash of movement. It could have been a deer. Chris raised his rifle again and peered through the scope. He fixed his eyes on the animal.

But this was no deer. This was something else entirely.

The creature was bigger than any person Chris had ever seen, over seven feet tall. Long wavy brown hair flowed down around the face, which was pale and symmetrical. It was a clean-shaven human face yet at the same time somehow not quite human. It seemed brighter, as if there was a light source radiating from underneath the skin. *And cleaner too*, Chris thought. There wasn't a single scratch or speck of dirt anywhere. There should have been.

Chris was sweaty and dirty all over after just a couple of hours scrabbling in and out of the brush. Unlike Chris, this creature looked like it had never seen the inside of a suburban ranch house. It looked like it lived here in the wild, judging from its clothes. It was wearing a rough tunic made of some kind of dark bearlike fur. At its waist was a thick ropy vine fashioned into a belt, which had a worn leather pouch tied to it. A large golden key hung from a heavy chain around its neck. The top part of the key was ornamented with an insignia that depicted a boar with a large Celtic-style *C* in the center.

Chris took all this in very quickly, but his mind was much slower at making sense of it. He just stood there, frozen and staring. In one arm, the creature carried a bundle of berry plants and flowers. It held the forefinger of its free hand up to its lips, in a "shh" gesture. It was looking right at Chris.

Strangely, Chris didn't feel afraid. In fact, he felt oddly relaxed, almost dreamy. It didn't even occur to him to call out for help or try to run away. For some reason, he felt compelled to walk toward the creature. He started to do so. The creature leaned down slowly, as if to set its armload of plants onto the ground. As it did, Chris saw the most stunning thing of all: a massive pair of wings emerging from two slits in the back of the creature's tunic. They were made of pearly off-white feathers flecked with gold. Folded down, their tips reached just below his waist.

Suddenly, a rifle shot cut through the air, followed by another. Chris jumped, startled. He turned around instinctively in the direction of the rifle shot. His dad must have shot at something. When Chris turned back to the creature, it was gone.

What just happened? he thought. *Was that thing real? Have I been reading too many books? Man, I know Justin would say: "Cut it out with all the science fiction and fantasy! Read something useful for a change."* Then he'd toss Chris a book on the history of the Black Plague or the engineering science of building skyscrapers. And maybe he'd be right. Could reading too much fiction start to affect your brain? Because that was what this was for sure—something right out of a fantasy novel or an episode of *Star Trek*.

Chris tried to shake it off. He took a deep breath and looked around. The dense vines looked undisturbed. He walked back and forth over the ground where the creature had stood. There were no footprints. In fact, there was no evidence at all that a giant nonhuman creature with enormous wings had just walked into the clearing then disappeared.

Was it a mountain man, a caveman, or an angel? Surely, it would have left something behind? But there was nothing. The berry bushes looked unscathed by its departure. They were quite still, barely moving with the morning breeze. A solitary long-stemmed flower lay on the ground next to the bush where the creature had stood.

The flower was a vivid rosy pink, tiny petals gathered in tight clusters along the length of the dark-green stem. That flower didn't belong there. Chris had noticed bunches of them growing down the front side of the mountain when they were hiking up, but there were no similar plants in this clearing. Chris kneeled, lifting the flower and inspecting it closely. There was a very fine golden dust clinging to the bottom of the stem.

The creature must have dropped it. Chris really had seen something; he was sure of it. It couldn't have been a dream.

"What are you daydreaming about?" Todd's voice cut into his scattered thoughts.

Chris turned to see his dad jogging into the clearing. "Oh, uh... nothing," Chris stammered. "I mean, just—what's this?" He lifted up the flower that seemed so out of place, hoping to change the subject. His dad knew just about every plant in the world it seemed and what was edible and what wasn't. Their family had lived so many generations in this part of California that Todd was especially familiar with the local flora.

Todd walked over and took a glance. "It's a rhubarb plant," he said. "They're good to eat when you cook them, kind of sweet and sour at the same time. Good for pies and tarts."

"So we should take it home and plant it then?" Chris suggested.

"Sure," Todd said. "In a year or so, we'll have some rhubarb pie. Now help me take care of this buck."

As they dressed the animal, Chris couldn't stop thinking about what he'd seen, wondering if he was going crazy or something. If Justin had been around, Chris knew there was no way he could tell his story without getting teased. *But Justin isn't here*, Chris reminded himself. *And Dad appreciates honesty.*

Chris didn't want his dad thinking he was crazy and maybe not letting him handle a rifle anymore. But Todd had never made his sons feel like they had to hide anything from him. The more Chris thought about it, the more it seemed wrong to keep quiet.

He took a deep breath. "Hey, Dad, I wasn't just interested in the rhubarb plant back there. I...saw something."

Todd glanced up sharply from his work. Chris was startled by the intense look in his father's usually mild friendly brown eyes. "What did you see?" he demanded.

For a moment, Chris doubted his decision to tell his dad about the creature, but there was no going back now. "It's...hard to describe," he began. "It was some kind of creature. It looked like a human but with a brighter face. Cleaner." He stopped. That sounded weird. *Brighter? Cleaner? What did that even mean exactly?*

"Well, it was too tall to be human anyway," he added. "Probably eight feet tall, and it was wearing a tunic made out of fur, and it had a vine for a belt and a big key around its neck..." Chris trailed off. He felt like every word out of his mouth sounded more ridiculous than the last. How was he going to explain it had wings?

Todd looked closely at his son, with a thoughtful look that Chris knew very well. It was the expression his dad always had when he was analyzing something, weighing things up.

"Were you scared?" Todd asked after a moment. "Did you feel threatened by it?"

He believes me, Chris thought. "No, I didn't feel scared. You know, it's funny, but I didn't feel like there was any danger. You would think I'd be a little afraid, but actually it was just kind of fascinating. I had the feeling I wanted to walk toward it. That's strange, right?"

"Not necessarily," Todd said with a chuckle. "You've always been pretty curious. What happened? Anything else?"

"No, not really," said Chris. "I turned away when I heard you shoot the buck, and when I looked again, it was just gone. Without a trace, no footprints or anything. Only that plant on the ground was left." Chris gestured toward the rhubarb.

Todd nodded slowly. "Well, all right then."

In thoughtful silence, they finished dressing the deer and loading up the truck. Chris was relieved that his dad wasn't going to check him into a mental hospital, at least. But he was still confused by the whole thing and wondered if they would talk about it again.

Todd put the pickup truck in gear and started the drive home. Chris gazed out his window and watched as the sun slowly dipped farther down the sky. He made an effort to picture the creature again in his mind in detail, in case he wanted to draw it later.

Suddenly, his dad spoke again. "I know what you saw," he said. "A creature, too tall to be a man but shaped like a man. Not an animal. A man with bright pale skin, long flowing brown hair, wearing a big key around his neck. But you forgot to mention the wings, didn't you? The giant wings coming out of his back."

"What?" Chris felt a chill run down his back. "Did you see it too? Or are you messing with me?"

"No to both questions," Todd said. "I didn't see it just now. But I have seen it before. And I recognized that look on your face. I must have looked the exact same way when I saw it…more than twenty years ago."

Chris felt a huge rush of relief. He really wasn't crazy. That was something to be grateful for, at least. "Wow" was all he could say. "But okay, so what is it then? Is it, like, some kind of…*Bigfoot*, or what is it?"

Todd chuckled. He pulled off his hat and tossed it on the bench seat between them. He ran a calloused hand through his brown hair. Then his expression grew serious again.

"Well, Chris, to be honest with you, I don't know what it is any more than you do," he said. "When I was in my early twenties, Grandpa Jim took me and my brothers on a hunting trip to this same mountain. It turned out to be our last outing like that. I know I've told you before that my dad had a long battle with cancer, and this was right toward the end of his life."

Chris had never met Grandpa Jim, but he felt like he knew him anyway. His dad often told Chris and Justin stories about their grandfather.

Todd continued with his story. "It was a lot like today actually, about the same time of year. It was one of my first chances to go hunting. I was nervous, like you probably were today. I wanted to do a good job and everything. And like today, we went off in different directions for a bit. That's when I saw it. Pretty much the same way you described. It just appeared out of nowhere. I looked away from it for a moment—I don't remember exactly why, I must have heard a sound or something, or maybe I just wasn't as deeply curious as you. But anyway, when I looked again, it was gone."

"Did you tell anyone?" Chris asked.

"Yes, I did," said Todd. "I told my dad and my brothers that very night when we were sitting around the campfire." He shook his head ruefully. "Maybe that was my mistake, telling the story around the campfire because they all just got a good laugh out of it and decided I'd made it up. They thought it was a great campfire story."

"I guess it'd be a good joke to scare someone who was new to the mountain," said Chris. "I mean, it's hard to believe something like that could exist, right?"

"It is," his dad agreed. "But here's the really interesting thing. After we got back from that camping trip, my dad pulled me aside and asked me a very strange question. He asked, 'Did the Caretaker have the key?' Of course I knew he was asking about the creature I'd seen. You know how big that key is—it really jumps out at you. All I could say was 'Yes, it had the key, but what is *the Caretaker*?' I had no idea what he meant by calling it that. Well, he just told me he'd explain later. That it wasn't the right time yet. But unfortunately, he never got the chance. We never talked about it again. He got very sick again right after that conversation and was gone two weeks later."

They drove in silence for a few minutes. Chris tried to make sense of the story his father had just told him. When had Grandpa

Jim seen the creature? What would he have said if he'd lived long enough to explain what "the Caretaker" was? Why had he pretended not to know about it in the first place when Chris's dad first told the story in front of his brothers?

That idea made Chris curious about something else. He broke into his dad's thoughts with another question. "Dad, do you think Justin has ever seen it? Or did you ever hear about anyone else seeing this...*creature*, or Caretaker, whatever it is?"

"No, I don't think so," Todd answered thoughtfully. "I've taken your brother hunting here before, and I think he would've told me if he'd seen it. Or I would've guessed anyway. He wouldn't have been able to hide his reaction."

"That's true," Chris agreed. "Justin would have been pretty freaked out too, just like I was. Did you ever see it again?"

"Yes, one other time," his dad answered. "At least I think I did. It was a couple of years after your grandpa died. I was by myself, deer hunting at the creek down by our house. I saw it step out of the woods several yards away from me. I don't know if it was going to approach me or not. Just then, I spotted a buck running up to the creek, so like a good hunter, I instinctively took aim and fired. When I looked back for the creature, it was gone. I never told anyone about seeing it that time. I guess I was afraid no one would believe me anyway."

"Well," Chris said, "I believe you."

His dad laughed. "Yes, I guess you have to. Or else we'd both have to be crazy."

"That's true." Chris had to laugh too. "But then all three of us—you, me, and Grandpa Jim—we can't all be crazy, right?"

"Good point," said Todd. "It's interesting, isn't it? Three generations of Cochranes now have seen this...*Caretaker*, always with the big key that has the letter *C* on it. I wonder why that is." He lapsed into thoughtful silence again.

Chris was wondering the exact same thing. What was the significance of that key? And what did it mean that he and his dad and grandfather had all seen this same mysterious being but had never heard anyone else talk about it ever?

They pulled up the long driveway leading to their house just as the sun sank below the horizon. It was odd to come home at this hour and not see any lights coming through the large front windows of the low-slung rambling ranch house. *Of course*, Chris remembered, *Mom's not here.*

Normally at this time of day, Chris's mom would be at the center of activity in the brightly lit open kitchen. She might be cooking or working on a spreadsheet or on the phone with a neighbor, giving advice about a construction project or the handling of a certain animal—or maybe all three at once. She'd grown up on a ranch herself and didn't shy away from any kind of work. Chris felt a pang of sadness, realizing that his mom and Justin wouldn't be inside to greet them.

As if reading his thoughts, Chris's dad said, "Hey, why don't we go ahead and get this rhubarb plant in the ground before it dries out. Your mom loves rhubarb pie—she'll be happy to see it in the garden when they get home."

Chris got some potting soil out of the garage and brought it around back. His dad quickly dug a hole, and Chris added the fresh soil, and the rhubarb was soon planted in one corner of the neat, well-maintained garden.

"It should be ready to harvest in a couple of years," his dad said as he doused the new plant with water. "Just imagine all the pies and tarts we'll be able to make from this one little plant."

Chris brushed his palms together to knock off the dirt and noticed a few fine specks of golden powder still clinging to his hands. *Yes, it was all real*, he thought.

CHAPTER 2

The next morning, Chris woke early and had the urge to sketch the creature from the hunting trip in one of his notebooks, but it didn't take long for his dad to realize that he was awake.

"Morning, Criffer Bob," Todd said. "Ready to help me on the ranch?"

Chris nodded and put down his pencil. He moved his sketching supplies to the bedside table and followed his dad downstairs.

"Right, I'm gonna water the nut and fruit tree orchard," Todd said, and Chris nodded. "After that, we can mend the fence out back and then make omelets for lunch with the chicken eggs."

"Sounds good, Dad," Chris said. "I'll just make some toast first."

While Chris loaded the toaster, he thought about his brother and his mom. "Do you think Mom and Justin got to Peru safely?" he asked.

"Oh yes, I forgot to tell you. Your mom called in the middle of the night to let us know that their journey to Lima went smoothly," Todd explained. "I would've woken you so you could speak to her, but she only had enough coins for a minute's use on the pay phone."

Chris smiled as he covered his toast with chocolate spread. "That's okay, I'm just glad to know they're safe. Hopefully, they can send us a letter soon."

15

Todd scratched his chin. "Just don't get your hopes too high, Criffer Bob. Peru's postal service struggle to afford shipping mail from the small villages, so we may not hear from them for a couple of months."

Chris nodded as he finished his toast. "I know, but we can hope. If only they had computers or telephones in the village."

"That would be ideal, but not being in constant communication with them will make their letters that bit more special," Todd replied. "Come on. Let's go and see our cows."

*****

After a long day of hard work, Chris decided to use the computer to look up the creature with the large golden key, but as soon as his fingers touched the keyboard, his mind went blank. He tried the terms "giant angel," "winged creature," and "caretaker with golden key," but they all belonged to the world of fantasy, not the real world.

Chris wished to return to the moment he'd first spotted the creature; he couldn't shake the feeling that it wanted to speak to him for some reason. Although he and his dad hadn't talked about the incident since the hunting trip, Chris secretly hoped he could go back to the mountain—not to hunt but just to speak to the creature he'd seen.

And as if by magic…

"I think we need to go hunting again tomorrow. I've been evaluating our supplies, and it would be good to get another buck before winter sets in. If it's a harsh winter like the last one, we'll want to be prepared."

"Yeah, of course!" Chris agreed eagerly. "Where should we go?"

"I think we'll go back up to the mountain," Todd said. "There was plenty of game up there. Maybe this time, you'll get a buck." He gave Chris a direct look and smiled slightly.

A spark of excitement shot through Chris. Was his dad thinking the same thing? Did he want to try and see *it* again?

"Yeah, I hope so," Chris said. "It would be good to have another chance—to go hunting, I mean."

"Of course, that's what you mean," his dad said with a chuckle. "Just remember to stay focused. Now let's get these dishes washed and get to bed. We'll have an early start tomorrow."

That night, Chris had to count about two thousand sheep before he could fall asleep. He was nervous and excited about the hunting trip, just like he'd been the first time. But now, there were two reasons for his excitement. Before he finally drifted off to sleep, he reminded himself: keep your sights on scouting deer tomorrow, not on scouting for the "Caretaker."

Shortly after dawn the next morning, Chris and his dad were hiking through the valley again. This time though, it felt very different. The first thing they noticed was that something big was missing. Very big. Last time, they'd hiked up to the top of a massive rock pile in the valley to do some scouting before going farther up the mountain. But today, the rock pile wasn't there.

"Hey, Dad," Chris said. "Wasn't there a huge pile of rocks right around here before? Remember, we climbed up to the top of it to get a better view of the area."

"Yes, there was," his dad agreed. "That's strange. It was right here on this side of the mountain. I remember because it was right at the spot where the river forks in two directions. It couldn't have just…disappeared, could it?"

They took the same hiking path up the mountain, traveling along the winding creek. The more they hiked and scouted, the more differences in the landscape they noticed. Just a few days before, there had been animal tracks everywhere. It was an ideal location for game, with the river and its smaller creeks providing plenty of water. There were many places for game to take shelter from the weather and predators too. That was why it was such good deer-hunting ground. But today, there didn't seem to be any deer. In fact, there didn't seem to be any animals at all to speak of. Even the birds weren't chirping. It was eerily quiet and empty, as if all the animals were just gone.

"It is getting to be late in the season," Todd said. "So it's possible that the animals have started to move farther down the mountain into the deeper thickets away from the hunters."

"But there aren't even any birds," Chris pointed out. "It's like there are no animals at all."

Todd looked troubled. "Yes," he agreed. "That does seem to be the size of it. Do you want to head back? I'll leave it up to you."

Chris felt the weight of the question. He knew his dad was asking more than just "Do you want to keep on trying to hunt?" He was letting Chris decide whether to stay here longer—whether to risk seeing the creature again.

Chris looked up and met his dad's direct gaze. "How about… we do some berry picking?" he suggested slowly.

His dad gave a short nod. "Sounds good," he said. They were on the same page. "It's blueberry season after all."

"Yeah," Chris said enthusiastically. "Going home empty-handed isn't an option, right?"

But berry picking turned out to be equally pointless. The berries had been packed and bursting on the previous trip, if not quite ripe yet. They should have been perfect now, and there should have been a lot of them. The weird thing was all the vines had been picked clean.

Chris and his dad zigged and zagged along the creek, all the way up one side of the mountain and back down again, but they found no berries, and no sign of what or who had harvested the berries either. There were no animal tracks. No deer tracks, no bear tracks, not even tracks of smaller animals. The ground was smooth, as if it had been swept with a broom.

What had eaten the berries? Had all the animals migrated from this spot to another, eating everything in their path, preparing for a long winter? Did they know something that humans did not?

Had the creature been here—the Caretaker? Had it scared all the animals away? If so, was it safe for Chris and his dad to be here? Chris didn't know. But one thing he did know was that he didn't want to leave. This was all very creepy, frightening even, but his curiosity was greater. He wanted to find out what was going on here even if it meant danger.

Yet somehow, Chris felt almost certain that this Caretaker—or whatever it was—did not mean to harm them. He felt somehow that it was a good creature, and there was something important that it had to tell them. He wanted more than anything to see it again.

Then as if some powerful force had read Chris's exact thoughts, there it was. As they came around a blind curve, returning to the fork in the river where the rock pile should have been, the towering creature with the large golden key stood not ten yards away. Without even looking at each other, Chris and his dad silently stopped and stood motionless. Their guns were slung over their shoulders, but they didn't reach back to grab them.

Then the creature spoke but not in English or any other language Chris recognized. It had a deep voice, and the syllables weren't harsh but musical. Just like the last time, a strangely calm feeling came over Chris. He didn't feel at all afraid, just curious. The creature walked toward them slowly, reaching into its pouch as it did so.

Chris glanced at his dad. Todd gave a small nod, which Chris knew meant everything was okay. Chris could see his dad wasn't tense or frightened either. His face and shoulders were relaxed, and he made no move to reach behind him for his gun. Chris followed his dad's lead and stayed relaxed too.

When the creature reached them, it extended its hand. It held two large ripe blueberries in its open palm. Again, Chris looked at his dad for confirmation. Todd nodded. The creature gestured that they should eat the berries.

As he put the berry to his lips, Chris felt a stab of worry, but he pushed away his fear. Something told him this was important and that he would be safe. There was just something about the creature. Chris trusted him without knowing why he trusted him.

The berries tasted just as they should, clean and delicious. The creature waited calmly for Chris and Todd to swallow, and then he spoke again. This time, his words were in English and perfectly clear.

He looked directly at Todd. "I know your face," he said. "My father saw your father on this mountain fifty cycles ago. That is fifty years to you. He was just a little boy then. Not long ago, I saw you and your son as well. You are descendants of Thomas Cochrane, are you not?"

"Yes, we are," said Todd. "He was our first ancestor to travel here from Scotland. But instead of asking how you know this, I think I would begin by asking, who are you?"

The creature smiled at Todd's choice of words. "I am Si, the Caretaker of Castle Forks," he answered.

"The Caretaker!" Chris exclaimed eagerly. "Dad, that's what Grandpa Jim called him, isn't it?"

Todd nodded slowly. "That's right." He glanced at Chris then back to the Caretaker. His expression was puzzled. "But what is this Castle Forks? And where is it?"

"Castle Forks is my home, and you are standing right in front of it," replied the Caretaker calmly.

What castle? There was no such thing in sight. Si saw the look of disbelief on their faces.

"The castle is very real," he said. "But to a normal person's eye, it's just a large pile of rocks overlooking the valley here, at the fork in the river. Do not tell me that you have not noticed the rocks? I saw both of you climb to the top the other day to get a better view of what was below."

"Yes, we were looking for it," Chris agreed. "But it isn't here now, is it? It's gone!"

Si laughed gently, the way a parent laughs at a small child who has just said something nonsensical. "No, it is very much still standing where it has always been," he said.

Is this guy crazy? Chris thought, but he stopped himself from saying anything out loud. He darted a glance at his dad, who was obviously wondering the same thing.

Their exchange of glances did not escape Si, who went on to explain.

"I understand your confusion," he said. "Castle Forks, which looks to you like a mere pile of rocks, can only be seen when a person is looking from the right place. There is a very specific spot you must be standing in to see it at all. The last time you were here, you happened to stand in that spot, just by chance. Therefore, you saw the pile of rocks and were able to climb up it. Today, you have simply failed to stumble into the exact right spot. From any other vantage point in the valley, there appears to be a continuous thicket of thorns and berry bushes here as far as the eye can see. But don't you find it strange that there are tall trees nearly covering the front side of the mountain? Whereas this side of the mountain appears to be treeless?" he asked.

As Si was speaking, Chris couldn't help darting his eyes all over the place, looking again for the mysterious rock pile. He saw nothing.

"Let me help you," said Si. "If you would both step just about two paces to the left."

They did so. "Still nothing," said Todd.

"And now, three paces forward...yes, another step to the right, and...one more step right," Si instructed them. "Ah, yes—now try turning around."

This time, when Chris turned to look behind him, the rock pile was there, only a few yards from where they stood. "Wow!" he said, startled.

"All right," said his dad, looking a little shocked. "Okay."

"There!" exclaimed Si. "Now you see what I mean. If you were standing anywhere else but precisely where you are, you would see only the brush and the vines."

"Well, I can see it, so I believe there's a big pile of rocks which can only be seen from this vantage point," Todd admitted. "But I still don't see a castle."

"Castle Forks only appears as a castle when the key unlocks the front gate or when someone inside lowers the front gate to welcome visitors approaching," Si explained.

As he said this, Si lifted the chain from around his neck. He inserted the large golden key into a crack in the rock face, then turned it clockwise. There was a loud cracking sound as if a massive lock being turned, then the metallic rattle of heavy chains banging together. The face of the rock began to move. It swung slowly outward like a giant gate made of many large stones, revealing a doorway through which light was pouring.

It's a different kind of light, Chris thought. *Light from another world.*

"Enter," said the Caretaker.

CHAPTER 3

The doorway opened onto a courtyard. This new place was drenched in bright sunlight and full of beautiful flowers of all colors. The gate through which they'd passed swung shut behind them instantly. As soon as it closed, all traces of it disappeared. There appeared to be only a smooth solid wall of stone where the gate had been.

Chris and his dad followed Si underneath a giant intricately carved stone archway and stood looking around in every direction. There was a lot to take in.

They appeared to be in the central courtyard of a massive castle made of gray stone. On every side of the courtyard were various stone archways similar to the one they'd just passed through, presumably leading into different areas of the castle. Looking upward, Chris could see that the dark gray walls rose hundreds of feet into the air all around them. There were a number of balconies, spiral staircases, and open archways placed along the many levels of the castle.

In all, Castle Forks must have been at least fifteen stories in height, and there was no way to tell how far back it went from where they stood. At regular outposts, there were archer towers with armed guards standing at attention. The guards wore what Chris could only think of as "medieval clothing"—tunics, boots, chain mail, and metal visors over parts of their faces. *There's no way we're in present-day northern California anymore*, Chris thought. *We must be in the past.*

"Who are the guards?" Chris asked. "I mean, are they people like us?"

"Yes, many of them are," said Si. "This place has been filled with deployed soldiers from all over the Old and New World since Castle Forks was built. Every civilization from the East to the West has had at least one occupant in the castle to protect this land."

"That explains why the guards aren't quite as tall as you are," Todd observed. "But if they're from all over the world, how does everyone communicate with one another?"

"There is no need to worry about speaking in different tongues here," Si explained. "As long as you are within these walls, you will understand and be understood by everyone, but outside, the language barrier will return until you ingest a single blueberry. The blueberries allow us to understand each other outside the walls of Castle Forks but only for one day."

Chris frowned. "Does that mean that blueberries are magical?"

"Only the ones around the castle," Si explained. "Novell, the former Caretaker, cast a language spell on them. We did not want random humans outside the castle to easily understand us, so Novell made the berries magic, only letting certain people past the barrier."

Todd nodded with great interest. "Ahh! Clever thinking. But what if random tourists or hikers just *happen* to eat the berries and then accidentally hear you? Wouldn't that be problematic?"

Si chuckled. "Well, yes, it would, but there is one main reason why random people would not be able to hear us. Because the berries are enchanted in such a way that only allows specific people to benefit from the magic—people whom we are trying to reach."

A large group of people approached. With them appeared to be a few humans who wore clothing like the guards in the towers. There were also several who were taller, resembling Si. Several members of the group carried large baskets that were full of flowers, fruits, nuts, and berries.

Now that Chris had spoken to Si, it was strange to think of him as "not human," but the fact was Si was eight feet tall and had wings—so he had to be something other. But Chris couldn't figure out a polite way to ask, "What are you?" It seemed like a rude thing to say to someone who was being so kind and hospitable. Chris decided he would just have to think of Si as a "Caretaker." Perhaps this was the name of his people, not just the name of his job description.

One of the Si-like creatures was a very serious and regal-looking older man with long flowing white hair. He wore a simple tunic as well, but it was made of a softer-looking golden fur-like material rather than dark-brown bear fur. Chris and Todd automatically looked to him first; he was clearly the senior member of the group.

Of the group, another of the figures stood out to Chris. He was younger than the rest, perhaps Chris's own age, and had bleached blond hair. Even though he was about a foot taller than Chris, there was something about his face and his wacky surfer-like haircut that made it obvious he wasn't yet fully grown. The shorter individual was smiling from ear to ear.

He definitely looks like a fun character, Chris thought.

The white-haired figure spoke first. "Welcometh," he said, opening his arms in a formal kind of gesture that reminded Chris of something he'd seen in movies about the legendary King Arthur and his knights. He had a large scar on the left side of his face, which continued down his entire arm, ending at his wrist.

Not sure how to respond to this greeting, Chris and his dad nodded somewhat awkwardly and said, "Hello."

The white-haired figure extended his right hand, shaking first Todd's hand then Chris's. "This is thy way of greeting, I understand. I am Novell, the former Caretaker of Castle Forks, now known as the Historian. Thou have already been introduced to my son and successor, Si, the current Caretaker of Castle Forks."

The resemblance between Si and Novell was striking. They had the same dark-brown eyes with heavy eyebrows, bright skin, and gentle smile. Chris had a sudden realization: *This must be the Caretaker that my father saw, not Si. Twenty years ago, he would have looked exactly like Si.* Just as with Si, Chris instantly felt an instinct to trust Novell.

"Welcometh back, Todd," Novell said to Chris's dad. "It is wonderful to see thee. I am sorry about thy father. I have not seen thee since his ceremony at the church and then the spreading of his ashes by the river."

After hearing Novell speak more, Chris felt relieved that he'd been forced to read Shakespeare at school despite his dislike for the language. He'd learned that a lot of words ended in "-eth," that "thee" and "thou" meant "you," and that "thy" meant "your."

Todd frowned in confusion. "Thank you for your condolences, but I have to admit that I don't remember meeting you at the funeral although I think I saw you on a hunting trip with my dad. But…we didn't speak, and I have definitely never been here before."

"Oh, but thou have been here before," Novell said. "Only I believe thou thought it was a dream."

Todd took a small step backward, as if shocked. He frowned. "Please, can you explain? This is all so strange."

Novell's expression was kind. "Thou were here just a few days, mayhap one of thy weeks, before thy father died," he explained gently. "Thy father brought thee, knowing it was his last chance to do so. But it was a hard time for thee, and thy father did not have the strength in those last days to fully explain everything about Castle Forks and his relationship to it. However, he did bring thee here. It was very important to him. Mayhap thou remember waking from a strange dream and finding a single blueberry sitting on thy nightstand?"

Chris watched his dad's face turn pale as Novell spoke. He looked unsteady on his feet for a second, and was that a glint of a tear in his eye? Todd raised his right hand to his forehead, as if he had a headache. Chris saw that his hand was shaking. It was strange seeing his dad, who was usually so calm and confident, seem so overcome by emotion.

Todd quickly recovered. "Yes, I remember that now," he said. "I thought it was a dream because of the way I woke up at home like nothing had happened. Due to my father's condition, he never got the chance to explain everything properly, and in those times, something so surreal never happened to ordinary people like me. But I thought nonstop about my first encounter with you on the mountain, waiting and hoping that my dad would explain what it all meant. But I didn't want to bother him with any questions in those last days."

For a few seconds, no one spoke. It felt like a moment of respectful silence. Then Todd smiled suddenly and continued, "I thought my dad died without ever being able to explain. But now, I see that he did find a way to show me. He brought me here. I remember this place."

"That is good," Novell said with approval. "I am glad thou are able to remember thy visit. I am sure more details of it will come back to thee with time. It has probably been many years since thou thought about that 'dream' which was not a dream."

"Yes, it has been," Todd admitted. "I haven't thought of that 'dream' in years or of the two times when I saw you out there, on the other side of Castle Forks. I actually put those memories out of my mind because there was no one to tell who wouldn't think I was crazy. But of course, when Chris saw Si the other day on the mountain…I started to remember some things…" His voice trailed off.

Chris was seeing a new side to his dad. Instead of being totally in charge and knowing exactly what to do, Todd looked uncertain and confused. So far, no one had been unkind to them, but Chris was starting to wish they would actually explain a few things. It wasn't fair to keep them in the dark anymore. He burst out suddenly, "Why has Si been following us? Why is our family so important to you?"

Instantly, Chris could tell that this was not the proper way to talk to Novell. There was an uncomfortable silence, and the younger blond guy's eyebrows went up, as if to say, "Uh-oh, you're in trouble now!"

Novell turned to look at Chris. His brown eyes looked into Chris's for a long moment, and Chris began to feel uncomfortable.

"I'm sorry," Chris said. "It's just that we've been brought here, and we still don't understand why. You have to realize, this isn't normal in Monument, California. It's like a whole other world here."

Todd nodded in agreement and said, "Yeah, you have to understand the frustration of being left in the dark."

Novell's stern look softened, and he smiled. "Yes, I know it is confusing for thee. I assure thee that everything will make sense soon enough. I will remind thee of many things that thy grandfather knew well, and thou will soon know everything. I give thee my word. But first, I ask for only a little more of thy patience."

Chris nodded. "Thank you," he said. He again felt the instinct to trust Novell, and he was glad he hadn't made a bigger scene by being rude to their host.

"Now as a routine matter," Novell said, "I must ask thee to hand over thy weapons to Whitethorn, our Castle Forks' head of security."

Another member of Novell's party stepped forward. He was taller than Novell and Si and very broad across the shoulders—definitely the largest person Chris had ever seen in his life. With his dark hair and black fur tunic, he reminded Chris of a grizzly bear.

Whitethorn held out his hands for their guns, which Chris and Todd quietly handed over. "I may be the 'ead of security, but I'm known to all 'ere as 'the Catapult,'" Whitethorn said. "You may call me by either name. As long as you are 'ere, your weapons will be kept in the armory. Only those on current guard duty are allowed to have weapons. This 'elps prevent accidents," he explained.

Chris instantly began speculating about how Whitethorn had gotten his nickname. Was he a decorated warrior with thousands of defeated foes? Or did he just really enjoy throwing things?

Whitethorn began walking toward the armory but turned back for a moment as if he'd heard Chris's thoughts. "I can throw any object of any size, just like a catapult," he said. "You don't wanna try me, boy," he added with smirk as he walked toward the armory door, chuckling.

Chris could tell that Whitethorn was joking, but he was definitely a fearsome being. Maybe there was a big soft teddy bear heart under the scary grizzly bear exterior? Either way, Chris decided to never get on his bad side.

The younger individual with the wacky haircut walked toward them and held out his right hand. "What's up, dude? My name's Valkyn, the Valiant," he introduced himself. "I'm Master General's nephew."

Several of the Castle Forks residents chuckled at Valkyn's introduction. Chris shot a puzzled glance in the direction of the laughter before looking back at Valkyn.

"Who's Master General?" Chris asked.

"Whitethorn, that's just what I call him. Everyone in my family has a nickname from their performance in battle," Valkyn explained. "Though I have yet to be in battle, I thought I would save all others the trouble by picking out my own nickname. There's no doubt that I'll make a name for myself and become a legendary figure like my descendants before me. It's in my blood."

Even though Valkyn's words sounded like bragging, Chris could tell there was a sense of humor behind them. He was obviously kind of a comedian, and he was being friendly.

"Well, it's nice to meet you, Valiant," Chris said with a smile as he shook Valkyn's hand. "Maybe you can help me come up with a good nickname for myself some time."

"Sure thing, dude," Valkyn agreed. "I'm pretty much good at everything, so I'll definitely be able to help."

"What's this?" Chris pointed at the strap that was slung over the shoulder of Valkyn's tunic.

With a grin, Valkyn turned around to reveal a longboard hanging from the strap.

"That's awesome!" Chris said. "I like skating too."

"Cool," Valkyn said. "Check this out." He pulled something out from under the belt of his tunic.

Chris couldn't help laughing when he saw that it was a BMX-branded T-shirt. "Nice," Chris said admiringly.

A polite cough interrupted them. "Ahem, Valkyn," Novell said pointedly. "I will need to show our guests around the castle now."

"Of course, Statman," Valkyn replied, and Chris assumed it was another nickname he'd made up.

He stepped back, then quickly dropped his longboard to the ground, and pulled the BMX shirt on over his tunic.

"Check out the recreation room when you can, man—it's full of pinball games, ping-pong tables, dartboards, and other sports equipment!" he called to Chris as he skated off through the courtyard.

All Chris could think in that moment was *This place is unbelievable. Wait a second—is this really happening?*

At first, it was like being inside King Arthur's Camelot or something, and then suddenly there was a kid with a surfer haircut skateboarding through a medieval courtyard? It seemed too good to be true.

His dad nudged him suddenly on the arm. "Criffer Bob, focus up," he whispered.

Chris jumped slightly. *Okay, I felt my dad do that, so I must be awake.* He jerked his attention back to what was happening.

Novell was talking. "Will explain the reason for thy invitation to Castle Forks at this particular time, but first, thou must be in need of refreshment. We have prepared a welcome feast for thee. Please, join us as our honored guests."

Chris and his dad followed their host, who led them deeper into the castle.

CHAPTER 4

Novell led them across the courtyard and down a long brightly lit corridor. There were numerous enclaves lining the walls that each held golden nuggets of all shapes and sizes. The high vaulted ceiling of the corridor was encrusted with jewels of every color imaginable. Sunlight streamed in from windows high up in the wall, glinting off the gold and jewels so brightly that Chris could hardly keep his eyes open from the glare.

They passed several arched doorways along the corridor, and Novell pointed to each one along the way. "This one leads to the Hall of Protectors…this one to the recreation room for the young ones…"

Chris zoned out. Novell's voice became a blur in the background as he gazed around the lengthy corridor in awe until Novell mentioned a particular room in the castle. "This one to the library…"

Chris broke from his amazement. "A library?"

Novell chuckled. "Why, of course. Every castle must have a library within its walls. Take a look before we move onto the Great Hall."

Chris gasped and looked at his dad for confirmation.

"Go on, but be quick," Todd replied, ruffling Chris's hair.

Chris grinned and pushed open the large wooden door that led to the grand library. He stopped in the entrance and gaped at the marvel before him. The spacious room had two floors, the bottom in the shape of a cross and the top laid out as a balcony that overlooked all below. Everything within the room had been carved from different types of wood: the floor, the arched ceiling, the towering bookshelves, and the circular desk at the back end of the bottom floor, giving the library an old but homely atmosphere.

"Dad! Come and look in here!" Chris called. In an instant, his dad appeared at the door and stepped inside the room.

"Wow, this is beautiful," Todd said, gazing around.

"I know, right?" Chris replied. "I already know I'll be coming back here...if we have time. Look at all these books!"

Todd gave a hearty laugh. "I love you, Criffer Bob. I love that you're not a typical boy. Not that there's anything wrong with typical, but most lads your age are all about football and video games, not books."

Chris smiled. Warmth filled his body. "I love you too, Dad. And well, books are a peaceful escape."

Chris strolled over to the closest bookshelf and glanced at one of the leather-bound books on display. "*The History of Castle Forks*," he said, reading the title. "Maybe I'll read that one first."

Todd stood beside his son and patted his shoulder. "Well, when we fully know what we're here for, we can ask the Caretakers if you can read some of these. Deal?"

Chris looked up at his dad and smiled. "Deal."

"Come on, let's get back to Novell," Todd said. "We don't want to leave him waiting for too long."

Chris and Todd left the library and rejoined Novell and the others in the hallway. Novell beamed and continued to lead the way, and at last, they arrived at a high-arched doorway leading into the Great Hall. Two large marble statues, carved with incredible detail and precision, flanked the entrance. Chris stopped short as the statues caught his attention. One depicted a Caretaker, wearing the familiar tunic and large golden key. In the face, it closely resembled Novell and Si. The other statue was more startling and actually caused Chris to gasp when he saw it. This figure was a human clad in battle armor and brandishing a long sword. In the other hand, it held a shield with the Celtic letter *C* engraved on it. In the face, this figure looked almost exactly like Chris's dad.

Novell saw Chris's stunned expression. "This statue is a likeness of thy ancestor, Michael Cochrane, the father of Thomas Cochrane," he explained. "The other is my grandfather's grandfather, Candar. These two fought side by side long ago."

So that's why we're here—because we're Cochranes. This has to do with our family. As Chris had this thought, he exchanged a look with his dad. He could tell his dad was thinking the same thing.

Even though the Cochranes' connection to Castle Forks was becoming more and more obvious, Chris still couldn't puzzle out exactly what he and his dad had to do with it or why they'd been brought here at this particular time. Chris didn't even know very much about his ancestor Thomas Cochrane, whom Si and Novell had both mentioned now. He made a mental note to look up this Thomas Cochrane on the Internet as soon as they got home—whenever that was. In the meantime, he realized, as his stomach grumbled, he was really hungry. This feast would definitely be welcome; whatever food they were about to eat smelled delicious.

Si, Whitethorn, and another called Thungor were there to greet them as they entered the Great Hall. The high vaulted ceilings of the massive rectangular room were adorned with dozens of chandeliers bearing lit torches. From the chandeliers hung animal antlers of all shapes and sizes. On the two longer sides of the room, two matching spiral-shaped staircases led up to a balcony that ran along the perimeter of the hall. At one end of the room stood a roaring fire encased in a boulder-stacked mantel and chimney. And at the head of the room, raised up on a dais, stood a lone chair carved from gray stone.

"That throne is for the Son of God," said Si. "He is the only one who will ever sit in that chair. He will return one day." Si's voice was somber. Chris bowed his head instinctively and said nothing.

Then Whitethorn spoke in a livelier tone. "And now am I the only one who can't stand these mouthwatering aromas any longer? I believe it's time to feast!"

"Yes," agreed Novell. "Please, fill thy plates and take a seat."

Three large circular tables were placed in the middle of the room. They were laid with plate settings covered with gold and flashy jewels. A large golden goblet was included at each plate setting. The center of each table was engraved with the Celtic *C* and boar insignia, exactly like the symbol on Si's key. The walls were lined with several long rectangular tables laden with food. There were all kinds of meat and vegetable dishes, breads of various shapes and textures, and plenty of desserts as well.

As he glanced over the dessert table, Chris began to see what had happened to all the berries he and his dad had been looking for earlier. *So this was why the bushes were picked clean*, he thought. The table was laden with every imaginable berry dish—cakes, pies, tortes, berries in cream—as well as numerous other dishes made of Chris's favorite things, including chocolate. There were berry dishes and chocolate dishes on the table that he'd never seen before. Everything looked so good that Chris couldn't decide where to begin.

"Boy, just take a little of everything so you can say you did," advised Whitethorn, loading his own plate high with slabs of beef, chicken legs, and a mountain of roasted red potatoes. "But leave room for dessert," he added. "You won't believe the desserts here." As he spoke, Whitethorn began to load up a second plate.

"Wow, that's a lot of food you have there," Chris commented.

Whitethorn laughed a big belly laugh. "This is just an appetizer. I'm comin' back for my meal and dessert next. The food goes fast 'ere. You should get it now before it's gone."

"Agreed!" Thungor said with amusement. "You need to act fast with him around, or you'll starve, kid."

Chris laughed and picked up a plate to begin serving himself as Whitethorn and Thungor walked off to set down their huge plates of food. The head of security was soon back, piling up another plate with steak and vegetables. Chris and his dad made their way over to the table with Whitethorn, Thungor, Si, and Novell and sat down.

"Try this," said Whitethorn, pushing a golden goblet toward Chris.

The drink was delicious, probably the best thing Chris had ever tasted. He couldn't quite identify the flavor, but he ventured a guess. "Is it apple cider?"

"Nope," said Thungor around a mouthful of food. "It's berry juice—elderberry combined with whitethorn berry."

Todd took a drink from his own goblet and looked up with surprise. "Delicious," he said. "But this isn't berry juice—it's wine!"

Whitethorn nodded. "Yeah, the cups are charmed," he explained. "The liquid inside each one turns into the desired drink of the cupbearer."

"Amazing," Todd said. "But in that case, I suppose I should take it easy on this one, delicious as it is."

Si chimed in. "The wine that you taste does not have alcohol. There is no alcohol allowed within these halls when the threat of enemy attack is present. We need to keep a clear head."

This caught Chris's attention. "Attack?" he echoed. "Is there a threat of enemy attack now?"

At that moment, a loud rattling sound caught everyone's attention, so Chris's question went unanswered. Valkyn and a giant were whizzing down on one of the spiral banisters on their longboards. Chris was impressed with the skill of this maneuver but the adults clearly were not. As they reached the bottom of the railing, a giant with a shock of bright-red hair caught them, one in each hand, and his expression was none too pleased. *I wonder if those two giants are related*, Chris thought.

Whitethorn rose from the table. "Valkyn and Dardush!" he said in a thunderous voice. "It's been made clear to you that you're only to use the ramps in the recreation room for this purpose. These off-road antics are much too dangerous."

Valkyn and Dardush looked down guiltily.

"Sorry, Master General," Valkyn said in a small voice.

"Yeah, sorry, Whitethorn," Dardush added.

The other giant, who acted like Dardush's dad, gave them a long stare as they bent down to gather up their longboards. The giant didn't need to say anything apparently. His eyes did the talking. The young ones left their longboards where they were and retreated from the room.

The thought of being in trouble with his own normal-sized dad was scary enough. Chris couldn't imagine what it would be like to have a twenty-foot-tall giant for a dad or Whitethorn for an uncle.

He felt bad for Valkyn and Dardush as he watched them leave the hall with their heads down.

"They're good young ones," said Whitethorn. "They just need to use the skateboard ramp and park that we had constructed for them in the recreation room."

"Yes," agreed Si. "It is much too dangerous for them to be playing like that. We cannot afford to have any broken arms right now—not when we may need them for more serious matters."

Chris was about to ask what Si meant by "more serious matters," but Novell cut him off.

"Thy nephew shows great promise," Novell said to Whitethorn. "He is not afraid of hard work. He is always on time to work in the gardens and was recently promoted to oversee the berry harvest."

"I hear that he sometimes refers to himself in the third person as the 'Hooded Hairy Skater King.'" Thungor chuckled. "He's quite a good athlete actually. If my kind is ever acknowledged in public again to your world, I'd assume that he'd like to compete as a professional longboarder. Do they have such a thing?" he asked, directing his question to Chris.

"Yes, definitely." Chris nodded. "And I bet he could do it. He's really good!"

Chris was beginning to feel like Novell, Whitethorn, and Thungor wanted to distract him from Si's mention of enemy attack. Chris took the hint, but he couldn't completely suppress his curiosity. He decided to try a less obvious approach. "When did you get that scar, Novell?" he asked, trying to sound casual.

"I was wounded in battle long ago," Novell answered. "It is a reminder to every person here that life cannot be taken for granted. I would gladly sacrifice my appearance again to help save the lives of innocent people from evildoers."

Everything Novell said just made Chris more and more curious. What was all this reference to being ready for battle? Chris had to bite his tongue to keep from blurting out a flood of questions. The last time he'd demanded answers from Novell, he had immediately regretted it. He would just have to trust that Novell would be as good as his word and reveal what was going on in due time. He struggled to be patient.

At last, all the plates were empty, and the goblets were drained. Chris couldn't eat another bite, and everyone else had slowed down too. Finally, Novell rose from the table.

"And now it is time for me to begin answering some of thy questions," he said.

Si, Whitethorn, and Thungor also rose from the table. Together with Chris and Todd, they followed Novell back down the long corridor. The sun must have gone down while they were feasting because moonlight was now shining through the high windows.

Novell stopped at one of the closed mahogany doors he'd indicated earlier. He took the great golden key from his neck and placed it in the lock, then pushed the door open to reveal a room that looked like a museum.

The room was full of clear glass cases, display cabinets, and pedestals holding a variety of antique-looking objects. The walls were lined with what appeared to be suits of armor and various types of weaponry. Next to each suit of armor was a portrait, presumably depicting the armor's previous wearers. There were swords and daggers of all shapes and sizes, some studded with jewels and some made of simple, unadorned metal. There were metal and bone-tipped spears, wooden clubs, crossbows, longbows, quivers full of arrows— just about every type of weapon Chris could imagine, all dating to various eras in history.

Todd immediately commented on this. "It looks like every era of weaponry is represented here," he said, looking around in fascination.

"That is very true," said Novell.

"We are in the Hall of Protectors," Si explained. "Every great leader from the beginning of time has his battle attire and weaponry here to honor their service."

"I can see that this is fascinating for thee. Please take a few moments to peruse the room," Novell invited.

Chris and his dad began to walk around the museum, trying to take it all in. One grouping of innocuous-looking objects caught

Chris's attention. It was a very battered-looking sling, displayed with a simple brown tunic which lacked any sort of flare. There was also a single lock of hair next to an unmarked shield of dull bronze that looked like it hadn't been polished in…centuries.

"Are those what I think they are?" Chris asked.

"Yes," said Novell. "There hangs King David's sling that defeated the giant Goliath, a lock of hair that belonged to Samson, and a bronze shield worn by Gideon."

"So when you said there were relics here from every era…you really meant it," said Todd.

"Yes," said Novell. "The Hall of Protectors acknowledges the service of many great leaders. They would be called heroes to thee. Many men and women whose names thou know fought to defend this world from pure evil. As thou can see, we have had some of the greatest warriors in history fight the Tourlt," said Novell.

A chill ran down Chris's spine at the way Novell said the word "Tourlt."

"What are the…Tourlt?" he asked.

"The Demon Shadows," rumbled Whitethorn. "The only enemy and always the enemy."

"You will soon know more than you may like about the Tourlt," said Si. "But first, you must learn the truth about your past."

"This is true," Novell agreed. "Thou are descendants of the great Cochrane clan of Scotland. Thy family has helped save everything as we know it from a very ruthless and formidable foe—a foe responsible for nearly every war in every known civilization from the beginning of time. Songs have been sung about thy family and the great victories over the Tourlt, the Demon Shadows."

"And now," said Si, "I am afraid we are going to need you once again."

Si's announcement was followed by a long silence. Chris wasn't sure exactly what to think. *Tourlt? Demon Shadows?* These words sounded like something from a fantasy novel he might read, but this was no novel. It was real life, and he sensed that everything in this world of Castle Forks wasn't just feasts and fun. It was beginning to sound dangerous.

Chris's dad broke the silence. "This is all very interesting, but I have to admit, I'm still pretty confused. You say you're going to need us—do you mean in some kind of battle against this... *Tourlt*, is it? But what are they exactly? And why do you need us?"

Chris could tell his dad was starting to feel impatient. It was time to get some real answers.

"Have you ever heard stories in the Bible of when God allowed some to see both the physical world and spiritual world?" asked Thungor.

Chris nodded. He had read stories of the Israelites being surrounded by enemies and God telling them to have faith and that he would protect them. In such moments, the Israelites were protected by armies of angels with shields and flaming swords. He also knew the story of Ezekiel, who was told by God what was going to happen before many battles had even taken place. Because Ezekiel was able to see the spiritual world, he saw the armies that protected his land while others had no idea how safe they truly were from their enemies.

Whenever Chris had thought about those stories, he always felt thankful that he couldn't see the invisible spiritual battles going on. It seemed like a burden.

"All the people thou see honored here in our Hall of Heroes are those who fought in both worlds—the physical and the spiritual," said Novell. "They earned their fame from the successes thou have heard about in history books and legends alike. What thou have not heard about are the battles that took place in the spiritual world—the world that most humans do not see. Most would see a flood, a fire, a tornado, or a plague of disease. Those things were a distraction in the physical world, concealing a deeper reality and a deeper truth. The people of Castle Forks have always been fighting the unknown and unseen battles of the world. This is the purpose of Castle Forks. It is a stronghold, a kind of barricade."

"Only a few humans have ever known of it," said Si. "Most importantly, the hero Thomas Cochrane, not only did he have the special gift that allowed him to see both worlds, but he had other unique gifts as well, without which we would not have won the last great battle against the Tourlt."

"You see," said Novell, "the Tourlt have caused nearly every war that man has ever known. Thy history was rewritten to hide the truth. Thou know of tyrants, dictators, and ruthless rulers throughout time, but many were given credit for things they had not done themselves. Also there were instances when the Tourlt actively helped some of the most terrible people in your history."

"Perhaps I can give a few examples to make sure they understand?" Si suggested.

Novell nodded.

"This is likely to take longer than a few minutes," rumbled Thungor. "We'd best have a seat." He headed to a cluster of plain wooden furniture that was arranged in the middle of the room and chose the biggest chair. The others settled themselves as Si continued speaking.

"Your history tells the tale of Alexander the Great defeating the Persians in the Battle of Thermopylae," he said. "But before Alexander came to the fight, the Persians had a million warriors armed to the teeth to protect Persia from the Tourlt. King Darius sent the famous marathon soldier to request Alexander's help. Though Alexander's and Darius's countries had been at war for years, they set aside their differences for the common good—survival. Alexander was prideful, so he never admitted to his people that he had aided Darius.

"The Roman Colosseum was built by the Caesars, but it was the Tourlt who oversaw the slaughter of thousands in that place until the Saxons destroyed it. The Tourlt had been attacking the Saxons from the east and north until the Saxons retreated south and claimed Rome, the capital of the collapsing Roman Empire. The Romans lacked the leadership to mobilize and defend their lands. The Saxons easily claimed Rome and its surrounding lands and absorbed the Roman people as their own. They did away with the slavery that had held the former Roman Empire together."

Wow, this actually seems totally possible, Chris was thinking. He'd read about Alexander the Great and about the fall of the Roman Empire but never from this perspective. Yet it made sense. In both cases, there could have been another factor, a secret enemy that was not in his history books.

Thungor stepped in this time. "Another example from Asia. Genghis Khan and Attila the Hun are credited for the construction of the Great Wall of China. But that's not actually how it was. You see, their forces were outnumbered, overrun by the Tourlt in every direction. They had no choice but to retreat east to China. The people of China believed that they could avoid more fighting by building a great wall, thinking the Tourlt wouldn't be able to breach their defenses. And in Japan, a special type of soldier was specially trained to fight the Tourlt. You may have heard of the samurai, kiddo?"

"Of course I have…wow!" was all Chris could say.

Whitethorn laughed. "You like the samurai, eh, boy?"

"Yes, they were impressive," said Si. "And in fact, they had better success in fighting the Tourlt than most other types of warriors. This is because they were trained by Caretakers."

"And don't forget, we 'airy People helped with that training a little bit too," Whitethorn was quick to add.

"Hairy People?" echoed Chris.

"Whitethorn can tell thee both about that later," Novell replied. "But for now, the Tourlt."

When he had their attention again, Si continued, "The Black Plague in Europe was actually the Tourlt. You may have learned that it was a sickness caused by the overabundance of rodents. Yes, there were rodents—but in fact, it was the Tourlt who killed so many in Europe that they earned the name 'the Black Plague.' Death followed wherever they went. There was no stopping their destruction."

Novell picked up the story from here. "And then, thy people came," he said, directing his statement straight to Todd. "The Cochrane clan was able to help us and many other people and creatures from around the world to defeat the Tourlt. The final stand happened here, at the Great Battle of Castle Forks. It was a yearlong siege, and thousands perished on each side. If we had not won, with the help of thy clan, Castle Forks would not be standing here today. And one cannot imagine what kind of wasteland thy own world would be. I do know that it would not be the world that thou know. It would be a barren and desolate world, ruled over by the Tourlt."

"Wait, so the Tourlt are responsible for *every* bad thing that's happened in our history?" Chris asked, scratching his head.

"Indeed, young boy," Novell clarified.

"So, for example, the Second World War…that *wasn't* solely Hitler and the Nazis?"

Everyone in the room bar Chris and his dad shook their heads.

"No, I am afraid not, Chris," Si said. "Of course, the Tourlt did not possess Hitler completely. They just needed to find a man evil enough to agree to cover up their bidding."

Todd rubbed his chin. "So they worked together?"

"Sort of," Si replied. "The Tourlt would have put an idea within Hitler's head and made him believe that it was his idea from the beginning, therefore, planting the seed for such a horrific event in history."

"On the other hand, the Tourlt also work by giving wrongdoers the tools to commit their crimes and atrocities," Novell added. "For example, I am horrified to tell thee that the destruction of Hiroshima and Nagasaki would not have occurred if not for the Tourlt."

"No? Good God! How?" Todd exclaimed.

"Well, unlike their involvement with Hitler, planting the seed in his head, the Tourlt actually created the atomic bombs that caused the blast."

Chris had never heard of Hiroshima or Nagasaki, but atomic bombs, destruction, and his dad's reaction told him that the bombing was a serious point in history, and he planned to look it up on the Internet the next chance he got.

"Not forgettin' other points in 'istory, such as the assassination of JFK," Whitethorn piped up. "That was all planned and carried out by the Tourlt, which is why no one knows who killed him even to this day!"

"And Julius Caesar getting stabbed in the back," Thungor said. "He would've survived, but one of the Tourlt disguised themselves to get close enough to him, and his thrust was the one that did it."

"Jeez, it's scary how we're led to believe one thing about our history when the complete opposite has happened," Chris said.

41

His dad nodded. "Hmm, I'm starting to think that we've never been safe."

A tense silence filled the room, but Chris's next question broke the atmosphere.

"But what if the Tourlt kill our family, leaving no one to stop them?"

"I've often wondered that myself, but your family seems to be invincible against the Tourlt, lad," Whitethorn said.

Todd dipped his brow. "Don't you have a backup plan in case the Cochrane bloodline ever ceases to exist?"

"We do, and it involves retracing thy family tree, which we keep locked in our highest security vaults," Novell revealed. "But for now, we need to build up an army of fighters within Castle Forks, including thee."

Chris nodded, and Todd scratched his chin, frowning in thought. "But does that mean our family are forever destined to fight the Tourlt? There will always be wars, natural disasters, and diseases even without the Tourlt."

"Unfortunately, it is not about defeating the Tourlt indefinitely because of the reason you have just mentioned—there will always be bad things in the physical world," Si explained. "Instead, our job is to prevent, delay, and help ease the disasters the Tourlt cause."

"So like Dad said, our family will always be fighting them?" Chris asked, wide-eyed.

Thungor nodded. "That's why the Cochrane bloodline is so important, son."

"Isn't it possible to ever defeat them?" Todd questioned.

"I am afraid not," Novell replied. "We call them Demon Shadows for a reason—because they are dark spirits of evil that linger in the shadows, negatively influencing and controlling the physical world. Let me ask thee, young one, does thou think thou could ever kill a ghost?"

Chris shook his head. "No, of course not. Now that makes sense."

Novell walked over to the far wall and pointed up at a sword mounted there. It appeared to be made of some golden-red metal that caught even the dim light from the candles and blazed with color. It was almost as though it wasn't made of metal at all but fire itself, Chris thought.

"This sword was created by one of my kin, and it is one of the things that binds thy clan to us," said Novell.

"The sword is named Valor, after the name of its maker," Si explained. "A flaming sword entrusted to King Juniper of Sandal. King Juniper and your ancestor Thomas Cochrane were cousins. Their mothers were sisters."

"Like all swords of this kind, it was created by Valor, brother of Candar, who is my great-great-grandfather," Novell said. "Valor was always a Caretaker though he did not often come to Castle Forks. He was bonded to Juniper's mother and her family, and it was his life's work to watch over them. He traveled between Castle Cochrane and Sandal and looked after the people there."

"King Juniper was the one who could wield the sword, as was Thomas. Only the one for whom the sword was forged may touch it or another person of the same bloodline—but even then, only if the sword permits it. In the case of Thomas, the sword permitted it."

"This was our first indication that Thomas was selected as one of our warriors," explained Novell.

"And what was your second indication?" Todd asked.

In unison, Novell and Si each looked down at the large golden keys that hung around their necks.

Novell lifted his into the air and said, "Our second indication was his ability to be a key bearer even though he was not a Caretaker."

Whitethorn jumped in. "Just to ease your suspense," he said in his deep, rumbling voice, "I'll let you know that that's not something humans can do usually, nor my people either, without special protections. But humans, only a few of them in all your history 'ave ever been able to bear one of those keys without it burnin' the skin right off their hand or worse."

"That is right," said Si. "Unfortunately, the Tourlt also have the capacity to bear and to use the three keys. And if they gain possession of one, they can enter Castle Forks as easily as I can."

"So thou can see, that is why the keys must be so carefully guarded. They are passed down to each generation's selected Caretaker," said Novell, holding up his key again. "This one here is for Castle Cochrane in Scotland. We continue to protect the last survivors of the Cochrane clan there, as well as here. And of course, Si bears the key for Castle Forks."

"But you mentioned three keys," Chris said.

"That's right," said Todd. "Where is the third key?"

"That is a good question," said Novell. "The third key went missing during the Black Plague. We sent two ships to Europe to deliver instructions to Thomas Cochrane and also to bring back some of his army here to Castle Forks. The third key went on that voyage, carried by a Caretaker who was kin to me. On the return journey, the ships were besieged by the Tourlt, and one of them was lost entirely—along with the Caretaker and his key."

"It has never been found to our knowledge," said Si.

"But doesn't that mean it could have fallen into the wrong hands? I mean, like into the hands of the Tourlt?" Chris asked.

"Smart lad," Thungor said approvingly.

"Yes," Novell said. "It may be lying innocently at the bottom of the ocean, or it may, as thou say, have fallen into the wrong hands."

Todd stood up from his chair suddenly and paced a few yards. "I'm beginning to see where this is going," he said. "You need us to... to find this key or something like that?"

"No, not exactly," Novell said slowly. "But I will not deceive thee, and I will not try thy patience any longer. We do need thy help, as I have said. But it is not to go looking for anything. Rather, I believe we are going to need thy help here, defending Castle Forks."

"We do not know exactly when," said Si. "It could be a day, a week, a year from now. But we do know that the Tourlt are stirring again and that Banlin still lives—"

"Banlin?" Todd said sharply. "That's a new name. I mean, it's true we've heard a lot of unusual names today, but I'm pretty sure that's a new one. Who is this Banlin?"

Si darted a guilty look at Novell. Chris recognized that look— he had made it himself in the past. It meant Si had just let something slip that he wasn't supposed to and that his father was going to be annoyed about it.

Novell's calm expression didn't change though. "Banlin is my brother," he said. "*Was* my brother. He is no one's brother any longer. He is one of the Tourlt, and it is believed that he is also a Seer, one with the second sight. This means he is the most dangerous and powerful of them all. He retreated into hiding after the Last Battle for the Forks. We had hoped…"

Novell's voice trailed off, and he had a faraway look in his eyes for a moment. Chris thought he looked very sad, but Novell shook it off quickly.

"We had hoped he would not return," Novell said simply. "But he is in the process of gathering his forces again. I do not know what he is planning or when it will happen, but I know that a battle is coming. And I know that it cannot be won without the Cochranes."

Novell stood up from his chair and walked over to face Todd. He spoke in a sympathetic tone of voice. "I am sorry that some of the choices have already been taken from thee," Novell said. "In the usual course of events, thou would have been able to pass this information onto thy sons in thy own time. Chris, too, would have been given the choice about whether he wanted to come here, as would thy elder son, Justin. But this is not the usual course of events. For centuries, we have kept the Tourlt at bay, and there has been relative safety. But they are once again a direct threat to Castle Forks—which means a direct threat to everything as thou know it."

"I don't know," Todd said, looking suddenly very tired. "My son is only twelve. Surely he's too young for this kind of thing."

"If I might interrupt for a moment, good sir?" said Whitethorn. "It's true that in your world, twelve is young to be a warrior, but it's not the case 'ere. Our people 'ave a special ritual that brings young men of your son's age into the rank of warrior."

"Will Valkyn be doing the ritual?" Chris asked.

Whitethorn shook his head. "He's one of the only kids who isn't takin' part. Valkyn's true passion lies with skatin', so he's off to compete in a few competitions."

Todd scoffed. "Like any child should at that age!"

"Every other young one of twelve will be taking part in the ritual," Thungor explained. "That's why it's difficult for us to understand that your young man wouldn't be willing and able to fight."

"However, we do understand the differences between thy world and this one, and we know that it is difficult," added Novell.

Silence fell on the group. Chris could tell his dad was struggling to figure out how to respond.

For his own part, Chris felt a bit insulted about the discussion happening as if he wasn't even there.

Impulsively, Chris spoke up. "Dad," he said. "I want to help. I want to fight...or whatever is needed. I know I can do it. I'm not a fan of hunting innocent animals in our world. I do it because we need to eat, but I really like the sound of putting my skills to a good cause here."

Todd looked sharply at his son, frowning. But before Todd could speak, Si eagerly jumped in. "He has already learned to use guns, and we have observed that he is efficient with your hunting rifle," said Si. "He is a good marksman."

"And he's not afraid to shoot his mark," Whitethorn added quickly. "I've noticed that, which is good because in this fight, he'll have to aim and fire, not just at wildlife but at the Tourlt themselves."

Chris felt a surge of pride hearing his hunting skills described this way, but his dad was not so pleased.

"Look," said Todd. "I just don't like it. Maybe...maybe I can help you...but not Chris."

His dad was speaking in a tone now that told Chris he shouldn't argue. It was final. Chris felt disappointed and kind of sulky. He sank back into his chair and stared sullenly at the flagstone floor.

"You don't understand, Criffer Bob," Todd said in a gentler tone. "You have no idea what fighting in war does. You don't understand the impact it has on people."

Novell's calm, powerful voice chimed in at this moment. "It is true," he said to Todd. "It is true that in the world thou know, there can be a great deal of trouble later for those who fight. It can weigh heavy on the mind. But our purpose is just, and thou must understand something—the Tourlt are not a human enemy. They are corrupted creatures whose only purpose is to serve evil."

Todd wasn't convinced. "That may be true. But that doesn't make me feel better. If they aren't even human, how can my twelve-year-old son be expected to fight them and win?"

Before anyone could answer that question, Chris jumped in. He couldn't stop himself. "If they aren't human, then what exactly are they? You said they're *Demon Shadows*, but what does that look like?"

Novell and Si looked at each other for a moment. They were obviously communicating something, but only they knew what it was. Si gave a short quick nod. When Novell looked back at Chris, his brown eyes were bright and piercing, almost glowing with a golden light.

"Instead of telling thee, I will show thee," he said.

CHAPTER 5

Si passed around a bowl of bright red berries that Chris recognized from the trees around his home in the physical world.

"Are they edible?" Chris asked, taking one and rolling it between his finger and thumb. "I've only ever seen birds eat them."

Si nodded. "Yes, they are edible but also magical. As well as their impressive health benefits, these enchanted ones will act as a window to the past."

Todd frowned. "What does that mean?"

Thungor chuckled and said, "It's about to blow your minds. It still amazes me!"

Novell smiled. "Thou will see. On the count of three, we shall all eat our berries and close our eyes."

Chris and Todd nodded and waited for the countdown.

"One...two...three," Si counted, and Chris watched everyone chew their berries and close their eyes.

Chris snapped his eyes shut at the last minute. The room fell away. The Hall of Heroes wobbled and faded, and Chris felt a chill wind rise up, blowing all around them. He stood on a fragment of the flagstone floor, but everything around had become a dark void, almost empty of light. Disoriented, he looked around frantically for his father.

Across an abyss of darkness, he saw his father standing on a similar fragment of the stone floor, apparently floating in midair. Whitethorn, Thungor, Novell, and Si were still there too, each standing on his own separate slab of stone.

Out of the darkness, a spiral of red and green light emerged. Before Chris could gather his wits enough to call out to his dad, the spiral of light exploded into fragments, and the darkness was replaced by a warm golden light. The light filled Chris with a feeling of peace. His fear retreated.

Then Chris heard Novell's voice, but it didn't seem to be coming from Novell. It was as though Novell was speaking quietly inside his own mind.

"Do not fear," said Novell. "Thou are safe. What thou see has already happened and will not happen again, and we are not a part of it nor can we change it. This is the story of Jerg, the first of the Fallen, the first of the Tourlt. The world had never known war until Jerg came. It had known only peace."

As Novell spoke, the light around them flickered, wavered, and materialized into another setting.

They were now standing in the courtyard of Castle Forks, the same courtyard Todd and Chris had entered just hours ago. It was bustling with Caretakers of all ages, laughing, talking, and playing. Many of them were carrying baskets of flowers, fruits, and vegetables as they crossed the busy courtyard.

"We are a mere breeze to those of the past," said Novell. "They cannot see or hear us. Ah, here comes Candar."

A powerful-looking Caretaker with golden hair entered through one of the arched doorways at that moment. His resemblance to Novell and Si was noticeable, but this Caretaker was even taller than his descendants, and his face was smooth and serene. By comparison, Chris thought, Si had more of a frowning face, and Novell's face was more serious. Candar seemed completely free of worry.

At this moment, Candar was laughing at something that had just been said to him. He was walking with a young-looking giant with red hair and a very stout woman who looked related to Whitethorn.

She wore a simple brown tunic of rough cotton and carried a basket overflowing with ripe red tomatoes. Her large leathery feet were bare.

"Yes, Valleria," Candar was saying to the Kiern woman. "You have outdone yourself with the tomatoes this year. We'll have fresh for the next three months and enough to preserve for the next year."

"Hmph," said Valleria gruffly. "Try the next three years if I have any say in it. Just make sure I have the right help when canning time comes. Don't send me any of your daydreamers!" She shot a look up at the red-haired giant beside her.

"Me?" said the giant, offended. "Madame Valleria, I only let that pot boil over last year because I was too busy helping everyone who needed me to get things down from the high shelves. A giant's work is never done!"

"Hmph! Well, at least you're helpful, Dandok. That's a lesson your brother could use, Candar."

"Yes, I notice Jerg has been avoiding his duties of late," said Candar, no longer laughing.

"It's worse than that," Valleria said bluntly. "He's sabotaging other people's work too. The other day, I found him slipping a toxic herb into a batch of wound balm I was making. If I hadn't discovered it and the balm had been applied to a human or to a giant or Kiern injury, it would have caused infection and decay. Limbs could have been lost, maybe even lives."

"This is a very serious charge, Valleria," said Candar. "You suggest that Jerg wishes harm to others? This is the opposite of what we Caretakers wish. It is counter to our purpose."

"Exactly," said Valleria quietly. "I know it's painful to hear, but you know as I do that it's the truth."

Candar sighed. "I do know my younger brother is not...as I had hoped he would be."

Dandok shyly interrupted. "Candar, sir, if I may, I wanted to tell you something as well."

"Yes?" Candar looked up at the young giant, fixing him with a serious stare.

"Well," stammered Dandok. "I saw...the other day, I saw... your brother was laughing at a young Kiern boy who had fallen from the pillar, there." He walked over to the support pillar and indicated how far the boy had fallen. "It was several feet, and the boy's ankle was broken."

"He's fine now," added Valleria. "The boy was fixed up, and his ankle will mend. But Dandok's story is true, I'm afraid. Instead of helping the boy, the moment he was hurt, instead of offering comfort, Jerg mocked the boy and laughed at him. It was Dandok who picked up the child and carried him to the infirmary."

"Valleria, my dear friend," said Candar, "I don't have to tell you how troubling this is. I have long feared that Jerg was…different. He does not have compassion and care as he should. Instead of helping others, he prefers to see them suffer. I do not know of any Caretaker that has ever been this way. I do not know what to do."

"Well, one thing is certain," said Valleria. "He cannot be named as your successor to Castle Forks."

Candar nodded gravely. "I know."

At that moment, the scenery around Chris began to waver and flicker once again. As the courtyard dissolved, it was replaced by what appeared to be a throne room. It was a very humble room, almost completely bare of furnishings. A long golden rug ran from one end to the other, beginning at the heavy oaken doors and ending at the foot of a simple wooden throne, which was situated on a low platform. The stone walls of the room were sparsely decorated, holding just a few flaming swords and shields. Chris and his friends were standing midway between the entrance and the throne, beneath the room's single large window.

Candar sat alone on his humble wooden throne, bathed in the light that poured in through the window. The sunlight dappled the tips of his bright folded wings, making them glitter like gold. He sat very upright, with his elbows resting on the arms of the throne and the fingertips of each hand pressed together in a steeple shape. He was sunk deep in thought, gazing quietly at his hands.

The heavy oak doors swung open, and a Caretaker entered. His face was unlike any Caretaker face Chris had seen yet; it was dark, twisted, and devoid of light whereas Si, Novell, and the others all had a bright inner light shining upward from underneath their skin. This

Caretaker seemed to suck all the light out of the very air around him. He was like a shadow, casting another shadow of itself in a world without a sun. Chris did not need to be told his name. This was Jerg.

Jerg strode quickly down the long golden rug and stood in front of his brother. "Candar," he rasped. His voice came out low and growling, without any of the music or gentleness of Candar's voice. "Today you will tell me. When will you name me as your successor? When will I be the Caretaker of Castle Forks?"

Candar slowly raised his eyes from their meditative gaze. For a long moment, he gazed into the dark eyes of his brother. Finally he said, "You know the answer to this, my brother. You have written this answer yourself. A Caretaker of Castle Forks must care for humanity and all other beings. A Caretaker of Castle Forks must protect others from harm, not do harm. He must forsake envy and the desire for personal power. You are envious. You desire personal power. You harm others and do not protect. You are no Caretaker of Castle Forks, and you will never be its keeper."

In one swift movement, Jerg reached back between his wings, drawing his flaming sword, and lunged at Candar. In a movement that was even swifter, Candar crossed his forearms to block the flaming sword, then knocked the sword from Jerg's hand with his right arm. He pinned Jerg to the ground in front of the throne.

Jerg's look of bitter hatred met Candar's look of grief and pity.

"You are a Seer," Jerg spat angrily. "You knew what I would do. That is the only reason I am here now, pinned to the ground, at your mercy. Release me or kill me. I do not want your mercy!"

"But mercy is all I have," said Candar quietly. He released his grip on Jerg and stood up. "And you will not be killed. You are banished from Castle Forks forever."

With a hideous laugh, Jerg gathered himself and stood up. "You will regret your mercy," he rasped, leaning close to Candar's face. "For I am not your only enemy."

As he turned toward the door, Jerg unfolded the giant wings from his back. As the wings opened, their brown feathers began to shed and morph into something else. The soft feathers were replaced by leathery opaque wings, like the wings of a bat.

As Jerg spun around in front of them on his monstrous new wings, Chris almost forgot that Jerg couldn't see them. For one horrible moment, Chris saw into the monster's eyes at close range. They were the eyes of a demon: dark, poisonous green and red, with no whites left at all, and full of burning hatred.

Swooping out of the throne room, Jerg screamed to his companions, "Now come, all who would leave with me! You who would not be prisoners of Castle Forks! You who would rather rule than serve! Come with me and forsake your bondage!"

A terrible flapping sound arose all at once, like a sudden windstorm sweeping through the castle.

Candar strode to the open door and stepped onto the balcony overlooking the central courtyard of the Forks. "You will live forever among the shadows!" he cried as a mob of fallen Caretakers swept into the courtyard on their new featherless wings. There were maybe two dozen who chose to follow Jerg. Their dark leathery wings flapped and fluttered ominously as they flew into formation behind him.

"You will wander the world and forever be afraid of the light!" Candar's booming voice thundered after them. "The sun's rays will be your torment and bring your death. You will be trapped by the sun and by your own shame. You do not escape bondage. You will live forever in bondage!"

The scenery began to flicker and waver again. As their location changed, Chris heard Novell's voice, reciting these words: "The Tourlt would live in the shadows, trapped by the rays of sunlight. The sun would burn their skin, so they would stay hidden. They would only be able to come out of the shadows at the last fading light of day, and with the sunrise, they would have to return. Those who chose to follow Jerg and give up the life of a Caretaker would forever mark themselves as a sign of their betrayal. With white-hot iron, they branded dark symbols into the skin of the face, arms, and torso. Their brown irises turned to a dark, murky green, and the whites of their eyes became red because of their hatred for the light in the world. Their bright feathery wings became dark and leathery, like the wings of a bat."

By the end of Novell's speech, the scene had resolved itself once again. This time, they were standing outside the front gate of Castle Forks. An army of hundreds was arrayed in a defensive formation along the castle walls and in front of the gate. There were Caretakers, giants, and humans in their various battle armor, all standing with swords and axes in hand. Archers with their bows at the ready were strategically arranged along the wall of the castle. The scene was eerily quiet. Although there were hundreds of soldiers prepared to fight, no one spoke. They stood like statues, watching the sun's slow descent behind the mountain.

"The Dark Skirmishes of Windy Nip Glen," Novell whispered in the silence of the hall.

As Novell's words faded into the still air, the sun took its final dip behind the mountain. In the last rays of fading light, Chris saw something that took his breath away.

Over the brow of the mountain came a dark army, swarming over the ridge like a plague of locusts. Some were on foot, some rode skeletal horses, and some flew above the others on their giant bat-like wings. The earth rumbled, and the still air was shattered by the terrible flapping sound. Their wings blotted out the light from the early evening stars as they grew closer. *The Demon Shadows*, Chris thought to himself in horror.

As the Tourlt made their steady approach, the silent defenders of Castle Forks swallowed their fear and raised their weapons.

CHAPTER 6

Chris and his dad watched in helpless fascination as the age-old battle played out all around them.

Storms of arrows descended from the walls and towers of the castle. In the open field, giants bludgeoned the Tourlt army with clubs and fists. Both sides were fully engaged in bloody sword fights and hand-to-hand combat with knives and axes. Screams of soldiers facing their doom and new blood being drawn fueled the fury on both sides.

Chris had seen similar things in films, but that was nothing compared to being on the battlefield. He felt a little sick as he watched the fighting but did his best to shove down the feeling. He didn't want his dad to be concerned about him or to think he wasn't ready for this kind of thing. Chris was determined to be as brave and calm as possible and to observe the mechanics of the battle. This could be very educational after all.

"The fighting went on through the night," said Novell. "But I will not make thou watch every moment of it. However, there are one or two more things that I would like thee to see."

Suddenly, it seemed as though Novell had hit a fast forward button on this strange memory playback of his. The scene around them sped up and became a blur. When the details became clear again, it was terrible.

The ground and the walls of the castle were strewn with the dead of both sides.

Among the bodies of humans, giants, and Caretakers lay many bodies of the Tourlt as well, their leathery wings broken and smoldering as if in the aftermath of a fire.

Among the dead and wounded, the battle continued. The defenders of Castle Forks were much fewer in number, but they were still holding their own against the enemy. It was clear that the Tourlt had not managed to overtake the castle.

The sun was just beginning to rise. As the first light of day came up over the mountain, a very strange thing happened. The Tourlt made a sudden and hasty retreat, some of them taking to flight or riding quickly away. Many of them seemed to simply disappear into thin air. It was impossible to tell where they went, impossible to trace the path of their retreat. Within moments of the sun's first flickering light, they were all simply gone.

"Charles Christopher Cochrane, the elder brother of Thomas Cochrane, led this first stand against the Tourlt, side by side with his parents," Novell told them. "Sadly, both parents were killed in the Dark Skirmishes, but Charles survived. The death toll on both sides was great, but Charles prevailed. He maintained his defenses for several days and prevented the Tourlt from overtaking the castle walls. They could not get through his defenses."

"Charles and his people spent the second day removing their fallen brethren as well as the wounded that needed to be tended to," continued Novell. "But they would not have time for a break. The Tourlt appeared again at the fading light of the day, catching the host army nearly off guard. Charles scrambled to gather his forces to confront the return of the opposing force.

"The enemy kept up their onslaught. They left again at sunrise and returned the next day. Several days of this was starting to take a toll on the people at Castle Forks. They would have only a few hours to collect the fallen, tend to their wounded, then prepare for the returning enemy. The home army was nearly overrun on the fifth day by the impending force. Yet the enemy did not manage to break through our defenses and overtake the castle. And that is when your ancestor Thomas arrived, just in time for the final defense of Castle Forks."

As Novell spoke these words, the scene flickered once more. In the next moment, they were standing on top of the highest part of the castle wall. Below them was the interior courtyard. From this new vantage point, they could see inside the castle as well as outside.

The flowers in the courtyard were gone and replaced with soldiers. Every square inch of the wall and towers was filled with soldiers and archers. The army stretched out in front of the castle gate in ranks that reached nearly a quarter of a mile into Windy Nip Glen.

Something was different about this army of soldiers from that in the last battle. While there were still many Caretakers and giants, there were hundreds more human soldiers than there had been before. Their shields and breastplates were adorned with the Cochrane insignia. A flag bearing the same symbol flapped in the breeze from the highest guard tower.

Standing at the top of the wall just to their left was a group of four commanders, deeply engaged in conversation. Two of them were wearing the Cochrane armor with their visors off, so their faces were visible.

Chris was struck by their physical resemblance to his dad and his older brother Justin.

Both men were of strong, slender build and slightly above-average height. They had the same straight medium-brown hair and even features with dark-brown eyes.

"Those are thy ancestors, Thomas and his older brother Charles," announced Novell. "Thomas is the slightly taller one. He has just arrived with his army from Scotland, where Castle Cochrane tragically was taken by the Tourlt. Castle Forks is now the last barrier of defense against the Tourlt, the only thing keeping them from completely overtaking your world."

Thomas and Charles were talking earnestly with a Caretaker and a brawny ginger-bearded man. The Caretaker had the same build and face as Novell, minus the facial scars and white hair. His long hair was a light-colored brown that glowed in the sunlight.

"Is that you, Novell?" Chris asked.

"Yes, that was me," Novell said. "And that is Sun Shadow beside me," he added.

A tall, broad-shouldered, and barrel-chested figure stood next to Novell. His size and his bushy ginger beard gave him away as one of the Kiern. He wielded a large club in one hand. He also had something slung over his shoulder that looked like a deer antler but not like any antler Chris had seen before. It was of the deepest black and shined as if it had been carefully polished.

"That's the 'orn of Unity over his shoulder, lad," Whitethorn said gruffly. "This 'orn 'as 'elped create an alliance between the Caretakers and my people, the Kiern. Sun Shadow was my grandfather's grandfather, and he 'arvested the antler from a dying black stag. Once blown, the sound of the 'orn calls all the 'airy People to honor their alliance."

"The horn was instrumental in the Battle for the Forks," said Novell. "Once heard, each member of the Kiern repeats the call in every direction, notifying all Kiern within hundreds, even thousands of miles away. Their call can sound like a shriek, a caw, or a scream in a variety of tones. If thou have heard any sound like that before, then thou have heard one of the Kiern."

"You may 'ave even 'eard me makin' the screechin' call," added Whitethorn. "I 'ave spent my entire life on this very mountain. The Battle for the Forks was the last time my people stood alongside the Caretakers and giants in such large numbers."

"Yes, it is true," said Novell. "The Kiern made a huge sacrifice in defending the Forks. They still exist to this day, but sadly their numbers were nearly wiped out in the last stand against the Tourlt... in the final surprise attack which was spearheaded by my former brother, Banlin."

Novell spoke his brother's name with bitterness, and a look of great sadness crossed his face once again.

"Thou might refer to the Kiern as a legend now as their numbers are spread out and only a few hundred exist to this day," continued Novell. "They rarely come into contact with other peoples. With the exception of Whitethorn and a few dozen of his closest friends and family, most feel their alliance was fulfilled during the Battle for the Forks. Understandably, they prefer to live among themselves with little contact from the outside world. So we try to respect their wishes for solitude."

"But the 'orn of Unity still has the power to call the Kiern," said Whitethorn. "We are an honorable people to the last, and I'm sure my brethren would return if the time came."

Chris turned to the vision. At that moment, Sun Shadow took up the horn and blew it. Three short blasts erupted from the horn and echoed through the valley. Within a few seconds, a reply came in the form of several screeching cries that seemed to come from all directions.

Sun Shadow turned to Novell's past self and said, "Reinforcements from my people will be here by tomorrow morning. Let's hope they get here in time."

"The enemy is not far off," said the younger Novell. They could hear the sound of war drums beating in the distance.

"With my brother's reinforcements, we'll hold them off until the Kiern arrive," Charles said fiercely.

"My few remaining men are weary, it's true, but their determination is undimmed."

"They've reached the outer settlements," said Sun Shadow, pointing down at the river.

Along with everyone else, Chris turned his head in the direction of Sun Shadow's gesture. The winding river, clearly visible from their high vantage point, was slowly turning from a clear blue to a crimson red.

"Is that...what I think it is?" Chris heard his dad ask with a slight tremble in his voice.

"Yes," said Si. "Blood. The blood of the villagers."

Chris watched as Thomas directed a question to the young Novell. "How many were in the villages?"

"No more than a few dozen able-bodied folk who could wield a weapon. The rest were children and elders who had lived too many seasons to fight. We could not spare..." Here, the young Novell's voice cracked with grief. "We could not...spare any soldiers to defend the settlements, I am afraid. They are surely destroyed now, beyond hope."

"Do not blame yourself," said Thomas quietly. "We are serving an even greater purpose, one that will save millions more than those who were in the villages."

The drums continued beating more and more loudly as the enemy approached.

Within minutes, the Tourlt ranks began to swell over the mountaintop. This time, there were even more of them than had attacked Windy Nip Glen. Just as before, they swarmed in a dark wave over the mountain, many of them in flight and just as many riding or on foot. The hideous sound of their flapping wings and the steady beat of their war drums filled the air.

"I thought it was horrible last time," Todd whispered in a tone of wonder. "There must be twice as many of them now."

"Yes," agreed Si bitterly. "Now they are joined by Banlin and his fighters as well."

It was almost impossible to distinguish an individual Tourlt soldier from the oncoming horde. The army had reached full strength. The closer they got, the more the ground shook, and the castle walls began to shake as well.

The two facing armies were nearly within striking distance of one another. Suddenly, the air was shattered by several ear-piercing shrieks that came from all directions.

The shrieking was a familiar sound to Chris now. "The Kiern must be coming!" he exclaimed, as a warm surge of hope cut through the cold feeling that the Tourlt army created in his chest. Even though he'd already known that Whitethorn's people were on their way, Chris was relieved to hear their calls.

"Look to the trees," said Novell, pointing toward the stands of forest that surrounded three sides of the bald mountaintop.

A sudden wave of movement shuddered through all the trees and brush at once, as if a strong steady wind had blown through them, but there was no breeze. In the next moment, the mountaintop was swarming with another army. This time, it was the Kiern.

There must have been thousands of them, emerging from the forest not even half a mile behind the Tourlt hordes.

Then he appeared, a creature whose appearance chilled Chris to the bone. Emerging at the front of the swarm of Tourlt came a man who was not quite one of them but not a Caretaker either. He had long flowing brown hair, like Si. His features were similar to Novell's, and the wings folded over his shoulders were soft and feathery still, like one of the Caretakers. But his eyes burned with the red hue of the Tourlt.

"Who is that?" Chris asked, but in his heart, he already knew the answer.

"That was Banlin—my kin, my brother. My other me," Novell replied.

Banlin uttered a loud terrible war cry as he drew his flaming sword. It was not the kind of sound a Caretaker would make. It was a cry of bloodthirsty rage, like the scream of one of the Tourlt. The sound roused his army to a frenzy. They erupted in anticipation of the battle. They were horribly eager to fight.

"They've come to destroy Castle Forks, just like their kind has destroyed Castle Cochrane," Thomas said bitterly to his brother.

"But they will not succeed," Charles replied with determination.

The younger Novell turned back toward the courtyard and raised an arm with an open hand. The enemy erupted into another furious war cry. Large contraptions emerged from the shadows of the Tourlt army as they began mobilizing giant catapults and siege towers.

Banlin waved his flaming sword in the air. The fighting was about to begin. Novell and Sun Shadow raised their arms in unison. All bows were fully drawn as the archers waited for the signal to release their arrows. A handful of Kiern stood at the ready within the courtyard behind piles of large boulders. On the mountaintop, the full Kiern army was continuing to emerge from the trees. Their front ranks were steadily closing the distance between the back line of the Tourlt army, but the Tourlt still seemed unaware of their presence. At the castle, the war drums and battle cries had come to a sudden stop.

There was an eerie silence, an air of complete focus as soldiers on both sides waited for their generals' commands to begin the attack.

A solitary man's scream pierced the stillness. All eyes within the castle gates followed the sound of the scream to a high corner of the wall, where a soldier was falling, having been knocked from his post by something. It was not clear what had hit him. Then there was another scream from the opposite corner, and another soldier plummeted to his death. Yet another soldier cried out in pain and slumped to the ground. The third soldier wasn't stationed on one of the walls but had been well within the protected courtyard of Castle Forks.

"They must have gotten inside!" exclaimed Chris. "But where are they?"

Charles Cochrane was dashing down the stairs to where the third soldier had fallen, near the armory door. He had nearly reached the fallen soldier when a sword came out of nowhere, stabbing at his shoulder. As Charles ducked the attack and drew his own sword, the twang of an arrow being released from its bow could be heard. The arrow flew across the courtyard and found its mark. There was a shriek of pain from the unseen assailant and then a heavy thud as a body fell to the ground.

"Novell, how is that possible? How can they be using invisibility?" Chris asked. "And if the Tourlt can be invisible, does that mean the Caretakers have this power too?"

Novell shook his head gravely. "No, Chris, a true warrior does not need to hide himself to fight his battles."

"But they did it!" Chris protested.

"It is not honorable," said Novell. "The Caretakers are already fighting a battle that cannot be seen by the physical world. We refuse to fight unseen in an unseen battle. This is not our purpose."

"Yes, but shouldn't a person use their strengths and exploit their enemies' weaknesses in a fight?" Chris argued.

"It is not done," said Novell firmly. Chris said no more but returned his attention to the battle.

From across the courtyard, Thomas Cochrane saw his brother suddenly fall into the armory door.

With lightning speed, Thomas grabbed an arrow from his quiver and locked it onto his bow, pulling back and letting it fly all in one smooth motion. As the arrow arced across the courtyard, a sword appeared out of thin air and plunged into Charles's shoulder a second time. Thomas sprinted over and pulled the sword from his brother's shoulder, tossing it to the side.

"Thanks, brother," said Charles. "Now I just need bandaging, and I'll be fine to soldier on."

Thomas laughed at that, then let out a loud whistle. Two soldiers carrying black satchels appeared and quickly began to dress Charles's wounded shoulder.

Thomas looked around to see where his arrow had landed. It was hanging point down, about six inches off the ground in what appeared to be midair. Thomas placed both hands around the arrow and felt down along the length of it toward the arrowhead. Then his palms went flat, and he moved his hands over what appeared to be nothing at all. After a moment, his fingers curled around something, and he pulled upward with all his might. Suddenly, he held a bloody helmet in his hands, and a body materialized on the ground. It was pierced through the throat with Thomas's arrow, which must have hit a main artery. The dead Tourlt was drenched in blood. Its red eyes stared out of its heavily scarred and tattooed face.

"Cowards!" Thomas muttered. He spat at the ground where his enemy lay dead and then sprinted back up to his position on the wall, drawing an arrow from his quiver as he ran.

The bombardment commenced. The younger Novell and Sun Shadow raised their hands in unison and then thrust them down. The archers released arrow after arrow into the moonlight. The Kiern began lifting their massive boulders and launching them over the wall onto the enemy. The air was filled with thuds and screams and all the other dreadful sounds of battle.

Banlin swooped into the air above his army and began shouting commands down at them. His orders were impossible for Chris to understand, as they were spoken in some harsh, unfamiliar language. Like a terrible bat, Banlin swooped here and there over and among his ranks, issuing commands. The Tourlt began firing their own catapults and arrows as well. It was mayhem, a chaos of arrows and boulders and blades.

Outside the heavily defended walls of the castle, forces were falling on both sides. Many of the Tourlt were knocked out of the sky by arrows and boulders and fell to the ground, either wounded or dying. But for as many that fell, more kept coming.

Chris wondered how long the invisible soldiers had been present inside the castle and what kind of information they'd gathered. Were they able to relay messages to Banlin and his army? And just how many of them were there inside? It was impossible to tell.

Banlin must have retained some of his honor as a former Caretaker, Chris thought, because at least he was facing his former brethren face-to-face without using the invisibility.

A loud snap sounded overhead. The great Cochrane flag that had flown from the highest tower had been snapped off its post and thrown out over the wall of the castle. Another invisible soldier was inside! That must have been some kind of signal for the enemy because their ranks erupted with cheers. Banlin shouted a command, and his forces surged in a new charge.

The Castle Forks defenders in front of the wall were fewer in number now, and the Tourlt had just enough of an opening to close the distance to the castle wall. Their siege towers were getting closer. They managed to prop several tall ladders against the wall and began to swarm over the top of it.

"That's clever," Todd observed. "When they just use their wings to fly over the wall, your archers pick them off more easily. Swarming the wall this way makes it harder for the archers."

Now the wall was engulfed with soldiers on both sides. There were swords, spears, clubs, and shields banging and clanging, spraying blood and sweat into the air. Soldiers were dropping like flies as the enemy swarmed over the castle wall. Reinforcements sprinted up the stairways, attempting to fill the void of their fallen brethren.

The warriors inside the courtyard were maintaining their defense somehow. The Tourlt who managed to escape the archers and make it all the way over the wall were being slain at a steady pace.

Sun Shadow and Novell were fighting two, three, four, and five at a time. Chris's attention was riveted on the young Novell, who moved so fast it was incredible. Novell was always just one step ahead of his foe, almost as if he could predict their next move and prevent it before they had a chance to strike.

It reminded Chris of how Candar had evaded his brother Jerg's attack in the throne room, and Chris began to suspect that Novell was also a Seer.

Sun Shadow's fighting style was a little different than Novell's but equally effective. He overpowered his foes with brute force and incredible rage.

Were they afraid of him? It sure looked like they were, Chris thought. The Tourlt soldiers were no match for Sun Shadow. He dropped his foes like he was picking daisies. There were so many of them, but he easily bested each of their advances. Chris watched in amazement as Sun Shadow took out five of his assailants with a single swing of his huge club. In the split second before those five were replaced with new foes, Sun Shadow put the Horn of Unity to his lips and blew it once more.

Novell followed the call with another loud whoop. There were two loud shrieks in response, one after the other. And then, the surprise attack of the Kiern was on.

Chris returned his attention to what was going on outside the castle wall.

The Kiern had stealthily surrounded the enemy from behind. Now fresh volleys of arrows and boulders were raining down on the Tourlt from all sides. Flying boulders filled the night sky. Even larger rocks and boulders came rolling down the mountainside, crushing the enemy in their path.

Just when it seemed that this new dual bombardment was going to force the Tourlt to retreat, Banlin charged into the courtyard. Chris watched in wonder as he leaped over the wall effortlessly and began slaying everyone in his path. Three, four, five, six soldiers engaged Banlin, but they were no match for him. He fought just like Novell. No foe could touch him. He seemed to know where they were going to attack before they even knew themselves, so they were dead before they could lift their weapons to strike.

Then Banlin charged at Novell. He leaped high into the sky, drawing back his flaming sword in preparation to strike. Novell was fighting seven foes, so occupied by the mayhem that he didn't notice Banlin. As Banlin surged down from above, he struck his brother with all his might.

The flaming sword cut into Novell just below his left eye and continued in a steady slash all the way down to his left wrist.

"He nearly split you in two pieces." Todd gasped.

Banlin stood over Novell and smirked at the sight of his former kin, now wounded on the ground.

Novell was too injured to stand, but he met Banlin's gaze without fear. "I did not expect to see thou leading the charge, Banlin," said Novell in a tone of perfect calm. "Although I should not be surprised that thou have joined with Jerg. I had hoped for better."

Chris couldn't believe Novell was even conscious after that injury, much less able to speak without screaming.

"And I had hoped for better from you than this sneak attack of yours!" Banlin replied. "What are these, these *hairy, loathsome monsters* of the woods who crept up behind us?"

"Those are the Kiern, of course," said Novell.

"Not as peaceful as they once were, eh? Filthy sneaks!" Banlin spat.

"Watch thyself, Banlin," Novell snapped. "It is incredible thou would find our tactics lacking in honor when thou thyself have sent invisible spies among us. At least the Kiern fight face-to-face with courage."

By the end of this speech, Novell's strength was beginning to fade. With his right hand, he was twisting the fabric of his tunic into a very rough tourniquet near the top of his left arm. It staunched the flow of blood slightly, but he was unable to stand.

Banlin paced the ground in front of Novell, showing no pity for his brother's suffering. "You think this surprise attack will keep us from occupying the castle," he said. "But it won't. We will find our way in somehow, but I am not sure you will be alive to see my victory."

Novell met Banlin's gaze directly, no trace of fear showing in his face.

"Well, do thou plan to finish the job?" he asked. "Is that not what Jerg sent thee here to do?"

In reply, Banlin lifted his sword in both hands and aimed the tip of it at Novell's chest. But just before he could strike, a terrible shiver overtook his body. The sun was beginning to rise. Banlin looked at the horizon once and then back at Novell.

"I'll be back, brother" was all he said. Then Banlin vanished, along with the rest of his army.

CHAPTER 7

T he sun was up, and the enemy was gone. The ground was littered with dead and wounded. Those who were still on their feet tended to their fallen brethren, administering what aid and comfort they could. A group of Caretakers who carried black satchels moved carefully among the wounded, issuing instructions to the surviving soldiers as to how they could assist.

"Those Caretakers with the black bags, are they like paramedics?" Chris asked.

Thungor nodded. "Indeed. They're healers. And they've a few tricks up their sleeve that your paramedics don't."

"Fortunately, for me, that is true," Novell said. "Otherwise, I would not have survived. As it was, my wound was too severe to heal entirely. It remains a live scar, which does not threaten my life but still causes pain."

"I have a question," Todd said. "It sounded like, just now, that your brother—I mean, Banlin—didn't recognize the Kiern at first. Why was he so surprised that they came to your aid? I mean, haven't the Caretakers and the Kiern always been allies?"

"It is true that we were always friends," said Si. "But the Kiern were not always warriors. In the long-ago days before Jerg betrayed Candar, before the Tourlt existed, the Kiern were farmers, hunters, and gatherers. They lived peaceably, caring for the land. But once the

Demon Shadows became a threat to the world, the Kiern began to adapt."

"Yes," Novell agreed. "And because of their natural physical strength, they evolved to be strong fighters and defenders of Castle Forks. All this happened quietly and almost in secret. The Tourlt did not know of the Kiern's transformation."

"You see, lad, we Kiern were the secret weapon," said Whitethorn with satisfaction. "We were the fightin' force that even Jerg and his 'enchman Banlin never knew about."

"Without the Kiern, Banlin would no doubt have occupied Castle Forks that day," said Novell. "But as thou see, their forces were terribly diminished. However, they were not retreating for good. We knew the Tourlt would return the next day. And we knew that when they did, we needed something more—another secret weapon."

As Novell finished speaking, the scenery around them flickered and shifted once again.

This time, they found themselves in a private bedroom. The younger wounded Novell was lying in bed, propped up on pillows with bandages wrapped around his head and nearly half of his body. In spite of the bandages, he looked strong and healthy. Standing at the room's single window was Sun Shadow.

"So he must have joined with Jerg sometime recently," Sun Shadow was saying.

"Yes, he is not full Tourlt yet," said the young Novell. "Thou saw that? His eyes and wings were not completely transformed."

"Even half formed, he is more powerful than any of the others," said Sun Shadow. He turned away from the window and, gesturing toward Novell's bandages, added, "I know I don't have to tell you that."

"It is true. It appears that Banlin is a Seer, unlike Jerg. One must admit, I was not sure if he was a Seer before…he left," Novell trailed off, gazing into the distance with a puzzled frown. "I wondered all these years whether he had turned out to have the gift," he went on after a moment. Novell shook his head. "I really did not think he had it when we were younger. But thou saw him fight. It must be the case. And with Banlin on his side, Jerg will be more powerful than ever."

"And they will be back soon enough to continue the siege," said Sun Shadow grimly. "We'll be seeing them again at sundown."

Sun Shadow walked toward Novell's bed and sat down heavily in a nearby chair. He appeared to have emerged from the battle without any injuries but was obviously very tired.

"Thy people have fought bravely," Novell said. "We would never have been able to resist the last attack without thee."

"It is as much our duty to defend the Forks as it is yours," Sun Shadow replied. "For the sake of all our people, this castle must never fall to the Tourlt. It must never be occupied by these...*demons*. Unfortunately, so many of my people have fallen. And our secret weapon is no longer secret. I don't know how many more nights of this we'll be able to hold off."

"I understand," Novell nodded. "Yes, I think it is time. We must rely on our final secret weapon. Do thou know which one I mean?"

Sun Shadow straightened in his chair, suddenly looking more alert. "You mean the legacy of Juniper's sword? You mean the Cochranes?"

"Yes, we must test them both," said Novell. "We must discover whether either of them has the ability to wield Juniper's flaming sword."

"Yes," said Sun Shadow. "If so, he might have the power to banish the Tourlt back into the shadows where they belong."

Novell sighed. "It may not work even then," he said, frowning. "But there is a chance, at least."

"And if there is any chance at all, I think we have to take it," said Sun Shadow. "But what about the consequences?"

"We will have to tell them what might happen," said Novell. "They must be given the chance to decide for themselves. But I think—"

There was a knock at the door. Sun Shadow and Novell looked at each other in silence for a moment before Novell called out: "Enter."

Charles and Thomas Cochrane came into the room. They were both bandaged in various places but still dressed for battle.

"Novell, Sun Shadow." Charles nodded to each of them as he walked over.

"Novell, what a relief to see you looking so well!" Thomas exclaimed.

Novell nodded. "And I am glad to see the two of thee in relatively good health."

"Yes, we're patched up and ready for the next attack," said Charles. "Which will no doubt come again at sundown."

"We must count on it," said Sun Shadow.

"I am really amazed at your recovery, Novell," Thomas continued. "But not as amazed as I was at the nature of your injury. That was…your own brother? Your own brother was capable of doing this to you?"

"I'm sorry to say that is true," Novell said with a sigh. "And though it may not have been obvious to thee, I was very surprised to see him myself. I did not expect to see Banlin leading the Tourlt into battle. It has been many years since he left Castle Forks, and I was unsure where he went. However, I must admit that it makes sense, in a way, that he would join with Jerg and his army."

"Banlin chose to leave Castle Forks long ago," said Sun Shadow. "But we did not know what had become of him. You see, he wanted to become the leader of the Caretakers at Castle Forks. But it wasn't his decision to make. That was up to Novell's predecessor, and he chose Novell."

"Banlin knew that he would forever be in my shadow," Novell explained. "He would never be the leader. He could become head of security and even one of the battle generals, but that was all. So like Jerg before him, Banlin decided to leave the castle. It was a huge loss to us for many reasons. Before his departure, Banlin fought alongside me against the Demon Shadows. He was a true thinker and expert tactician. Many of our victories would not have been possible without him. He was a natural-born leader, but his ambition exceeded his grasp."

"Did he try to harm you before? Or did he leave peacefully?" Thomas asked.

"No, he did not try to kill me before he left," Novell answered. "What thou saw yesterday was his first attempt at that," he added with a trace of bitterness.

"In the intervening years, he must have been enticed by Jerg," Sun Shadow said. "He has joined with the Tourlt, and together they are an even more powerful force than either of them could be on their own. You see, it appears that Banlin has the 'gift'—the Seer's gift that Candar had and that Jerg lacked."

"This is Jerg's way," Novell said. "He managed to amass his army of Demon Shadows by playing on their desire for power. When he betrayed Candar, many Caretakers willingly followed him. They left behind their noble ways and their goodness and transformed into the monsters we are now fighting. Jerg is always on the lookout for those whose hearts are full of envy, like his own. He manipulates them with false promises of power or riches. Who knows what has been promised to Banlin."

As he finished speaking, Novell began to pull himself out of the bed. He drew a dark-green tunic over his bandages and walked to the window with a surprising show of strength. "It is true that Banlin was once a good brother," Novell said, looking out of the window. "I believe he had a good heart, but his desire to become a leader was too great. When a person wants something so badly, it becomes an obsession. Their mind begins to play tricks on them, and they become vulnerable to something that is not true."

"Of course Jerg took advantage of it," said Sun Shadow gruffly.

"Yes," Novell agreed. "And he must have known that Banlin was a powerful weapon to have. My brother was very good at coming up with battle strategies. The formations he used all over the world against the Tourlt would have caught the attention of Jerg. He must have known he was losing to someone not only smarter than himself but who was also a Seer."

"What is a Seer capable of exactly?" Charles asked.

"Seers are not able to perceive the distant future, but they can see a few moments into the immediate future, which always gives them a competitive advantage in battle," explained Sun Shadow. "It's not a complete gift of future vision, but it is certainly a powerful edge. With this gift comes incredible tactical skill in general. Seers are better able to strategize and come up with effective battle plans, and they are almost impossible to defeat personally in moments of direct conflict. They're always one or two steps ahead of you, no matter what, always ready for the very next thing."

"Long ago, Jerg lost his battle to Candar because of this," Novell added. "Jerg was not a Seer, but Candar was. When Jerg attacked his brother, Candar immobilized him instantly. The fight was over before it had even begun. I am sure Jerg has bitterly regretted his own lack of the gift. In Banlin, it looks like Jerg may finally have a henchman with the gift. With Banlin on his side, he stands a chance of winning."

"But he must not win!" Charles exclaimed. "How can you say that? There must be some way."

A determined look came into Thomas's face. "Yes, I agree with my brother. There must be some way. What can we do? What is our strategy now?"

Sun Shadow and Novell looked at each other for a moment. "There is one thing..." said Sun Shadow finally.

"Yes, but both of thou must agree to it," said Novell. "Our last chance lies in the Hall of Heroes, and it lies with the Cochrane clan. It is not a certainty, but it may be the only chance we have."

Thomas and Charles both stood up from their chairs immediately. "Please, show us," Charles said.

Without another word, Novell got up and walked to the door. The others followed him down the hallway.

Everything wavered and flickered once more. The next thing Chris knew, they were standing in the large interior courtyard of Castle Forks again, but it was different than the last time. The sunlight was shining brightly on abundant masses of flowers, and there was no more death. Gone were the bodies of the dead and dying. The only soldiers that remained were the few who stood at regular watch posts along the wall, but the battle was over.

"And now, it is time for thee to return home," said Novell. "But please consider what thou have seen. Please consider making the choice to aid us in this battle."

"But what happened with Charles and Thomas?" Chris asked quickly. He was disappointed that Novell had not chosen to take them to the Hall of Heroes so they could see the end of that story.

"Thomas was able to wield the sword," Novell replied simply.

"Aye, and Charles wasn't," added Whitethorn. "But nonetheless, both were able to fight bravely that night, from all I've heard of it."

"They both fought valiantly," Novell said. "In the end, the scheme worked as we had hoped. When Banlin returned the next time, Thomas was there to do battle with him. The Sword of Juniper burned him, weakened him terribly. Banlin retreated into darkness for these many centuries, taking what remained of his devastated army with him."

"For many years now, we have continued to guard the Forks while the Tourlt nurse their wounds," said Si. "And restore their army, no doubt," he added grimly.

"So Thomas defeated him, but Banlin didn't die?" Chris asked.

"Thomas's attack on Banlin weakened him horribly, but we did not see him die," said Novell. "He went off to nurse his wounds in secret. We do not know where."

"No one knows where the Tourlt retreat to when the sun rises," Thungor grumbled. "It always has us at a disadvantage."

"But we know that Banlin is on the move again," said Novell. "Recently, we have spotted his invisible soldiers among us. There is that and a terrible feeling that binds me to my lost brother. I can never tell exactly where he is…but I know when he is alive and active. His armies are on the move. His spies are in place."

"And when he returns," said Si, "we will have to call on all our allies again. If he has returned to his former strength…" As Si's voice trailed off, he looked over at his father.

"If he has returned to his former strength," Novell continued bluntly, "we will once again have to call on the special bond between the Cochrane clan…and the Sword of Juniper."

"I see," said Todd. "But I have more than a few questions about this. First of all, what was it Sun Shadow said? Something about 'consequences'? Is there some dark side to this Sword of Juniper or what?"

Todd opened his mouth to ask another question, but a loud *crack* filled the silence, and Novell grabbed his sword from his side. He wielded it before him and shoved Chris out the way.

"Get down!" Novell bellowed.

Chris lost his balance and stumbled to the ground, and Novell thrust his sword into the empty space in which Chris had stood. Chris thought Novell had struck at thin air, but suddenly, his blade made contact with something solid.

Novell reached down with his other hand and jerked at something, and when his hand came away, it was holding a metal helmet. A wounded Tourlt soldier lay visible on the ground. He made another swing at Novell's head, but Novell blocked the weak attempt with his sword and swung down hard at the ground near Chris's head.

For a moment, Chris thought he was a goner. He heard the *clang* of two swords making contact and felt the heat against his skin as they collided. Then there was a burning sensation in his temple as the tip of one sword glanced off his head. Warm sticky blood began to flow from a surface wound near his hairline. Chris climbed to his feet, clutching at the wound in confusion. Then his dad was there, grabbing his arm and running him toward the now-open gate leading back outside, back to the normal world.

As the gate clanged shut behind them, they could hear Si calling one final time: "Consider your choice well for you may soon lose the ability to choose!"

CHAPTER 8

Chris and Todd stumbled into the clearing in front of Castle Forks. The castle and its gate were no longer visible to the eye.

Todd instantly inspected the wound on Chris's temple. "It's a clean cut," he said. "Not too bad. It tends to bleed a lot when you get cut on the head, but it's nothing to worry about. When we get back to the truck, I'll swab it with some iodine to make sure there's no chance of infection."

Todd ripped off a strip of his flannel shirt and wrapped it around Chris's head. His actions were quick and sure, but he was frowning.

"Don't worry, Dad," Chris said. "I feel fine. I don't really think it's a big deal."

That wasn't exactly true. Chris's head was throbbing in pain, but he didn't like seeing the worried look on his dad's face.

"Sure, not a big deal," Todd said with a sarcastic shrug. "Some angel creatures from another world want to draft you as a child soldier into their invisible army. Not a big deal!"

"No, Dad, you got it wrong. The Tourlt are the ones who use invisible soldiers, not the Caretakers."

Todd scoffed. "You know what I mean."

"Don't be like that, Dad," Chris said.

"How do you expect me to be, Chris!" Todd yelled. "You have to be *seventeen* to join the army here, yet they think you can fight as a warrior at *twelve!*"

"But I can!" Chris shouted. "Why don't you have any faith in me?"

"You've only just learned how to hunt! Why do you suddenly think you can fight against demons?"

Chris didn't have an answer, so he remained silent and crossed his arms, sulking.

After a moment of heavy silence, Todd sighed and said, "I'm sorry, Criffer Bob. It's been a long day, and I don't want to lose you."

"I'm sure they'll look after us, Dad," Chris said. "They'll be fighting too."

Todd nodded, but Chris knew it wasn't out of understanding.

Chris looked around, finding it hard to believe that they were back out in the clearing where they'd first met Si. It seemed like ages ago, but it had really only been a few hours. He reached out his hand and placed it against the tower of gray rocks next to him. Those rocks had opened into a different world when Si was with them. Castle Forks was right there, behind them. Now pressing his ear to the rock, Chris couldn't hear a thing: no voices, no fighting, nothing. It was so strange that he'd seen and heard so much just past that pile of rock, and now it was silent.

Then Chris remembered the situation they'd just escaped from. "Dad! What about Novell and Si and the others? What about the fight just now? Banlin's spies must have been inside Castle Forks the whole time. What if they heard everything? What if they know about all of it—everything Si told us? The sword and everything?"

"Try not to get too worked up right now, Chris," his dad said. "You did lose some blood just now, and we've got a long hike back to the truck. It's best if we focus on our own situation for the moment and don't spend a lot of energy worrying about what's going on back there. I'm sure they've got it covered."

There's that word again—focus! Chris thought. His dad was always telling him to focus. Chris knew his dad was right, but that didn't make it any easier. His mind was filled with questions, not to mention concerns. Had Si and Novell and Whitethorn gotten rid of the spies? Were any of them injured? And what if Banlin's attack was coming sooner than they thought? What if it was happening right now, just on the other side of that silent, innocent-looking pile of rocks?

Todd stood up and started looking around. "Our guns," he said. "I just remembered that Whitethorn took our guns when we got there. I guess there was no time to give them back."

Chris got to his feet. "I'm sure they'll find a way to get them back to us," he said. Secretly, he was thinking: *We'll get them back the next time we go there.* But he didn't say anything about going back out loud. His dad was obviously not in the mood to talk about there being a "next time."

Todd could practically read his son's mind though. He laughed. "Well, maybe it's worth taking a look around anyway since we're not sure when that will be. And who knows? Maybe they found a way to leave them out here for us."

They walked carefully around the clearing, looking for any glint of metal in the brush. As soon as Chris moved away from the large pile of rocks, he could no longer see it. He remembered Si explaining that you could only see the rocks from one specific vantage point; when you weren't in exactly the right place, it just looked like an unbroken thicket of thorny green vines at that moment, bursting with fruit. Chris had just reached out and picked a couple of berries when a very strange realization hit him.

"Dad! The berry bushes are all full!" Chris looked around at the familiar features of the mountaintop clearing. A chill ran down his spine in spite of the sun's warmth. Everything was lush and green as it would be in spring, not fall. When they'd entered Castle Forks, it had been a cool October day. There hadn't been a single ripe berry left on any of the vines, and now they were full to bursting again.

"Yes, and everything's green!" Todd panicked. "It's not October anymore, Criffer Bob. If I had to guess, I'd say it's more like April."

"But I thought we were only gone for a few hours!" Chris exclaimed. "It doesn't make sense."

"So did I," Todd replied. "The ranch has been unattended for six months, and no one would have heard from us!"

Chris's heart sank. "What are we gonna do?"

"We need to go back. Now," Todd said.

Chris and Todd turned to leave the area when Chris seemed to notice something near the place where he'd first noticed the ripe berries. "Our guns!" He pulled the two rifles out from a tangle of brush.

"Whitethorn must have slipped them back out here for us somehow," said Chris.

"Well, that was good of him," said Todd. "Let's get back to the truck. Do you feel okay about walking?"

"Definitely." Chris was determined not to show any sign of weakness. After seeing Charles and Thomas Cochrane fight in the Battle for the Forks, he felt stronger somehow. Charles Cochrane had taken an arrow clean through the shoulder, and it hadn't slowed him down. Chris couldn't imagine what his ancestors would say if they heard him complaining about a little scratch on the head.

The hike back out was relatively easy, and they helped themselves to several handfuls of berries along the way. Within an hour, the truck was visible through the trees, parked right where they'd left it.

Chris was very thirsty by this time although he was careful not to complain about it. He hoped that some of the drinks he'd packed in the cooler would still be okay to drink.

Just as they neared the truck, an oddly familiar shrieking sound echoed through the valley. Chris and his dad looked at each other. Without thinking about it too much, Chris turned and made a loud shriek of his own in the direction of the call. A single short shriek came back.

"That's Whitethorn, right?" Chris said. "I know it is. That's the call the Kiern make."

"Yes, and I think that last one sounded like a goodbye," Todd answered firmly. "So let's see about clearing this truck out and getting home."

The bed of the pickup was full of fallen tree branches and pine needles. It took half an hour or so to clear it out. They also had to drag several fallen branches off the trail to clear their way out of the woods.

Chris pulled the cooler out of the truck's cab and opened it. The foulest smell greeted him: rotten milk. "Ugh, I forgot I put some milk in there." He gasped, turning his face away. Of course, all the ice was gone. Fortunately, there were a couple of canned sodas and a bottle of water. All the drinks were very warm, but Chris and his dad were both too thirsty to care. They shared the water, then cracked open the sodas for the drive home.

The sky became overcast while they cleared out the truck. The rain hit as soon as they started driving, and it didn't let up until they were almost home. There wasn't much conversation during the two-hour drive. Todd was focused on the road as the rain came down harder and harder in fat drops.

"It's like a monsoon," he commented at one point. "A big spring storm is what this is. No, it's definitely not October anymore."

Chris just watched the windshield wipers going left to right, left to right, over and over again. Their steady rhythm might have lulled him to sleep if he wasn't so preoccupied with his thoughts. His mind was swirling with questions about Castle Forks, about everything Novell had shown them, and about what was happening back there right now. He wished there was some way of finding out.

Even though he'd met them only hours ago, Chris felt like Novell, Si, and Whitethorn were his old friends. He didn't like running away right when they were being attacked, but the choice hadn't been his. Besides, he wasn't prepared to help. He'd had no weapons, and he had no hand-to-hand combat skills.

But I could learn! Chris thought. Something had happened inside Chris when he saw his ancestors, Charles and Thomas Cochrane, fighting off those demons. Something had changed. He felt brave and eager to fight. Even though the Tourlt had been terrifying, he knew somehow he could confront them if he had to. Part of him envied Valkyn attending all those skating competitions, but Chris couldn't skate to save his life even though he enjoyed messing around on a board; he was better with a bow and arrow.

Besides that, he couldn't stop thinking about Juniper's sword now. Who would be able to wield the sword and save Castle Forks? he wondered. Was it him, Chris? Or was it his dad? Or was it Justin?

Novell had said it had to be one of them. Novell seemed very sure of that.

Chris knew there must be other descendants of Thomas or Charles somewhere, but maybe it had to be someone in Grandpa Jim's direct line. After all, Novell had known Chris's grandfather pretty well.

Grandpa Jim had been to Castle Forks more than once. There had to be something special about this particular Cochrane family and that meant Chris, his dad, or his brother. Who was it? There was no way to know without going back.

Chris looked over at his dad and felt a brief stab of resentment. Why was his dad being so hesitant about all this? He'd repeatedly said he didn't want Chris to be involved in any fighting, but that didn't seem fair. There was so much at stake—maybe even the future of the whole human race! How could a decision like that be up to his dad alone? Why wasn't Chris able to make the choice for himself?

Chris had never questioned his dad's decisions before. It was a strange feeling. He tried to shake it off. *Just focus on what's actually in front of you*, he reminded himself. First things first, they'd have to figure out exactly how much time had passed at home since they'd left Castle Forks that morning.

Chris expected the house to look abandoned and unkempt, but the lawn had been freshly cut and several lights were on within their home.

"If we've been gone for six months, surely the grass outside would be overgrown?" Chris said.

Todd nodded. "Yes, you'd think so, but it looks like someone's tended to it while we've been away. And from the lights on, I can only assume they're still here."

The windows and front porch had been kept clean and free of cobwebs, and the concrete path leading to the garage door had been cleared of leaves. Chris stepped out of the truck and opened the garage with the automatic opener. As his dad pulled in, Chris eyed his dad's Harley-Davidson parked at the end of the garage, its burgundy fuel tank cover and fenders shining bright in the natural light that beamed inside.

Todd had once shown him some old pictures of him and his biker friends "back in the day." They had worn thick leather jackets, trousers, and boots, which Chris always thought looked *so cool.*

In the house, Chris flipped the light switch next to the door that led into the kitchen, but the fuse went and the bulb burst, plunging the living room into darkness.

"Dad, the lights have gone out!" Chris shouted back into the garage. But as Chris crept into the dark kitchen, he noticed a male figure sitting at the table in the corner of the room. A wave of terror surged through his body, but he was too scared to move.

"Dad!" Chris yelled. "Dad! There's someone in here!"

The figure rose from the table, and Chris's knees weakened.

"Dad!" he shouted again. "Dad!"

The person slowly approached Chris. Todd appeared at his side, his eyes wide and his rifle raised. But as the calm individual got closer with a warm smile on his face, Chris recognized him and instantly knew that he was no foe but a friend.

The man smiling before them had pale skin that glowed in the darkness and long brown hair with giant wings—a Caretaker.

"Who are you, and why are you here?" Todd questioned.

"Dad, I know who he is," Chris said. "After the flood that drowned all our crops, I saw him outside the window. *He* made everything grow again!"

Todd kept his eyes on him, and the pair of them waited for the creature to speak.

"That is right, young Chris," he said in a soft voice. "Novell instructed me to assist after your land became flooded all those years ago, and he instructed me again this time…to watch over your home while you were away. I am Vannsd, one of the Caretakers."

Chris and Todd paused for a moment, digesting the new information.

"You've been here since we left?" Todd asked, lowering his rifle.

"Since you left in October," Vannsd confirmed. "It is now April."

"So we *have* been gone for six months!" Chris exclaimed.

Todd sighed, but Vannsd smiled again. "Do not worry. I have tended to everything as if you were here the whole time. The crops have been harvested and replanted. You have plenty of food in the freezer. Your family in Peru know you're safe, and your school think you're away because of an urgent family matter."

Todd exhaled a long deep breath, the kind he usually made in relief. "Er…um…thank you."

"It is my pleasure, Todd Cochrane," Vannsd replied. "Novell has asked me to watch over your home for the foreseeable future, as it is likely that you will be needed again at Castle Forks very soon. So while you both get used to being back again, I will be on the grounds, tending to your orchard trees."

Vannsd bowed and departed from the kitchen, leaving Chris and Todd speechless.

"I-I'll go and put this away then," Todd stuttered, looking at the rifle in his hands.

"Yeah, and the lights need fixing," Chris said.

While his dad locked the rifle up in the cabinet and flipped the trip switch, Chris walked over to the garden. The beds were neat and free of weeds, and the rhubarb plant in the corner was thriving. It had grown over a foot in height and circumference, and there were light-red stalks of fruit visible among the wide green leaves, definitely way more than one week of growth.

After a few minutes, Chris decided to made a beeline for the laptop his mom always kept in the kitchen, but his dad had already beat him to it. Todd was sitting at the little built-in desk that held the computer and answering machine. He was shaking his head.

"It's a good thing your mother set up all the utilities on auto-payment," Todd commented. "Otherwise, there'd be no electricity, definitely no Internet. Look at this, the computer says today is April 10. Vannsd was right."

The calendar hanging on the wall was still open on October.

Todd turned his attention to the answering machine. He pushed the button, and a robotic voice said, "You have no new messages."

"Wow, Vannsd has actually dealt with *all* the messages!" Todd exclaimed.

"Imagine if he hadn't been looking after everything," Chris said. "They would have sent search parties looking for us."

Todd sighed. "I dread to think, but I'll definitely be treating Vannsd for all his help, even just for making sure that your mom and brother knew we were safe."

The mention of Chris's mom made both of them feel her absence. The house felt especially empty.

"Your mom would've been out of her mind with worry if not for Vannsd," Todd went on. "And she definitely would have contacted the police, sent out search parties, the whole nine yards. As it is, Vannsd has saved her from worrying, but I should write to her myself. Then sort through today's mail and errands."

Todd picked up a pen and started jotting down some notes, and after a few moments, he set the pen down with a sigh. "Why has so much time gone by while we were in there? Poor Vannsd wouldn't have had to slave away for all this time, and it would be so much easier to deal with if the time scale were the same. But I guess it proves the whole thing wasn't just a dream."

"Yeah, well it couldn't have been a dream anyway because we were both there, and I have this cut on my forehead to prove it too," said Chris, carefully peeling off the strip of flannel that was serving as a bandage.

Todd got to his feet. "Let's get that properly dressed."

After Todd had cleaned Chris's cut and dressed the wound in a fresh plaster and bandage, Todd started working through the day's errands to take the load off Vannsd. And while his dad busied himself with loud '80s rock blasting throughout the living room, Chris took the chance to go into his bedroom with the laptop. He eagerly typed "Thomas Cochrane, Scotland, Black Plague Era" into the search engine. Only a few sources popped up that might be the Thomas Cochrane he was looking for, and none of them were Wikipedia. He tried a few other searches: "Caretakers," "Charles Cochrane,

Scotland, brother of Thomas," "the Kiern," and "the Tourlt." He was just guessing at the spelling for the last two, but no results came back no matter what spelling he tried. He got practically nothing on the other searches either, and what did pop up didn't seem relevant. He went back to his original search phrase and read what he could find on Thomas Cochrane.

The most promising website was called Medieval Celtic Diaries. It was a very basic, low-budget website that didn't have much going on in the way of design. There weren't a lot of pictures, and Chris thought the writing could use a good proofreading. There was nothing on the "About" page or anywhere else to show who had made the website. Chris knew he should be skeptical of any website that claimed to have historical information but didn't have any sources or scholarly research to back it up. But it was hard to remain skeptical once he came across the portrait of Thomas Cochrane.

It was a color photograph of an old painting, and it was a very realistic portrait. Chris knew that painters had once made very detailed and accurate portraits of important people back before cameras existed. The painters knew they had to capture the person's image accurately, so there was no embellishment. In this one, the man standing in battle armor looked just like the Thomas Cochrane Chris had seen with his own eyes. He was the same man Novell had shown them. Chris was sure of that. The caption read: "portrait of Thomas Cochrane, artist unknown."

Around his neck, Thomas wore a large golden key hanging from a gold chain. It looked like the same key that Si had worn, engraved with the Celtic *C* and boar insignia. Chris tried to recall what Novell had said about the keys. One of the things that made Thomas special, Chris remembered, was that he was able to touch and carry the key to Castle Forks. But did that mean he'd been given one?

Chris was pretty sure that only the Caretakers actually held onto the keys. Si had one now, and Novell had the other. The third key, Novell had said, was lost at sea while his ancestor's ship was on the way to rally Thomas Cochrane and his forces. Why and when had Thomas been given one? If the key had been lost on the way to Scotland, as Novell had said, then it never would have made it to

Thomas Cochrane. Could this be the missing third key that Novell had mentioned? Had it made its way to Thomas after all? Or had one of the Caretakers just loaned Thomas a key to wear while posing for this portrait? That seemed unlikely. The keys were too precious to be loaned out for something like that.

Beneath the portrait was a photograph of an old battered leather journal. The caption read: "diary of Thomas Cochrane." Beneath it, the author of the website had apparently just typed out several pages of the diary itself. None of them were dated, so it was impossible to tell if they were in the right order.

Chris quickly scrolled down to the bottom of the web page. There were too few entries to include the entire diary, which was disappointing. The author must have just selected a few. Chris scrolled back to the top and eagerly read through each entry, scanning quickly for any reference to Castle Forks, the Caretakers, or the Tourlt.

To his disappointment, Chris found only a few scraps of the kind of information he was looking for.

Thomas was vague on details in his writing, and some of the diary entries weren't about anything interesting at all. There were whole paragraphs on the scenery of Scotland and some boring mentions of "lovely maidens." But Chris picked out a few points of interest in Thomas's mention of "an eastern voyage" during which both of his parents were killed "by bandits."

Novell had said that Thomas's parents died defending the Forks, in the Skirmishes of Windy Nip Glen. This "killed by bandits" excuse came up in another entry too: "I am returning to Castle Cochrane now after these many years' absence, but my return will bring great sadness. Most of my crew has been lost to murderous bandits, and I must carry this news to their families."

The diary didn't explain where Thomas was returning from, but Chris had a pretty good idea who the "bandits" were. Just like his parents, Thomas's men must have been killed by the Tourlt.

There was only one specific mention of Castle Forks, which Thomas referred to as the "sister" of Castle Cochrane. He didn't name the location of Castle Forks, just that it was "far away, across the water." When Chris tried a search for "Castle Forks," the only thing that came up was Thomas's diary entry.

The diary said: "Charles will lead the defense at Castle Forks while I battle the enemy's creeping arm elsewhere. I have sent forces to Jerusalem. The Caretakers will send for me if I am needed across the water."

Chris was frustrated with the lack of detail in the diary and wished there were more entries.

"Thanks, Thomas!" he muttered to himself. "You're really not much help here."

In the same entry that mentioned Castle Forks, Chris was sure that Thomas also described the Tourlt. The passage read: "There is a plague upon Europe, and I fear how far it may spread. It is an enemy that appears out of nowhere like a swarm of locusts, destroying everything in its path. It attacks with ruthless brutality, night after night, retreating only briefly when the sun is high in the sky. It does not accept surrender or compromise, only complete annihilation."

Thomas must have been talking about the Tourlt, the Demon Shadows. He even used the word *plague*, Chris noticed. That backed up what Si had been telling them about the Black Plague in Europe being attributed to disease when really it was a plague of Demon Shadows.

Novell said that human history had been rewritten to hide the truth about the Tourlt. Chris completely understood why that was. The world did not need to know. Most people would go insane if they could see what was going on in both worlds: the physical and the spiritual. While the Caretakers and their allies succeeded in containing the Tourlt and keeping them few in number, their attacks could easily be attributed to regional skirmishes or even disease. Humans would be making wars among themselves till the end of days. The Caretakers could hide the truth about the Tourlt within those stories. But if the Tourlt ever found a way to grow their numbers again as they had during the Black Plague era, the whole world would be vulnerable. *We'd probably have to just nuke ourselves and start over*, Chris thought. And that was what Novell was afraid of.

If Banlin had managed to return to his full strength, then that was exactly what they were facing.

Chris and his dad had been called upon to stop that from happening. Didn't they have an obligation to do that no matter what? Chris knew his dad was good. He knew he'd do the right thing eventually, no matter what he was saying at the moment. Maybe Chris just needed to try harder to convince his dad that he was ready to be a warrior too.

With that in mind, Chris grabbed the laptop and hurried back downstairs to show his dad the information he'd found online, but as he entered the living room, he spotted Todd on the sofa with his face in his hands, a folded note poking through his fingers and the '80s rock music blaring from the stereo.

"Dad?" Chris called out, edging toward him.

Todd lifted his head with a start and wiped his face with his sleeve. "Sorry, Criffer Bob, I didn't know you were there," his dad replied, and he reached up to turn off the stereo.

"What's wrong?" Chris asked. "And who's the note from?"

Todd smiled, but his eyes were full of tears. "I just miss your mom and brother, that's all. Our time in Castle Forks has been a little overwhelming, but it's usually your mom who comforts me, so I'm feeling her absence. The music helps though, so don't worry about me. I'll be all right."

Chris sat beside his dad on the sofa and wrapped an arm around him. He sighed. "Yeah, I miss them too. I wish they could be here. Is that a letter from them?" Chris nodded toward the piece of folded paper in his dad's hand.

"It's an old letter from your mom, one she wrote before you and Justin were born," Todd explained. "She used to go on family mission trips to Peru as a teenager, which is how we met, so writing letters to each other was the only way we could communicate."

"Can I read it?" Chris asked.

Todd chuckled. "Sure, here you go."

Todd handed Chris the letter, and he read the neat handwriting that didn't look much different from his mom's handwriting now.

Dear Todd,

I hope this letter reaches you. The Christian missionaries in the village helped me to send it, and they promised to make sure your letters get to me safety.

Anyway, I'm loving it here! We're living with a friendly Peruvian family, and they've been teaching us how to speak the language and introducing us to lots of traditional food. Life is so much slower down here compared to North America, which makes all the tasks feel relaxing even though we're technically working. Tomorrow we're helping to make textiles for the local people to sell at the market.

Wish you were here,
Cyndee x

Chris smiled. "She never lost her love for Peru then."

"No, she loves it down there," Todd said. "It's a wonder we don't all live there."

"That wouldn't be so bad," Chris said.

Todd chuckled. "Maybe one day, if your mom has her way. Anyway, enough Internet time for you, Criffer Bob. I've just realized tomorrow's Tuesday, and we've got a big day ahead of us, getting all this stuff sorted out. Time to get some shut-eye."

"Okay, Dad. But look at this first," Chris said, opening the laptop back up. "I found some information about Thomas Cochrane." Todd leaned over and looked at the computer screen. "See, this is the guy Novell showed us, right?" Chris expanded the Thomas Cochrane portrait to full screen.

"I'd say so," agreed his dad.

"Well, there are some of his diary entries here." Chris scrolled down slowly, pointing to the screen at the relevant points. "He mentions Castle Forks and his brother Charles and even the Caretakers, and look, he's wearing the key to Castle Forks in this picture! And I'm sure he's describing the Tourlt right here, see? Even though he doesn't mention them by name. If all this is true, then everything else Novell told us must be true too, right? And that means we have to go back, we have to help!" Chris hadn't intended to say so much, but the words came rushing out before he could stop them.

Todd rested his elbows on his knees and looked thoughtfully at the carpet for a moment. He sighed.

"Here's the thing, Criffer Bob," he said finally. "I was there too. It isn't that I don't believe this stuff is real. I just have a lot of unanswered questions still, and it's no good rushing into a situation without all the facts. Besides that, you've already been injured as it is. What do you think your mom would say if she were here? I promise you, she wouldn't just say, 'Sure, give my youngest son a sword he doesn't know how to use and send him off to battle!' You see where I'm coming from?"

Chris nodded but didn't trust himself to say anything. He could tell when it was time to just listen.

"Good." Todd looked thoughtfully at the computer screen. He frowned for a minute, then his expression softened. With a slight smile, he added, "Look, I'll give you this much. If they send for us, I mean if a messenger comes, I'll consider the situation again. I'll keep an open mind. I'm just not going out of my way to go back there. I'm sure if Novell really needs us, he'll find a way to get in touch. He can do a lot of things we can't, wouldn't you agree?"

Chris really couldn't argue with that.

"So we'll talk about this again if something happens." As Chris walked to the door, Todd added, "And I mean talk about it. I'm not promising you anything about what decision I will make. But we're not going back there on purpose now, just looking for trouble. Deal?"

Chris grinned and nodded. That was actually more than fair, he thought. "Deal," he said.

As he got into bed, Chris thought about school for the first time that day. He cringed at the thought. His classmates would be months into the spring semester of school by now, learning about Socrates and Hamlet and trigonometry. Meanwhile, Chris was trying to sort out real life from fantasy.

I can't tell anyone about this, he realized suddenly. His last thought before sleep washed over him was *Unless I want everyone to think I'm crazy.*

CHAPTER 9

C hris woke up soaked in sweat. He flung the covers back, sat up, and quickly turned on the light next to his bed to dispel the darkness. The nightmare had seemed so real. *But it couldn't have been*, he said to himself.

Si and Novell had been walking in the courtyard at Castle Forks. They were conversing about something, but he couldn't hear what they were saying. Everything was calm. Suddenly, out of nowhere, came an arrow. It hit Novell's right side, and he went down. Si turned in the direction of the arrow's origin, only to have a giant wooden club meet his face and knock him to the ground. He was out cold.

A storm of arrows came out of nowhere, flying at the soldiers in the watchtowers along the castle wall. One soldier went down, crashing into the courtyard, then another, then another. They didn't have time to defend themselves because the arrows all came at once. Novell's unconscious body was lifted into the air by an invisible being. In one bound, the creature leaped over the castle wall and disappeared with Novell.

"It was just a nightmare," Chris assured himself out loud. "It couldn't have been real."

Novell had quicker reflexes than any human. He could see things right before they happened. He was a Seer. If that scenario had been real, Novell would have reacted in time. He would've been able to dodge the arrow somehow, as Chris had seen him do before. Even if the archer was invisible, Novell could have sensed the arrow before it hit, right? Unless the attacker had been lying in wait, so close to Novell that he'd all but eliminated any possibility of reaction time. But even then, why would Novell have been knocked unconscious after a single arrow hit? Chris had seen him remain conscious enough to exchange words after nearly being cleaved in half!

Chris sat puzzling over the dream for several minutes. Of course it was just a bunch of random images—his subconscious mind working something out while he slept. It couldn't have been a *vision*. Chris laughed at the thought, but some part of him remained unsure.

He got up and walked down the hall to use the bathroom, then went to the kitchen for a glass of water. As he drank his water, Chris stood in front of the French doors and looked out into the darkness of the backyard.

The moon was a thin crescent, casting very little light. The long expanse of yard ended in a thick line of trees that separated them by at least an acre from the nearest house. Without the porch lights on and so little moonlight, the yard was inked in darkness. Chris could barely make out the outline of the trees, swaying slightly in the wind.

In the two weeks since they'd returned from Castle Forks, Chris had found himself waking up a lot at night. It wasn't always a nightmare, and his dreams were not always as vivid as the one he'd just had. As much as he tried to keep his attention on school and normal life, Castle Forks and his friends there crept continually into his thoughts. Maybe it was because he tried to push the thoughts away during the daytime that they had to come out at night.

Suddenly there was a flicker of light out near the garden. It disappeared as quickly as it had come. Chris watched for a few more moments to see if it happened again, but there was nothing. *Could have been my eyes playing tricks on me*, he thought. *Maybe I'm still sleeping. Could have just been a firefly even.*

Chris headed back to bed. He was really very tired. As he pulled the covers up again, the back porch creaked. After a few seconds, the creaking sound came again. Something was definitely on the back porch. *It must be that dumb fox again*, Chris thought. He'd seen the fox several times lately on his midnight trips to the kitchen. It had claimed a corner of the porch as its nightly pee spot. "Find your own place to go to the bathroom. Leave my house alone," Chris grumbled as he laid his head back down on the pillow.

Then there was the unmistakable sound of something tapping against the glass of the French doors. This was no fox. Something— or someone—was on the back porch, knocking deliberately on the door. A shock of excitement mixed with anxiety shot through Chris. What if it was Si or some other messenger from Castle Forks? It had to be. Who else would be knocking at this hour? Chris rolled out of bed and pulled on his jeans and a T-shirt.

When he reached the kitchen doorway, he hesitated slightly in spite of his excitement. There was the remote chance that whatever had tapped on the French doors wasn't friendly, he realized. He shouldn't just run in there and blindly open the back door.

Chris looked around for some kind of weapon. His eyes landed on an antique iron candle sconce that was hanging on the wall. Holding the sconce firmly in his right hand, he slid down to the floor and crept quietly into the kitchen on hands and knees, leaving the lights off. He crawled over to the island in the middle of the room where the cabinet would shield his body but still allow him to have a good view of the French doors.

There was no one at the door. The back porch looked just as he'd left it: empty and dark with only the barest hint of moonlight casting formless shadows. Chris crept across the floor until he reached the French doors. The tapping had stopped, and there was nothing at the door. He strained to see anything in the dark yard.

Suddenly the silence was pierced by a scream of pain. There was a heavy thud near Chris's head, and he instinctively rolled backward, away from the door. The tip of a dagger protruded through the doorframe, shining where it sat embedded in the wood.

Chris saw a large figure detach itself from the shadows near the garden shed. Something about the shape was familiar. Wait! Could it be? The figure strode quickly onto the back porch, which creaked loudly under the weight.

Chris watched as the massive, bulky figure yanked the dagger from the doorframe. As the blade was withdrawn, a leather-clad body materialized and slid down the wall. With one quick flick of his wrist, the dark figure separated the head of the corpse from its body. Chris caught a glimpse of the victim's twisted face and its wide staring red eyes before the head bounced twice and rolled off the porch into the rose bushes. That brief glimpse of the dead one's face was enough to prove its identity: only the Tourlt had those horrible red eyes. One of Banlin's spies, cloaked in invisibility, had just been killed right outside the kitchen door.

By now, Chris was certain he knew the identity of his visitor. Even in the darkness, the towering broad-shouldered Kiern warrior with his full bushy beard was unmistakable. It was Whitethorn. As Chris stood up from his crouching position, Whitethorn raised one large hand in greeting while tapping lightly on the glass door with his other hand.

All traces of fear left Chris's body. He eagerly unbolted the latch and slid the door open. "Whitethorn! What are you doing here?"

The big Kiern soldier remained silent. He reached into his leather belt pouch and pulled out two blueberries. He ate one and handed the other to Chris. *That's right!* Chris remembered. *We can't understand each other until we eat the blueberries.* He gulped his down.

"Hello, lad," Whitethorn said with a smile.

"Hello!" Chris exclaimed. He reached out and enthusiastically shook Whitethorn's hand.

"I'm glad to see you came prepared when you 'eard a suspicious noise," Whitethorn said approvingly, gesturing to the iron candlestick in Chris's left hand.

"Of course!" Chris said and set the candlestick down on the countertop. "But I'm glad I didn't have to use it."

"Yeah, it's just as well I got to him first," Whitethorn said grimly. He placed his dagger back into the folds of his tunic. "The bad news is, where there's one of Banlin's cursed spies, there're probably others. Can we talk inside?"

"Yeah, sure. Come in." Chris gestured his friend into the kitchen and slid the French door shut behind him, instinctively bolting it shut again. "Uh, do you want to have a seat?" He gestured to the kitchen table. "Would you like some water?"

"Aye, a drink of water would be most welcome," replied Whitethorn, gingerly sinking his big frame down into one of the wooden kitchen chairs. The chair creaked loudly under his weight, threatening to break. Whitethorn rose to his feet again.

"On second thoughts, we might be more comfortable in the living room," Chris said quickly. "I'm sorry, those chairs weren't really made for Kiern." He filled a large pitcher with water and grabbed a glass.

They walked through to the living room, and Whitethorn sat down on the couch. The springs squeaked a bit, but it looked like the couch would survive.

Whitethorn downed one glass of water without pausing to breathe. As he reached for the pitcher to pour another glass, he said, "I've worked up quite a thirst. While I slake it, why don't you go wake your father, lad? What I've come to tell involves both of you. And I won't beat around the bush—I've come because I need your help."

Chris hurried down the hallway to his parents' room and nudged his dad on the shoulder.

Todd awoke with a start. "What's going on?" he asked quickly, sitting straight up in bed.

"It's okay," Chris assured him. "It's just Whitethorn. He's here. He's in the living room, and he says…he says he needs our help."

Todd nodded, rubbing the sleep from his eyes. "Right. Of course. I'll be right there."

Chris went back out to the living room, where Whitethorn had finished the pitcher of water. The shaggy-haired warrior was studying a very old well-worn parchment paper with what appeared to be some kind of map on it. Chris caught a glimpse of some spidery lines marked with a flourishy cursive that looked like calligraphy. Not wanting to be nosy, Chris chose an armchair across the coffee table from Whitethorn and sat quietly. The parchment had obviously been folded up into a very small square and unfolded several times, judging from the thin, worn look of the paper and the various stains and watermarks. Whitethorn was bent over the paper with a frown on his face.

A moment later, Todd walked into the living room in his bathrobe. Whitethorn looked up with a friendly smile. He pulled a blueberry out of his pouch and handed it to Todd, who ate it instantly then said, "Welcome to our home, Whitethorn."

"Thank you, Todd Cochrane," Whitethorn said formally. "I'm grateful for the welcome, especially considerin' that I 'aven't come for pleasure but because we're in great need of your 'elp."

"No need for formalities then," Todd said brusquely, taking a seat in the armchair next to Chris's. "Please, fill us in on what's happening."

Whitethorn nodded and began bluntly. "Novell's been captured. Two days ago. We were ambushed by at least three, possibly more, of Banlin's invisible soldiers. Novell was wounded with an arrow and taken away by the enemy while Si was knocked out with a club. It all 'appened very quickly. I arrived on the scene right after Si had been knocked out, and I'm 'appy to say I was able to kill two of those filthy spies. At least one must have escaped with Novell, however."

As Whitethorn spoke, Chris's dream came back to him vividly. Whitethorn's report fit almost exactly with what had happened in the dream. Chris fought the urge to tell Whitethorn and his dad about the dream. There wasn't time to go into all of that. Also, on some deeper level, Chris was a little afraid of the can of worms that would be opened if he told them he'd dreamed about things he couldn't possibly have seen. It would freak his dad out, to say the least. It was better to file this away for later, he decided, and stay focused on what Whitethorn had come to tell them. He contented himself with asking, "Is Si okay?"

Whitethorn nodded. "He was fine when I last saw him yesterday. He went in search of his father. But he 'asn't returned yet, and there's been no message."

Whitethorn paused. He looked down at the paper in his hand thoughtfully, as if getting his thoughts in order. Then he took a moment to look Chris directly in the eye, then did the same with Todd.

"When you were at Castle Forks recently, many things were told to you. A few of the things you were told were not entirely true. We had to be deceptive on one or two points. I apologize, but there was no other way. We knew there were spies among us. There always are. Even outside your 'ome just now I killed one."

Todd sat forward suddenly in his chair. "What? A spy was here?"

"It's true, Dad," Chris said. "I saw it. After Whitethorn killed it with his dagger, it became visible. It was definitely one of the Tourlt. I could tell by the red eyes."

"All right," Todd said. "Go on please, Whitethorn."

"There was a second one as well," Whitethorn continued. "But he ran away. A gutless coward that lacked the honor to face the wrath of the Catapult." His free hand clenched into a fist as he snarled the last sentence.

"I suppose we're not exactly safe here then," Todd said quietly.

Chris hadn't even had a chance to think about that yet. As his dad spoke the words, he realized they were true. What would he have done if Whitethorn hadn't been there to kill the spy? His iron candlestick would have been of little use against an invisible Demon Shadow, he realized.

"I'm afraid you 'avent really been safe 'ere for some time," Whitethorn said. "Since you left Castle Forks, Novell has instructed me to check on your home nightly. This is actually the third time I've caught Banlin's spies lurkin' around 'ere."

The back of Chris's neck tingled uncomfortably at the thought. Maybe that fox he thought he'd been hearing had actually been an invisible spy, or maybe it had been Whitethorn checking on the house.

Todd was troubled too. "But why didn't you announce yourself before? I mean, shouldn't we have been told our home was in danger?"

"Again, I apologize," Whitethorn said sincerely. "But I had strict orders from Novell. 'Patrol the Cochrane home,' he said, 'but do not let them know you're doing it.' He said he wanted you to have a little time to yourselves to think about everything you were told during your visit to Castle Forks. He didn't want to frighten you or force you into a decision too quickly. Alas, he thought we had more time. But now that Novell has been captured, there is no more time."

Todd sighed and nodded. "Yes, I recall Si's last words to us. He said, 'You may soon lose the ability to choose.' I suppose that time has come." As he spoke, a look of fierce determination came into his face.

Whitethorn nodded in agreement. "Before you left Castle Forks, we were attacked by one of Banlin's spies. I'm sure you remember," he said, pointing to the cut above Chris's eye.

It had healed over the last two weeks, and now Chris didn't even have a bandage over it. A stab of pain shot through the wound. Chris lifted his hand to it. As quickly as the pain had come, it was gone again.

"This wound will heal into a scar, but the pain will never go away completely," Whitethorn continued. "It will become a live scar where pain will always exist as long as evil does. Because you were touched by one of the enemies' weapons, a kind of blood bond was formed. That's how they were able to track you. Until we defeat Banlin and drive the Tourlt back into the shadows where they belong, they will always be able to track your whereabouts outside of Castle Forks. It's more dangerous for you 'ere than if you return with me, where we can help protect you."

"Yes, I understand," Todd said quietly. "Enough chitchat then, I suppose. Let's get to the point." The determined look had not left his eyes.

Chris was startled to hear his dad speak so bluntly to the massive Kiern warrior, but it didn't seem to bother Whitethorn at all. A low rumbling laugh emerged from the thicket of his black beard.

"I respect that, Todd Cochrane," he said. "And I'll try to get to the point as quickly as I can. The short version is this—I need both of you to come with me tonight on an expedition to find Novell. It will be a perilous journey, but I'm confident I know where Banlin has taken him. In a few moments, you'll understand why I say this, but there won't be time to answer every question you might 'ave. I must ask you to trust me. In exchange, I promise to defend you and your family with my very last breath."

As Whitethorn spoke, there was a fire in his eyes that almost defied anyone to accuse him of dishonesty. In Chris's heart, he felt that Whitethorn was completely trustworthy. One look at Todd was enough to convince Chris that his father felt the same way.

"There's another problem," Whitethorn continued. "The Sword of Juniper has gone missing as well. We 'ave no idea how the security of the Hall of Heroes was breached, but we 'ave to assume that a Caretaker was in on it. Or else Banlin has found some other way to lift the sword from its place. No one other than a Caretaker can lift or wield any of the flamin' swords with the exception of a few humans, such as your own ancestor Thomas Cochrane. This has been explained to you.

"Once a Caretaker has turned Tourlt, they are no longer able to touch the flamin' swords either. The swords know who is touchin' them. If no descendant of the Cochrane clan lifted the sword and took it away, then the only possible explanation is that…there's a traitor among the Caretakers. That brings me to my final point. You may recall some things we talked about regardin' keys? This is one of the points on which we were not entirely truthful."

Whitethorn reached behind the breastplate of his armor, and after digging in the folds of his tunic for a moment, he pulled out a large golden key attached to a very thin silver chain.

"Is it…the third key?" Chris asked in an awed tone.

Whitethorn simply nodded and stowed the key away again underneath his armor. He then reached into his pouch and pulled out a roll of parchment done up with a wax seal. Chris recognized the markings. It was the seal of the Cochrane clan. Whitethorn handed the letter to Todd.

"This letter is for the descendants of Thomas Cochrane alone," Whitethorn said. "There's no need to discuss it out loud. Simply read it."

Todd broke the wax seal and unrolled the parchment. Chris stood behind his dad's chair so he could read along with him.

Dear future Cochrane descendant,

I'm sure you are wondering why one of the Caretaker keys is in the possession of your Kiern companion. You may have been told that the third key went down with a former Caretaker on the high seas while on voyage to Castle Cochrane. However, neither the Caretaker nor

100

the key was lost at that time. This Caretaker and a few of his countrymen survived the attack of the Tourlt and reached the shore. On Candar's orders, they secretly entrusted me with the third key. Candar deliberately started the rumor of the lost key. As you may know by now, I was foolish in my youth and often boasted of things after a few too many glasses of wine. I even dared to get my first self-portrait done while wearing the key around my neck. Perhaps you have seen this gross display of my stupidity. Although I had that portrait destroyed later, some of the artist's studies may have survived.

Because of my foolishness, I decided that the true honor and protection of the so-called "lost" third key could not belong to me. It should be guarded by our most trusted allies, the Kiern. At Candar's direction, I handed over this key to Sun Shadow, the last great leader of their people in my time. I was instructed to never tell a soul, not even the Caretakers, what I had done with the key.

Candar gave me permission to write this letter and reveal the truth only to my descendants. He believed that one day you would need to hear the truth from me. If you are reading this now, then that time has come.

There are a few things that you'll need to know about the task that will be soon asked of you.

The Tourlt have a place they retreat to. Century after century, claims of a hidden city made of gold have attracted great explorers and swallowed whole all who dared to wander toward its beacon. The best of adventurers have sought to claim the great treasure of these untold riches.

Some claimed to have found the city once, but none ever returned. I have seen the place you must go. If you are reading this letter and have been shown the third key by your friendly long-haired companion, then one of the Caretakers must be in trouble.

You'll need to venture into the dark cave near the valley of Windy Nip Glen that overlooks the Forks. The path will be filled with danger at every turn and silent soldiers waiting in ambush. Take the descendant of Sun Shadow with you. He will be your guide. You must travel with great speed and remain unseen. The enemy will be expecting you. Sun Shadow and I found safe passage through the cave. His descendant knows the way. He will carry the key on your journey. This key is different from the other keys, and you will soon know why. It speeds your travel in many ways. However, even the key cannot hasten your journey to the City of Gold. That way must be traveled on foot.

Good luck,
Thomas Cochrane

"Wow," Chris said. "So you had the key this whole time, right under the nose of the enemy. Does Novell know about this too?"

"Novell is the only Caretaker who knows this," Whitethorn said. "And the spirit of his ancestor, Candar, who was even wiser than your Thomas Cochrane knew. I'm going to tell you something now that you must never speak of to another living soul, be they human, Kiern, or Caretaker. I do this only because we are to be comrades in arms, and I do not wish to have any more deception between us. Do I have your word?"

Chris and his dad both nodded silently.

"Candar's logic was even more complicated than your ancestor knew," Whitethorn said. "He wanted Thomas to have his portrait taken with the key to reinforce the image that the third key was in the 'ands of a human. He knew that the young Thomas Cochrane would probably be vain enough to do something like that. He also added the rumor about the key being 'lost at sea' to contribute to the confusion surrounding the third key. It was an insurance policy against treachery. Long ago, Candar resolved that the third key should be 'idden even from the Caretakers. Sadly, there is a history of treachery among the Caretakers. It is rare enough, but it has 'appened. You know the stories of Jerg and of Banlin.

"Candar decided that the third key should remain in the keeping of the Kiern, in case there should be another such traitor in future generations of Caretakers. There 'as never been any example in history of the Kiern betraying the righteous path. We are immune, it seems, to the false promises of Jerg. There is nothing in the Kiern's soul that craves power. We have always been a peaceful people and have peace in our 'earts to the last. As you know, we only became warriors out of necessity. It was thrust upon us. I understand that it may be difficult to believe me since I am the only one 'ere to back up my story. I did not even have to tell you all this, but I wanted there to be no more secrets between us. This, I hope, will ensure that you trust me."

Todd quickly rolled up Thomas's letter. As he stood up from his chair, he slipped the scroll into the pocket of his robe. "We trust you," he said simply. "Now what's next?"

"Now we go," said Whitethorn. "Get your things. Gather your knives and bows. Leave your rifles behind. They're too loud and will alert the enemy of our presence and exact location. We need to travel with great speed and stealth," he said. "You may each carry one of your backpacks—is that what you call them? Nothing too large. You'll need to maneuver through some tight spaces. Pack weapons mainly. You may bring one or two personal items if you can fit them."

"No problem," Todd said. "We know what to do. Right, Criffer Bob?"

In his mind, Chris already had his backpack ready to go: bottle of water, couple of granola bars, flashlight, an extra pair of socks, a T-shirt, one warm flannel shirt, and as many knives and projectile weapons as he could find.

"I'm sorry to rush you from your 'ome so quickly," Whitethorn said as they grabbed their backpacks from the hall closet. "But you're no longer safe 'ere, in any case. I understand the other members of your family are far away from here and will be gone for several more months. This is good. There should be no one in this 'ouse for the enemy has discovered it. You 'ave communicated with your mate?"

"Yes." Todd nodded. "I had a feeling. I have sent a letter that should arrive to her within the month. In it, I communicated as much as I could of the situation using a code language we developed a long time ago when we were dating. She'll know enough to stay away from here until further word reaches her."

"That is well," said Whitethorn with an approving nod. "You're a smart clan, truly the descendants of Thomas and Charles."

"Do you think Mom will be mad?" Chris asked as he started shoving things into his pack.

"No," his dad replied. "She'll understand because she'll know this is bigger than us. We always do what's right, I hope, even if it means making sacrifices. Otherwise, we wouldn't be Cochranes, right?"

Chris agreed with a nod. He felt a surge of pride hearing his dad say that, and he thought back to how Charles and Thomas Cochrane had so bravely defended Castle Forks in that ancient battle that Novell had shown them. He was determined to live up to that.

"But listen, this doesn't mean it's gonna be a free-for-all for you, all right?" Todd added. "I want you to stay close to me, no matter what. And I want you to stick with weapons you've actually got some experience with, like the bow and arrow. You're not to do anything brave or reckless. And as for this whole Juniper's sword thing…if we find it and they want you to try your hand at wielding it, well, don't go rushing into that. I suspect there's a dark side to that too. I want to know all the details before anyone goes touching it. Okay?"

Chris felt like there were a lot of rules and conditions to his coming along, but he didn't push his luck by pointing that out. He just nodded along with everything his dad said.

In less than an hour, they were ready. They met Whitethorn at the door leading from the kitchen into the garage. Fueled by the momentum of their rushed packing job, Todd grabbed his truck keys and pressed the button to open the garage door before Whitethorn could say anything. As he stepped outside, Whitethorn grabbed his shoulder and pulled him back inside. An arrow slammed into the wall right where Todd's head had been a moment before.

They heard a shrill quick scream, followed by the clanging sound of metal on metal. There was a heavy thud and a loud gasp, then nothing. After a moment, a tall, slender figure stepped out from behind the large elm tree at the end of the driveway. Even at a distance, Chris could tell that the bright winged figure was a Caretaker—and he was giving Whitethorn a thumbs-up sign. He must have killed the attacker.

The enemy truly had always been watching. Had this one been the other assailant—the one that had retreated from Whitethorn earlier? Had he come back to finish his task and have his vengeance on Whitethorn for killing his comrade? Or was it a new spy altogether? The thought made Chris's skin crawl. He was eager to get away.

"We always travel with a friend," said Whitethorn by way of explanation. "We never travel alone. It might appear that way, but there's always a protector watching over us wherever we go."

Chris looked back toward the elm tree, but the Caretaker was already gone. Before he could ask any more questions, Whitethorn took them back inside the kitchen and continued, "And we're not travelin' by truck tonight. We're travelin' by door. We need to get to Castle Forks now and not a moment later."

"Traveling by door?" said Todd.

Whitethorn reached behind his breastplate and pulled out the key. As he aimed it at the door, the key changed shape right in front of their eyes. The large golden key with the *C* insignia transformed into a typical house key.

"I believe Thomas mentioned to you in his letter that this key is different from the other two," Whitethorn said as he put the key into the lock of the kitchen door. "Castle Forks armory," he said quietly and turned the doorknob.

Whitethorn politely made the "after you" gesture to Chris and Todd. They walked through the door into what should have been the garage, but there was no truck, no tools, and no storage bins or fishing rods. In fact, they were as far from the garage as they could be. Whitethorn stepped out of the kitchen last and gently closed the door behind him.

CHAPTER 10

Castle Forks armory was a large room, its stone walls overlaid with planks of heavy dark wood. Nearly every inch of the walls was covered in weaponry of every imaginable kind, all hanging neatly from hooks driven into the wood. The room was dimly lit by four massive torches, one in each corner, and the low flames that crackled in a fireplace.

"Well, I guess you weren't kidding when you said this key was special," Todd said, shaking his head in wonder.

Chris was completely disoriented. "So somehow we just took about three steps out of our kitchen, and we're really here now, back at Castle Forks? And it's all because of that key?" It was almost impossible to believe.

"Yeah, it's quite a time-saver." Whitethorn chuckled gruffly, tucking the key back beneath his armor. "And now that we're 'ere and there aren't any arrows flying at our heads for the moment, allow me to reveal my friend, Thungor, who you met earlier at Castle Forks."

Whitethorn gestured to his left, and Thungor, who'd saved Todd's life moments before, appeared from the shadows behind him. As he stepped forward, Thungor nodded his head in greeting.

"So you can move back and forth between being visible and invisible?" Chris asked.

"Yes." Thungor nodded. "I'm what's known as a stealth warrior of the Caretakers. I go into stealth mode when a scout's needed—or a sniper."

"Well, I want to sincerely thank you for your help back there," Todd said.

"You're welcome, Todd Cochrane," Thungor said simply.

"Thungor's never out of earshot of me," Whitethorn said. "He's my protector and friend and bodyguard. Just as I've been actin' as your protector, he's mine. Every being has to have someone watchin' their back."

"I, too, have a protector," said Thungor. "And my protector has one of his own—and so on and so on."

"So there's another protector here that we can't see, the one protecting Thungor?" Chris asked. How many invisible protectors were surrounding them at this moment?

"Yep, that's correct," said Whitethorn. "I don't know their names or faces. Their identities are known only to the one they're protectin', and also to the Historian. That's Novell right now. If Novell were to disclose this information to the enemy, then we'd be in trouble. Just imagine that Thungor has a protector and so forth and so on."

"But wait," Chris said, frowning as he tried to wrap his head around the logic of this information. "Does that mean there are lots of invisible protectors? If that's true, why did Novell say that only the enemy used invisible soldiers? Why did he say that it wasn't honorable to use invisibility?"

"We don't make use of stealth warriors in the same way," Whitethorn answered. "They don't directly intervene unless it's a last resort. It's one of our greatest secrets over the enemy. Not even Banlin or Jerg know of this tactic. The Caretakers formed this level of stealth and secrecy when Jerg left Castle Forks."

"But that doesn't make sense," Chris said. "I saw the Battle for the Forks myself. So many of the Caretakers and their allies died. But you're saying that there were invisible scouts on all sides of the enemy that could have attacked them at any moment?"

Whitethorn sighed heavily. "I know this is difficult to understand. In one sense, aye, these protectors could've attacked the enemy all at once and turned the tide in the Battle for the Forks. But the protectors don't work in this way. We can't be responsible for the extinction of any being—even the Tourlt. We weren't created to decide who should be wiped out and who should be allowed to continue their existence. We're 'ere to ensure the survival of all beings and to stand between the evildoers and those who can't protect themselves."

"But if the Caretakers and Sun Shadow and all the invisible protectors had decided to, they could have ended the Tourlt? Banlin and his evil foes could be gone forever?" Chris said.

"No," said Whitethorn. "Evil will exist as long as good exists. Only durin' the end of time will evil be wiped out. Your good book does mention that evil will end only at the end, doesn't it?"

"Yes, it does," Todd said thoughtfully. "I think what he's saying, Chris, is that our job is to defend and protect—not to destroy. Nobody can make the choice to exterminate an entire people even if the enemy is serving evil."

Whitethorn nodded. "You're right, Todd Cochrane. There're many decisions we don't have the right to make. In the meantime, we must keep to the path of protection. And right now, that means findin' Novell and Si. That's why I've brought us to the armory. 'ere we can prepare ourselves for the journey and rescue mission."

Chris nodded. "So are both you and Thungor *Hairy People*?"

"No, I'm known as a Kiern, but 'airy People works too. Thungor's a stealth warrior," Whitethorn replied with a chuckle. "My kind have long been allies of Castle Forks and have always been instrumental in the fight against the Tourlt. There're several portraits in the castle of those who've fought to defend Castle Forks over the centuries."

Chris stroked his chin. "Oh yeah, I remember seeing those. They all looked like you with long dark hair, heavy-looking armor, and dangerous weapons!"

Whitethorn nodded. "Many of my relatives are in those portraits—my parents, grandparents. They all spent a big part of their life fightin' the Tourlt."

Chris got distracted by the sights of the armory, which was filled with weapons from every imaginable era, it seemed—including many weapons he didn't recognize at all. There were various kinds of swords, knives, daggers, bows, and quivers full of arrows, clubs, sling-shots, and even guns—every weapon Chris could imagine. Many of the items had a futuristic look—as in Chris had never even conceived of such a thing. One of these, which instantly caught his eye, looked like a cross between a bow and a Gatling gun.

"We'll 'ave to be quick," Whitethorn said as he pulled a long sword from its sheath and inspected the blade. "Every moment is precious. Select weapons for yourselves—bows, arrows, daggers—whatever you feel comfortable wieldin'. Whatever you 'ave packed with you from your 'ome, please leave it in this room. In order to use somethin' from this armory, you 'ave to leave something of equal value. So take your own knives and bows and arrows and place them on the table to our right. Trust me, the weapons 'ere will serve you better."

"Why is that?" Todd asked.

"The weapons in this place are much different than what you're used to," Whitethorn said. "For example, the bows. Every time you let an arrow fly from the bow and it hits its mark on the enemy, the next shot will be earmarked for the same destination. If the enemy is still within range of the bow's reach, then the second arrow will travel to the same destination as the first arrow."

"You mean, the bow will somehow know where the arrow hit and then send the next arrow to the same place?" Todd asked.

"Not exactly," Whitethorn said. "But somethin' like that. The arrow disappears instantly from the flesh of the enemy but leaves a tiny fragment of itself behind. It then reappears on the bow for another attempt to make the fatal shot. The second shot acts like a magnet being attracted to its opposite. It wants to be whole again. I know this may seem strange, but I ask once again for your trust since we don't have time for a demonstration."

"Fine with me," said Todd. "I'm happy to trade my bow for one of these. I'll take all the help I can get. You too, Criffer Bob."

"Good," Whitethorn said with a warm laugh. "And one final thing, please only take weapons from the past or present. Don't take anythin' that appears to be unknown to you or not from this place."

I was right! Chris thought. *There are weapons from the future here.*

As much as Chris wanted to pick up the Gatling gun–crossbow hybrid, he could tell that was exactly the kind of weapon Whitethorn was warning against.

Maybe if they saved the day on this adventure and had their portraits placed in the Hall of Protectors…then maybe Chris would have the chance to do some fun target-shooting with it. But he knew today was not the day, so he turned his attention back to something more realistic.

Chris was careful to select a bow that was just the right size for him. It was hanging next to a matching quiver of arrows. Both the bow and the arrows were incredibly light, almost as if they were made of air. He placed his own bow and arrows from home on the table that Whitethorn had indicated, then continued to browse among the other weapons.

"No swords," Todd reminded him. "And nothing crazy, period. Nothing you don't understand. I'd like you to have one up-close weapon, in case it comes to that, but mainly long-range choices would be good. I want you to do your best to stay out of close contact with danger, if you know what I mean. Choose things you can use at a safe distance. You can have one knife, a small one. Hide it inside your hiking boot, just in case you end up in a situation where danger does get close."

As Todd spoke, he was examining his own choices with a critical eye. There was a terribly serious look on his face. As Chris watched his dad choose his weaponry, he began to have a slightly sick feeling in his stomach. Suddenly, here in this place surrounded by blades, bullets, arrows, and every kind of weapon imaginable, Chris couldn't help thinking about the reality of what they faced. Who know what or who these weapons had killed, what they had seen?

Everything that was happening seemed a little less like a book. It was beginning to feel real. His dad didn't look so much like an outdoor gear salesman, a rancher, or even a hunter. He was beginning to look a little more like Charles or Thomas Cochrane. He had a tense look in his face: a furrow between his eyebrows and his jaw slightly clenched. Todd's friendly brown eyes were squinty as he frowned over the weapons and made his choices very deliberately. Even the way he was speaking to Chris seemed a little sterner and clipped, as if he didn't want to waste his words.

Is this what it looked like to switch your thinking to a battle mindset? Chris wondered. He tried to keep all these thoughts from his face. The last thing he wanted was for anyone to notice he was beginning to feel anxious, especially after all the enthusiasm to undertake this mission.

Chris added a humble-looking switchblade and slingshot to his arsenal. The switchblade was very small in its folded position, but when Chris pushed a small gold button at the back, a blade at least twice the expected length shot out. It was really a very long dagger but looked no bigger than a Swiss army knife. He thought that was a pretty neat trick.

Chris picked the slingshot because he knew he had good distance aim, and a slingshot could do some real damage if you had the right rock. Plus, he wouldn't have to worry about carrying all his ammunition for it. Surely there would always be a rock or something similar wherever they were going.

Whitethorn and Todd each approved of his choices. Within a few minutes, they were ready to leave.

"One final thing before we go," said Whitethorn. "If we become separated for any reason, Thungor may need to communicate with you in stealth mode. You'll know he's present by a certain question he'll ask you."

"Please tell me what your favorite thing is, young man," said Thungor.

"Thungor, my favorite dessert is anything with ice cream," Chris answered.

"Good," said Whitethorn. "If he's ever in stealth mode and you 'ear a voice mention ice cream, you'll know it's Thungor and not the enemy."

They exited the armory, crossed the empty dark courtyard, and descended a short flight of steps. At the bottom of the steps was a very long hallway. It was similar to a subway tunnel. There were no windows or furniture along the corridor, but it wound on for a long time. Chris began counting his footsteps. At around five hundred steps, they came to what looked like a wall made of dirty glass.

Whitethorn knocked on the wall several times. Apparently, it was not a solid wall at all. After knocking, Whitethorn stepped through the glass and disappeared. Todd followed immediately after, and Chris went after his dad. As Chris stepped toward the window, he felt a moment of hesitation, but the moment he put his foot through, he realized there was nothing of substance there at all. It felt just like walking through an open doorway.

Chris expected to find himself right outside the castle, perhaps in the clearing where they'd first discovered the front gate to Castle Forks. To his surprise, they were deep in the forest already. Chris turned around and saw the castle far across the valley behind them. The doorway they'd stepped through was no longer visible. All Chris saw directly behind him were the trees. There was no hint of the window.

Looking around, Chris saw Whitethorn and his dad. Thungor was no longer there. He must have gone back into stealth mode.

"We've come as far as the secret tunnel beneath the castle will take us," Whitethorn said. "We'll 'ave to walk the rest of the distance through the forest in the open. By my estimate, it shouldn't take more than an hour to reach the cave entrance. Stick close together and try not to talk much. We don't know who may be listenin'."

Under the weak light of the crescent moon, they trekked through the forest in silence. Whitethorn led the way. Periodically, he paused to look at the old yellowed square of parchment he'd been looking at earlier in the Cochranes' living room. Afterward, he would usually make a slight adjustment to their course. Often Whitethorn had to clear the trail using his sword, slicing easily through the foliage as if it were made of butter.

When they reached the cave entrance, Chris had a strange shock of recognition. He looked over at his dad. "This is the cave Grandpa Jim always warned about, right?" Chris whispered the question as quietly as he could. Todd nodded in reply.

Chris and his dad had passed this cave on scouting trips before. Todd had always been warned against going inside, and he had passed that message onto Chris and Justin. Grandpa Jim had referred to the cave as "the darkness that lies."

Chris had never been sure what that meant, but it had always given him a chill, spine-tingling feeling. Now he was on the verge of entering the one place he'd always been told to avoid. *At least I'm with Dad*, he thought. *Not to mention Whitethorn, Thungor, and a potential army of invisible soldiers standing at the ready.*

They had made the trek pretty much in silence, and nobody seemed inclined to talk now. Chris knew it was a good time to keep quiet. Whitethorn gestured for them to wait, then he entered the cave alone. Chris assumed Thungor went in as well, still in stealth mode.

The minutes ticked by as Chris and his dad waited for Whitethorn to return. Without speaking, they sat down on the ground to the right of the cave's entrance. Leaning against a tree root, Chris strained to hear any sounds he could from within. There were a few faint cracking, creaking sounds, like trees bending in the wind or the sound a house makes when it settles into its foundations. Once or twice, Chris thought he heard a cry or shriek. Could that be Whitethorn making one of his Kiern sounds?

Chris couldn't help thinking that every horror movie he'd seen had a scene like this one—a person going into a cave or cabin or empty house or something to see if it was safe. In the movies, they usually didn't return at all, or they came back running and screaming pursued by some terrible enemy. Or the enemy would appear silently at the mouth of the cave and snatch up the people waiting there before they had a chance to run. Regardless, the outcome was usually not good.

But that's just in the movies, Chris reminded himself. *And this is real life.*

Then Chris heard a voice. "Hey, guys," the voice said.

Chris and his dad both bolted to their feet and peered inside the cave entrance. There was no one there.

The voice came again. "Hey, guys," it said. "Would you ever eat ice cream on a Tuesday when it was no longer considered a Sunday?"

Chris knew instantly that it was Thungor. He exhaled in relief. Chris looked over at his dad, who nodded at him and shouldered his pack. Chris followed his dad's lead, and they walked together into the cave.

As soon as he stepped into the darkness, Chris felt two light taps on his shoulder. Somehow he knew it was Thungor, letting them know he was there, watching their backs.

There was almost no light in the cave. Chris accidentally kicked a few rocks, then tripped over a small boulder, nearly falling to the cave floor. A large hand on his shoulder caught him just in time to prevent a face plant. He could tell from the size of the hand that it was Whitethorn.

A low whisper of "It's me" indicated that the band was back together again.

"Hold onto the back of my tunic," said Whitethorn. "Todd, you hold onto Chris, and Thungor will walk behind you. It's nearly pitch black all the way to the center. We'll need to stick together by feel."

They filed into the cave. A very dim light occasionally filtered in through cracks high up in the walls of the cave, but it never got bright enough to really see anything. In near-total darkness they walked, Chris holding onto the back of Whitethorn's tunic. He could feel his dad's hand lightly holding onto the canvas loop on the top of his backpack. In single file, they walked for what felt like hours.

It was very disorienting. At first, Chris tried to keep track of the turns they were making: left, right, right, right, left. But there were too many to remember. He tried to note the changing of the ground, whether it was level or uphill or downhill, but after all that time in the darkness, he couldn't keep track. He wondered how he'd ever find his way out of here without a guide. It would be completely impossible. Well, hopefully they'd all be leaving together so the situation wouldn't arise.

Although their trek was long and dark, the path was remarkably clear. Rarely did anyone trip, and although Chris kept waiting for some kind of stealth attack from the enemy, somehow it never came. It occurred to him that Whitethorn and Thungor may have cleared the path in advance. Maybe that's why they'd been gone for so long while Chris and his dad had waited outside the cave entrance. The lack of enemy traps seemed almost too good to be true.

After about an hour, Chris felt safe enough to let his mind wander a bit. In his letter, Thomas Cochrane had said that he and Sun Shadow had been on this path before. Chris reflected that he was now walking the same path and taking the same steps as his famous relative of the past. Pretty cool.

He knew the situation was very dangerous still, with all the unknowns, but it was nevertheless exciting to be there. *Beats algebra,* he thought.

After some time, Chris became aware of a faint light up ahead. It was more light than they'd yet seen inside the cave. As they rounded a bend in the tunnel, Chris had to shut his eyes against the startling brightness. A single torch hung on the cave wall, shining a light onto their path.

Finally!

Blinking in the sudden glare, Chris tried to find the path forward—but there wasn't one. The cave had led them all the way to this point: a dead-end. They stood there for a few moments. Whitethorn pulled out his map again and looked at it for a long moment. Then he walked up to the dead-end and knocked lightly on the wall. The rock surface flickered for a moment, then became solid again. Whitethorn repeated his knock, and the wall flickered again before turning back to rock.

He knocked again as he spoke. "Downopensideuppetydownseytomorrow."

What? Chris thought. He had never heard Whitethorn speak such words before.

Whitethorn reached into his pouch for a blueberry and ate it. That made sense. It had been a while since they'd eaten the blueberries, so the language translation must have worn off.

116

Whitethorn passed each of them a single blueberry from his pouch, then held one into the air. It disappeared. Thungor must have taken that one.

Whitethorn knocked again. This time, he said, "I'm a mere traveler seeking riches. I've come to claim that which is rightfully mine."

His words must have been a secret code or password that somehow unlocked the wall. The wet gray rock flickered, and for a moment, it looked like a dirty window. Whitethorn stepped through it and disappeared. As before, Chris and Todd followed after him.

Chris flinched against the sudden blazing light. It was as if they'd stepped from midnight on one side of the wall into the full light of noon. As their eyes adjusted, they could see that the light was not coming from any sun. The path ahead was bright and glaring for two reasons. One, there were hundreds of lit torches shining from metal posts along what appeared to be an otherwise empty road. The other reason was at the end of that road.

The City of Gold—it was real. A shining collection of buildings, gates, bridges, towers, spires, and garrets—all made of gold. In the brilliant light of countless torches, the city was bathed in a reddish light. There was no sun, but the city was the color of sunsets Chris had seen on the ocean. It was the red-gold color of the sun just as it sank past the horizon on a clear day at the beach. Those kinds of sunsets were pretty though. Here, the red light was frightening. Chris couldn't help but think of blood.

The road upon which they stood led through a valley of dead trees and ended at the main castle's front gate. A red river forked around the castle—a mirror of the river that flowed around Castle Forks. In fact, the castle itself looked exactly like Castle Forks, Chris realized, except that it wasn't made of gray stone. It was a gold copy of Castle Forks—down to the front gate, the protective wall, and the towers.

The valley, too, was a bizarre copy of Windy Nip Glen. Except for the addition of the torch-lit road, it looked just like Windy Nip Glen—if Windy Nip Glen had been in the path of a forest fire. There was nothing green or alive in the valley. The ground was dry, red, and clay dotted with black leafless trees. The river was a copy of the two-pronged river that wound around Castle Forks, but its waters were bloodred instead of clear, bright blue.

Chris's mind was racing with questions. Had the Tourlt created this place as their interpretation of Castle Forks? Or was this the true opposite of Castle Forks—and had it been here just as long? And where was the enemy? The place looked deserted. Was the enemy lying in wait for them? Surely they must know of the intruders' presence by now. Chris shrank back against a skeletal tree, suddenly wanting some cover from all the light. He felt like they were totally exposed.

"Don't worry," Whitethorn whispered. "I'm beginnin' to think the enemy has badly underestimated me—which is perfect. That's how we'll get into the castle and how we'll get Novell and Si back."

Todd leaned in. "You mean, they're not sending any of their soldiers after us? Because they think we're not a real threat?"

Whitehorn nodded.

"I thought so too," Todd said. "Our path until now was too easy. They want us to make it all the way to the castle."

"That's right. We might as well just walk right up there, singin' loudly the whole way." Whitethorn laughed.

"Well, there's no need to press our luck," Todd said. "Maybe we should see how close we can get cautiously. We can take some beneath the dead trees if we walk through the valley off-road."

"Works for me," said Whitethorn.

They moved off the main road and began walking toward the castle.

"Uh, what are we gonna do when we get there though?" Chris asked after a few minutes. He was starting to feel like they needed a plan.

"Leave it to me," Whitethorn said. "All I want you to do is stay covered. We'll 'ave to improvise a bit, but I've got a theory. This place is a mirror of Castle Forks. It probably has the same tunnel system too. I know those tunnels like the back of my hand. I bet I can find a way into this castle, just like we found our way out of Castle Forks back there."

Just then, a loud bang sounded. They turned their heads in the direction of the sound—the highest peak of the tallest castle tower. The door at the top clanged open, as a sinister winged figure came swooping out of it. The dark figure flew to the balcony edge of the tower and alighted, perching himself there and looking out over the city. Chris and his friends were just close enough to see his face.

It was Banlin. He was alive after all these years.

"The time has come to witness the downfall of the Caretakers and their so-called legacy," Banlin roared. But who was he talking to? It looked like he was speaking to an empty city.

Chris felt a chill crawl up his spine. There was no way the city was empty. This place must be full of invisible Tourlt. They were surrounded by the enemy.

Chris could tell his dad was having a similar realization. Todd was looking around vigilantly with a narrow squint to his eyes, tracking for danger.

"We've got to get a better vantage point," said Whitethorn. "Somethin's about to 'appen. We're nearly at the castle, but I don't 'ave enough time to look for a tunnel. Look, we'll climb up into these trees. At least we'll be able to see better."

They quickly scrambled up the bare branches of two neighboring trees. Whitethorn (and presumably Thungor) went up to one tree while Chris and Todd climbed the one next to it. From about fifteen feet up, they had a clear view of what was happening on the platform of the tower.

Behind Banlin came six more figures: four of his soldiers and two masked figures with their hands tied behind their backs. These were thrown at the feet of Banlin and forced to their knees. A soldier pulled the masks from their faces.

"Behold! I give you the former Caretaker and the current Historian, Novell," Banlin announced, sneering. "And here lies another fool cowering on his knees in defeat. He's the weak link to my old friend and foe, Si the Caretaker, the leader of Castle Forks. Well, soon to be *former* leader. Bring out the last prisoner," he yelled.

Another bound prisoner was dragged through the tower doorway and thrown at Banlin's feet. This one didn't have the Caretaker wings. It looked like a man. Banlin leaned down and ripped off the man's mask. He had long unkempt brown hair and a bushy brown beard streaked with gray. His clothes were ragged and dirty, and his face was extremely pale as if he hadn't seen the sun in a long time.

The man's face was strangely familiar. *No way*, Chris thought, as the man's identity slowly dawned on him.

Whitethorn's low grumbling voice came from a foot or so above Chris's head and echoed Chris's thoughts exactly. "No…it can't be," said Whitethorn. "We thought by now…he must be dead."

"I give you Thomas Cochrane," Banlin roared again.

"How is that possible?" Todd turned to look up at Whitethorn, who was perched on a wide limb to their right and slightly above them. "How can he be alive?"

"The Sword of Juniper," Whitethorn whispered back. "That's the gift, or some might say the curse, of any human who wields that sword."

"You mean, he's…immortal?" Todd asked.

"It's not exactly immortality," Whitethorn answered. "All beings die sometime. But Novell was never sure what 'appened to him. After he banished Banlin back into the shadows with the sword…somehow Banlin must have taken Thomas with him. And without the Sword of Juniper, Thomas must be very weak. Almost defenseless."

"We'll start the show with you, Sir Thomas!" Banlin announced. "Why don't you stand up so we can all have a good view of your demise?"

Banlin gestured to one of his soldiers, who pulled Thomas up roughly by the back of his tattered tunic. Thomas barely had the strength to stand. His expression was defiant, but his knees buckled weakly. If it weren't for the Tourlt soldier holding him up, it looked like Thomas would have crumpled to the ground.

"If he's defenseless, then don't we have to do something? To protect him?" Todd said. Before the words were out of his mouth, he'd pulled an arrow from his quiver and fitted it into his bow. In one smooth motion, Todd lifted his bow, drew the string back with all his might, and let his arrow fly.

The arrow arched through the sky and hit its mark. But with a metallic clang, it bounced harmlessly off Banlin's chest and fell to the ground. The Tourlt leader swiveled his head instantly in the direction of the attacker. Even at this distance, Chris could feel those terrible red eyes burning into him as Banlin spotted their hiding place.

"Aha! I see our visitors have arrived in time for the show!" Banlin shouted gleefully. He leaped off the tower, his leathery wings beating the air as he sailed directly toward the tree where Chris and Todd were nestled. He drew up just a foot short of the tree and hovered in the air right in front of them.

"Ah, you must be the Cochranes!" Banlin said in a mock-friendly tone, slowly looking them up and down.

Chris felt his blood turn to ice.

"And one of you really is just a child. How sweet," Banlin went on in his mocking tone.

He's really taking his time to mess with us, Chris thought bitterly. He resisted the urge to look up in Whitethorn's direction. Maybe Banlin hadn't spotted the Kiern crouching just above their heads yet, and Chris didn't want to give him away.

Banlin was focused on Todd now. "And you, what a brave soldier, just like your kinsman up there in the tower!" He fixed his gaze on Todd's face. "You must be the one who sent that arrow my way. I wonder why you would do such a thing. Didn't Novell tell you I was a Seer? That I could detect danger before it happened? Why would you think you could harm me?"

Todd looked straight into Banlin's face, showing no sign of fear. "My goal wasn't to harm you. My goal was to protect a defenseless man."

"I see," Banlin said, narrowing his red eyes thoughtfully. He fixed Todd with his stare for one long moment, then threw his hands up in the air and shrugged. "Oh well, I hope you feel good about yourself either way. Because now you're a defenseless man too, and I don't think any of your friends are in a position to help you."

With a shriek, Whitethorn lunged down from the shadows. His left hand was wrapped around the tree branch as he swung with all his might and connected a right hook to Banlin's jaw.

Banlin dropped to the ground like lead. Whitethorn caught himself easily on a lower branch and stood looking down at his foe.

"Hello, Banlin, nice to see you again." He chuckled. "I take it you still can't dodge my punches. I've truly missed our old sparring sessions."

Banlin stood up, wiping the blood from his face. He launched into the air again and hovered in front of Whitethorn this time but made no move to retaliate.

"Of course I knew you were coming, my hairy old friend," Banlin said. "I left my entrance practically unguarded for you. I have welcomed you into my trap."

"Aye, I know," Whitethorn said calmly. "We're all surrounded by your invisible army, and you let us get all the way up 'ere so you could slaughter everybody at once. I get it. But it's funny, isn't it? You knew we were coming, but you didn't see that last little punch coming, did you? That took you by complete surprise, didn't it? Why is that, old friend?"

Whitethorn paused, waiting for an answer. Banlin just glared back at him but said nothing.

"That's what I thought," Whitethorn said with satisfaction. "I know your secret. I know about your little Ring of Detection. It's the only item that sets you apart from the rest of your scum. You can sense the presence of approachin' danger mere moments before it 'appens. But that does not make you a true Seer. And what's worse... your little ring doesn't work on me."

Banlin gritted his teeth and snarled. With a roar, he sharply raised his right arm high into the air, his hand clenched in a fist. A Tourlt soldier appeared out of thin air to his left...and then another to his right. A battalion of Tourlt, all standing at attention, sprang up out of the empty air behind him—every one of them fitted in their battle armor, flaming swords in hands, bows and arrows slung on their backs.

There were so many of them. Chris looked over at his dad, silently wondering: *What in the world does Whitethorn have in mind?* How could they possibly win this fight when their "army" consisted only of himself and his dad, Si, Novell, Thungor, and a very old weak-looking Thomas Cochrane?

Todd looked back at him. He seemed strangely calm. "Listen, Criffer Bob," he said. "I don't think the odds are as bad as they appear right now, okay?"

Appear! Chris remembered what Whitethorn and Thungor had said about the invisible army.

The protectors had never broken their invisibility presence to the enemy before. Why would they do it now? Maybe this wasn't the same as the battle at Castle Forks—because it wasn't a battle. It was a rescue mission! Maybe that meant the invisible protectors could intervene.

Chris's vision seemed very clear all of a sudden and the waves of fear retreated. He drew an arrow and fitted it into his bow. He wasn't sure who his first target would be, but he wanted to be ready. He looked over at the tower platform. Si, Novell, and Thomas were still there, surrounded by the enemy.

Flaming swords had been drawn and placed at each of their necks. Time seemed to stand still.

Whitethorn drew his steel sword, and Banlin hauled a golden mace from over his shoulder. The rest of Banlin's army unsheathed their weapons, and Chris's stomach coiled with a fear he'd never known before.

Thungor readied his axe, and Todd grabbed an arrow from his quiver. He looked back at Chris and gestured for him to crouch instead of stand, but Chris's fear had rooted him to the spot—he couldn't move forward or back.

After a few moments of dead silence, Banlin let out a deafening war cry and swung his mace at Whitethorn's stomach. Whitethorn dodged out of the way and swung his sword at Banlin's head as a flurry of arrows flew toward Thungor and Todd, but Banlin sidestepped and blocked Whitethorn's attack. The pair of them continued to strike and parry as Thungor fought off two of Banlin's followers with his axe. They tried to slash his neck with a series of quick attacks, but Thungor blocked them with the edge of his weapon.

Todd aimed his bow at an archer at the back who was causing damage from the shadows and released one of his new arrows. The tip pierced the archer in the calf and forced the solider to his knees, roaring in pain. Todd lifted his bow again and fired another arrow at the soldier's head, penetrating his skull and ending his evil life.

Chris admired his dad's archery skills and wished he could be as good as him, anything to get through this battle unscathed.

As Todd lifted his bow again and focused on another shadow enemy, Chris turned his attention back to Whitethorn and Banlin, who continued to clash weapons and dodge each other's attacks. He took a deep breath and jumped down from his branch, quickly hurrying to the nearby tunnel.

Just as Chris positioned himself, one of Banlin's soldiers collapsed to the ground just in front of Chris's spot in the tunnel. Blood poured from one of his ears and pooled on the floor. Chris assumed he'd been shot by one of Whitethorn or Thungor's protectors, but he struggled to have complete faith in a group of warriors he couldn't see, especially with his dad in the battle.

Banlin roared with rage and bellowed, "Die, you hairy cretin! Die!"

"Never!" Whitethorn yelled back over the clanking of metal that filled the vicinity.

Whitethorn swiped his sword at Banlin's head, and Banlin blocked him yet again, but Whitethorn used this opportunity to push him back into the jagged wall behind him, the rough surface jabbing into Banlin's back. Banlin tried to shove Whitethorn away and break free, but Whitethorn's strength kept him in place.

One of Banlin's troops aimed their bow at Whitethorn's back but Todd took aim and launched an arrow, striking the soldier in the ribs. Without wasting a second, Todd volleyed another arrow and shot the soldier in the temple, killing him instantly.

Todd continued firing arrows at various soldiers attacking Whitethorn from behind, and Thungor hurled a set of throwing knives at the onslaught of warriors advancing toward him at speed. Chris watched as the knives found each soldier's skull, neck, or chest, dropping to the ground with a loud *thud*. But one of Banlin's troops dodged Thungor's throwing knife and bolted toward him with a great axe in his hand, much bigger than Thungor's.

Thungor turned his axe sideways and blocked the soldier's attack, but more and more enemies raced in his direction. Todd turned away from Whitethorn and used his remaining arrows to defend Thungor. The invisible protectors shot as many troops down as possible.

One agile warrior slipped through the defenses and headed straight for Todd, his mace raised and ready for the kill. Everything moved in slow motion, but Chris's heart thumped like time had sped up.

Chris had been too scared to fight, not knowing who to attack or who to defend, but if he wanted his dad to survive, he *had* to act and fast.

As the soldier charged up to Todd's blind spot and lifted his weapon higher, Chris drew a deep breath and began to pull his arrow back.

A loud gunshot tore the air, deafening him. Everything went dark.

CHAPTER 11

His whole body ached. As consciousness returned, Chris realized he couldn't lift his arms or legs.

They were pinned down. Through blurry eyes, he could make out the bright lights and white walls of a hospital room. Instinctively, he began thrashing, fighting whatever it was restraining his ankles and wrists.

Chris sensed someone moving toward the bed. He turned his head and could just make out the shape of a person—a nurse?—wearing a white-and-blue uniform. His eyes were gummy and filled with sleep. He blinked rapidly, trying to clear his vision.

"Help! Let me up," he croaked. His voice came out in a cracked, throaty whisper.

Chris felt a cool palm against his forehead. "Shhh," said a woman's soothing voice. "You're all right, I promise. You're in the hospital, and we're taking care of you. I know you're confused, but please lie back. If you stop thrashing, I can release your ankles and wrists."

Chris's vision was beginning to clear. He saw a dark-haired woman, about forty years old, leaning over him with a comforting expression. He stopped thrashing and drew in a deep breath, trying to relax in spite of his confusion and fear.

"Okay," he said. "I'm okay, I'll stop thrashing."

"That's better," the nurse said. She began to release the straps that bound him. "I know this must be very confusing. You've been asleep for quite some time. I'm sorry we had to strap you down like this, but it was for the best. You must have been having some serious nightmares. We had to do this in order to keep you in bed, where you needed to be, and to keep your IV going."

As she continued talking in her calm way, Chris felt a little more relaxed, but he was no less confused.

Once the straps were released, he tried to pull himself up into a seated position. It wasn't as easy as it should have been; his muscles were stiff and sore, and his limbs felt weak. The nurse helped him by pulling up the back of the bed and arranging the pillows behind him.

"I'm Nurse Parish," she said. "You can call me Helen or Nurse Helen, if you like." She checked the machine next to the bed, jotting down notes onto a clipboard as she did so.

For the first time, Chris noticed the needle jutting out of his left forearm connected to a tube running from the machine.

"So how long have I been here?" he asked. His voice was still hoarse.

Before answering, Nurse Helen hooked the clipboard back onto the end of his bed and filled a cup with water from a cooler in the corner.

"Here, you must be thirsty," she said, handing him the water.

Chris realized he was incredibly thirsty. He gulped the water down and held the cup out again. The nurse refilled his cup and handed it back. As Chris drank it down, she walked over to a phone by the door and made a call. She spoke so quietly that Chris couldn't make out what she was saying. Then she hung up the phone and walked back over to his bed. She sat down in the chair and looked at him with an oddly sympathetic expression.

"You've been asleep for about six months," she said. "And I'm very sorry to do this to you right now, but I'll have to ask you a few quick questions to check your memory. Is that all right?"

Six months! Chris was stunned. But the only thing he could do was nod, numb with shock.

Nurse Helen picked up his chart again. "All right then, can you tell me your name?" she asked.

"Chris. Christopher Cochrane," he said.

"And your date of birth?"

He told her. She nodded, jotted something on the chart, and asked several more questions, including the names of his parents and brother, his home address, what school he attended, and other basic things like that. Chris answered the questions without hesitation. He could tell the nurse was pleased.

Finally, she asked, "Do you remember how you got injured?"

Chris didn't say anything right away. His mind was racing. In fact, he had no idea how he'd been injured. The last thing he remembered felt like it had happened just moments ago. He'd been holding a bow and arrow, preparing to defend himself and his dad in battle against the Tourlt.

Whitethorn had been there…and Novell…and Si. He remembered hearing a gunshot, but he didn't remember getting hit or feeling any pain. Chris simply could not answer the question. One thing he knew for sure though was that he couldn't tell Nurse Helen the truth about his memories. She would think he was crazy.

The moment stretched on. Chris knew he had to say something. At last, with a puzzled frown on his face, he simply said, "No, I don't remember."

"That's not unusual," Nurse Helen said reassuringly. "It was traumatic, so you may not be able to remember it right now. You were in a car accident, Chris, in your father's truck."

"I was?" Chris gasped. "A car accident? With my dad? And where's my dad?"

Nurse Helen's face grew very sympathetic. "We don't know, Chris," she said. "I'm sorry, but we just don't know where your father is. We've contacted your mother in Peru. I want you to know that she and your brother are just fine. It took us a couple of months to get in touch with her though, so they're not back in California yet. I understand they're making their way home now and should be here within a few days. I'm sure they'll be happy to see you've woken up," she added with a smile.

Chris could tell that the nurse was doing everything she could to make him feel better, but it wasn't helping. He felt like he was having a nightmare. Could this be real? None of it made sense. He knew there'd been no car accident, right? He would remember if there had been an accident, wouldn't he?

Chris was beginning to doubt his own memories all of a sudden even though he'd been so confident just moments before. He felt a panic rising in his chest. Looking at the nurse's sympathetic face, he had the urge to spill out the whole story to her—to tell her everything about the Tourlt and Whitethorn and Novell and Castle Forks and Thomas Cochrane. Then he could tell her, "You're wrong, see? My dad's not gone. He's in the City of Gold, fighting the Tourlt. In fact, I should be back there myself—helping him! I have to get out of this hospital and get back there right away!"

Even as the words raced through Chris's mind, he knew how nonsensical they would sound out loud. He knew he had to resist every instinct to tell the truth right now, or who knew where they'd put him. He tried to gather his thoughts. Drawing in a deep breath, he decided to find out what he could.

"You said I was in my dad's truck when the accident happened? Where was he? I mean, why couldn't they find him?"

"Now that's a question for someone else, I'm afraid," the nurse said. "All I'm aware of is that you were brought in with a head injury. No one else was found with you after the accident. I know that emergency responders scoured the area but didn't find your father or anyone else. You may have been alone in the truck. Is that possible?"

Chris shook his head numbly. "I…I don't think so. I'm only twelve, I don't drive…I don't remember anything about it…" He trailed off, confused.

"It's all right, Chris," Nurse Helen said gently. "Try not to worry. Maybe some things will come back to you after a while. In the meantime, you'll need to talk to a California Highway Patrol officer. He needs to ask you some questions. Do you want something to eat first?"

Chris shook his head. For someone who hadn't eaten solid food in three months, he had surprisingly little appetite. "No, it's fine. I'd rather just get the questions over with."

"I understand," the nurse said, standing up. "I'll send him in. And, Chris, there's the call button. Don't hesitate to call me if you need anything. I'll be on the floor for another hour. After that, the night staff will be here for you."

"Thank you," Chris said.

A moment after Nurse Helen left the room, the door opened again. A tall blond CHP officer in full uniform walked in. He was carrying a clipboard.

"I'm Officer Smith, California Highway Patrol," he said, walking over to Chris's bed.

The officer held out his hand, and Chris shook it. "Hi" was all Chris could think of to say. His mind was still racing, and he felt terribly nervous. Officer Smith was looking at him with a sympathetic expression, and Chris could tell he was trying to be kind. Nonetheless, Chris knew this was about to be a very strange conversation.

The officer sat down in the chair next to the bed. He took out a pen from his left shirt pocket and clicked it. He tapped his pen on the clipboard, apparently pondering how to begin. "I've been assigned to investigate the accident you were involved in," he said after a moment. "I've been told you don't remember anything about it yet. So I'm gonna tell you what we know, and we'll see if anything I say jogs your memory. All right?"

He looked up from his clipboard and waited for Chris to nod before continuing.

"You were in a vehicle crash on Route 36 in October, about six months ago," he said matter-of-factly. "The truck you were in went off a cliff during a rainstorm. It was a three-thousand-foot drop—it's a miracle you survived. The truck landed upside down. You were thrown clear of the vehicle and found unconscious about twenty feet away, still buckled into the passenger seat. You had a head injury—a gash above your left eyebrow, and there was glass embedded in the wound. There was also a small burn on your right forearm, but otherwise, you were uninjured. You've been in a coma since then. Now we traced the plates on the truck to your father, Todd Cochrane. But, Chris, the confusing thing is that your father was not found anywhere near the vehicle. He still hasn't been found. The bench seat of the truck was apparently torn in half, and the passenger side was thrown clear with you in it. The other half of the bench seat was still inside the truck, but it was empty."

The officer paused. He rubbed his forehead for a second then looked at Chris. "I have to ask you, is any of this jogging your memory yet?"

"No, sir," Chris said. "I'm...I'm sorry, but I don't remember anything about the accident. I...do remember I went on a hunting trip with my dad in October. We went to a mountain off Route 36, so I guess maybe that's where we were. But I just don't remember anything else."

"Okay," the officer said. He wrote something on his clipboard. "Is it possible you were driving the truck from the passenger's seat?" he asked next.

"What?" Chris asked in alarm. "No! I mean, no...I don't drive. I'm not sixteen yet, and besides, I mean, how could I drive from the passenger seat? That doesn't even make sense...I mean, it's not even possible, right?"

Chris realized he was starting to sound panicky and defensive, so he stopped talking. Officer Smith shot him a quick glance that looked more suspicious than kind. Was the officer starting to suspect he was lying or that there'd been some kind of foul play? Once again, Chris had the desperate urge to explain what had really happened... that he and his dad had been to the mountain in October twice and that they'd discovered the world of Castle Forks. He wanted to explain that his dad was there now, not missing at all. But his dad was in trouble! And he had to get back to him—he had to get out of this hospital room and help him.

Before any of these words could tumble out, Chris forced himself to take a deep breath. If he told the truth, there was no way he was going to be allowed to go back to the City of Gold or do anything to help his dad. He would be sent straight to a loony bin and locked up instead, probably.

He had to keep his mouth shut, even if it meant telling some white lies.

"Officer Smith," he said in a weak voice. "Is my dad...dead? I mean, do you all think my dad is dead?"

The officer's face became sympathetic once more. Chris breathed a silent sigh of relief. *Good,* he thought, *I need sympathy right now, not suspicion.*

"Look, Chris, I'm sorry," Officer Smith said. "It seems likely that he is. But we haven't found his body. If he was driving the truck…it's just a total mystery where he is. We scoured the area and found no sign of him or anyone else. That's why I had to ask you if there was any chance you were driving. The only other possibility is…not very nice either, I'm afraid. Maybe he disappeared some other way, like he was kidnapped. Or he disappeared on purpose."

Chris wanted to shout that there was no way any of those things had happened, but he knew he needed to play it cool. *Fine. If this cop wants to think my dad just abandoned our family or someone's kidnapped him or something—who cares? I don't have to tell him that's not true. I should let him think that. I need to bide my time until I can figure out a way to get back to Dad and the others.*

"Disappeared on purpose?" Chris said. "You mean, like he may have taken off or something, just leaving me there? That seems so crazy." He just shook his head. "But I don't know. I wish I could remember what happened before. You said the accident was in October?"

The officer nodded. "Yes. And it's April now."

A chill ran down Chris's spine. April. That was the same month he and his dad had returned from Castle Forks the first time—when they'd first lost six months. They had gone on the hunting trip in October. That was when they'd met Si and been taken inside Castle Forks and shown everything about the castle's history. They had returned in April. They had driven home from the mountain in a downpour, Chris remembered suddenly. A rainstorm. *The truck you were in went off a cliff in a rainstorm*—that's what the officer had just said.

Chris felt sick to his stomach. Was it possible there really had been an accident? Had he dreamed all of this stuff about Castle Forks while he was in a coma? Is that why his hands and ankles had been tied down? Had he just been having crazy dreams about giants and angels and Demon Shadows and terrible, bloody battles?

He needed to be alone. Chris had to get rid of Officer Smith. He simply couldn't think his way through all this with the officer sitting there, looking at him with those questioning eyes.

"Officer Smith, I'm...I'm not feeling very well," he said truthfully. "I think I need some more water and something to eat. I'm gonna call the nurse in. I'm sorry, I wish I could help more...I wish I could remember." He trailed off faintly as he reached for the nurse call button.

Officer Smith slipped his pen back into his shirt pocket. "It's all right," the officer said. "I don't have any more questions for now, and you should probably eat something. It's been a while." He smiled and stood up. "We'll be in touch though. Let your doctor or one of the nurses know if you do remember something. And, Chris, look, I just want to say, wherever your dad is...I'm sorry he's not here."

He reached out his hand, and Chris shook it numbly. The officer's last words drummed through his brain like a cold rain. *Maybe my dad really is gone. Maybe he's...dead. Maybe I'm just alone here, a crazy kid who's been having nightmares for six months after he went over a cliff in his dad's truck.*

A nurse came in as Officer Smith walked out. It wasn't Nurse Helen but a younger curly-haired guy.

"I'm Nurse Mike," he said in a friendly tone. "What can I do for you, Chris?"

"Oh, I'm just hungry, Mike. Can I get something to eat?"

"Sure thing," Mike said, picking up Chris's patient chart. "Cool, it says here your only allergy is to berries. I don't think there are any on the menu tonight. I'll be right back with some food for you."

"What?" Chris blurted. "I'm allergic to berries? No way!"

Mike glanced at the chart again. "Sorry, buddy, it says so right here. Could be a mistake, I guess. I'll check with the doctor, but in the meantime, I won't take any chances. I'll be right back with your dinner."

Allergic to berries? Chris thought. It didn't make sense. Berries were the one food that allowed him to understand Whitethorn and the others from Castle Forks. It was too much of a coincidence that he now had an allergy to them.

133

What if the magical mountain berries were something his mind had made up too because he had an allergy to them in real life? What if his dad really was dead? What if there had been a wreck for real in the truck and all this business with Castle Forks was just something his subconscious mind had made up to tell him while he slept? Could it all have been just one long coma-induced fantasy?

It couldn't be. There were too many details. It felt so real. He had to figure out a way to get out of here. If he could somehow slip away from the hospital undetected, then he could find his way back to Castle Forks.

He'd have to get a car or someone to drive him up there though. What was he going to do, call a cab? No. If he could get back to his house before his mom got home and pack a backpack, then he could hike all the way there. It might take a few days, but he could do it. And if they weren't at Castle Forks, he could hike to the cave and find his way back to the City of Gold. He could do it. He knew he could. But first he'd have to get some food in him and get this IV out of his arm. He'd wait until late at night when everyone thought he was asleep, and he'd sneak out of the hospital.

He saw that his regular clothes and boots were on a table across the room. It looked like his clothes had been washed and folded and his boots were intact. That was good. It'd be much easier to sneak away if he wasn't wearing a hospital gown. Now he just had to act normal and bide his time.

Mike returned with a tray of food, and Chris ate it ravenously. He was now totally focused on getting some food in his system and getting his energy back.

"Let me open these windows for you a little," Mike said as Chris devoured his tray of chicken, mashed potatoes, and vegetables. "It's kind of stuffy in here, right?"

The cool spring air blowing in through the half-opened windows was a welcome change. With his stomach full of food and the fresh air on his face, Chris felt more relaxed. Mike checked his vital signs and removed the IV.

"You're doing great, Chris," he said, placing a small bandage over the IV puncture in Chris's arm.

"You shouldn't be needing this anymore since you're able to eat solid food now. Here's the TV remote. I'm here all night. If you need anything, just press the call button."

The sun had set while Chris was eating, and the low light of dusk filled the room. After Mike left, Chris tried to watch a little television, but he couldn't find anything as interesting as his own thoughts. He switched the TV off and found his sketch pad in the top draw of the side table, so he decided to draw the Caretakers, or what he remembered of them, to keep them alive in his mind. While sketching, he gazed through half-shut eyes at the stiff white curtains moving slightly in the breeze. Judging from the view of the other buildings outside his window, Chris guessed his room was on the third or fourth floor of the hospital. Maybe there was a fire escape outside the window he could use to climb down. Or maybe he'd be fine just walking calmly out the front door. It was possible no one would notice, right?

Either way, he just needed to pretend to be asleep for a few hours. Then when nobody was expecting him to be up, he'd quietly get dressed and get out.

His thoughts drifted back to the journey he'd taken with his dad and Whitethorn to the City of Gold. It certainly didn't feel like a dream, but if it wasn't, then what was happening now? Had his dad and the others survived the fight with Banlin? How much time had gone by for them? The time changes between Castle Forks and the regular world were strange. Maybe a long time had passed in that world, or maybe it was only an hour later. It was frustrating not knowing. His resolution to go back grew stronger with every second.

Suddenly, right in front of his eyes, one of the windowpanes slowly slid up about a foot, all by itself.

Chris sat up straight. The curtain slid smoothly on its rod all the way over to the right.

"*Sspppt. Sspppt.*" Chris heard a faint whisper in his ear. A blueberry appeared out of thin air, just within reach. Instinctively, Chris reached out and took the berry, popping it into his mouth.

"Would you ever eat ice cream on a Tuesday when it was no longer considered a Sunday?" a voice said.

"Thungor!" Chris exclaimed in a hoarse whisper. "You're really here!"

"Yes, I'm here," Thungor's voice said.

Chris's body flooded with relief. He wasn't crazy! It had all been true. He flung the covers off the bed and stood up but had to catch himself on the bed rail as his weak knees buckled beneath him.

Two strong hands caught him under the arms and set him back down on the edge of the bed.

"Your body is weak from a long sleep," Thungor said. He had dropped his invisibility, and now Chris could see the Caretaker in his black tunic standing next to the bed. "I will help you find your strength."

Thungor placed one palm on the top of Chris's head. A warm glowing sensation traveled down through Chris's body, as if the sun were shining on him. Chris could feel strength and energy flooding back into his limbs. When the Caretaker took his hand away, Chris rose to his feet. His legs were perfectly steady now. In fact, he'd never felt better in his life. He walked quickly over to the table where his clothes were, then took off his hospital gown and began dressing.

"Do you know how I got here?" Chris asked. "What really happened at the City of Gold after I blacked out?"

Thungor sighed and prepared his answer.

"Terrible things, lad. Your father and Whitethorn fought with many Shadow Demons until your father got injured. Whitethorn barely managed to get both of you out without getting killed himself, and I would've died if not for my brother, Vannsd," Thungor explained. "Whitethorn requested that I protect you before he and your father were found and captured."

Thungor paused, and Chris waited for him to continue.

"I brought you to the hospital and tampered with the knowledge the nurses had about you and your father, making them believe you had both been in a car accident on Route 36."

Chris gasped. "*You* staged the car crash and brought me here?"

Thungor nodded. "Yes, but with Vannsd's assistance. When the police started investigating the crash site, I had to place an altered image in Officer Smith's mind too. Meanwhile, Jerg and Banlin attacked and took over Castle Forks. Many lives were lost, and many people were captured, including your father. I'm afraid they're to be used as sport, in the Jungle-Gym Ziggurat."

"What…what do you mean, Thungor?" Chris asked, wide-eyed with horror.

"While you were in the hospital, I received information that Banlin's crew were building an arena, and it was to be called the Jungle-Gym Ziggurat, which is where Banlin keeps his demonic beast," Thungor said. "Individuals who find themselves in the arena are to fight to the death or be killed by the beast. I'm afraid that the prisoners taken from Castle Forks will be put in the arena to fight to the death."

Chris's legs went numb, and his body seemed to drop in temperature. "No!"

Images of Novell, Si, and Whitethorn flashed through his mind, and he thought about his dad. How could everything just end like this after all they'd struggled to protect and fight for?

"This is wrong, so wrong!" Chris blurted out.

"We don't have any other choice, Chris Cochrane. We live to fight for another day. Castle Forks has fallen to the enemy, so it's too late now. Jerg has won."

"But we need to try and save them!" Chris exclaimed.

"Indeed," Thungor agreed. "Everyone is imprisoned at Forks, but thankfully, Whitethorn, Novell, Thomas Cochrane, your father, and many more are still alive. So for now, I've come to enlist your help. Plus, there's more."

"What is it?" Chris said frantically, lacing up his boots.

"Valor, the Sword of Juniper, has been recovered," Thungor said. "Your father has already tried his hand to see if he had the power to wield it, but he's not the one. We think you may be. Will you return with me now and try your hand? It must be a decision made by you alone. Think well. Remember what you know of the sword and its power."

Chris thought of Thomas Cochrane, a man who should have died centuries ago but who still lived. He had looked so weak and old after being kept prisoner by Banlin for possibly hundreds of years.

CHRIS COCHRANE

The Sword of Juniper, Whitethorn had told them, might give those who wielded it an unnaturally long life span and turn their hair white a few days after using it. On one hand, sure, that seemed kind of cool, but Chris thought of Thomas's haggard face, his tattered clothing. The once-great warrior was just a shadow of his former self after all these years.

Chris had to ask just one question before making his choice. "Is there any other way to take back the Forks and save our friends?" he asked.

"There may be another way to take back the Forks—in time," said Thungor. "But I fear we don't have time. Not enough time to save our friends as well."

That was all Chris needed to hear. He finished tying his bootlaces and stood up. "Then let's go," he said. "Before we lose any more precious time."

A very slight smile crossed Thungor's pale face. "We'll have to fly," he said. "Come, I'll show you."

Chris joined him at the window. Thungor pulled a long silk cloth from a pocket of his tunic. He wrapped it around Chris's waist and then tied the ends together around his own upper arm.

"You'll be carried along beneath my arm this way," Thungor explained. "And you'll be cloaked in invisibility, along with me, as long as we're connected this way. Don't worry, the cloth will not come undone. Just trust me, and enjoy the flight."

Thungor began to unfold his wings.

A moment later, the room was empty. An observer walking in at that moment might have noticed a brief strange movement of the curtains, but there was nothing else to see.

CHAPTER 12

The full moon was now at its peak, making the never-ending forest, over which Chris and Thungor were flying, an eerie sight. It was densely covered with fog, so much that even without Thungor's invisibility, they'd probably have made it just fine. *But precautions first*, Chris assumed.

"Thungor, shouldn't we be at the South Fork Mountain by now?" *We've been flying for what seems like forever, and calculating the distance from the hospital to South Fork Mountain, we should have been there by now*, Chris thought.

"We're not going there yet," Thungor said. "We're going to meet someone at the Fields of Flat Slope Gap."

"Where's that?" Chris pondered how overly familiar the name sounded, but he couldn't seem to recall where or how he'd come across it.

"It's near Machu Picchu in Peru," Thungor replied, breaking his chain of Chris's thoughts.

"Machu Picchu? That's where Mom and Justin are," Chris said, getting excited. "Why are we going all the way there? Are we gonna meet them?"

"I need to get you as far away from Castle Forks as possible after what happened," Thungor replied. "Banlin and Jerg will be looking for you, but they'll expect you to be at home, not in Peru."

Chris's stomach twisted. "But what about Dad and the others?"

"We'll go back for them, kid," Thungor assured. "We just need to train you up somewhere safe."

By dawn, the eerie sight of the forest was gone. Although Chris could barely see through the dense fog, he was able to see a swamp. *Must be the reason for the thick fog*, he thought, *but what's that?*

Underneath the fog, Chris looked more closely at what seemed like a pulsating glow. It seemed to be following them. Chris must have been exhausted from flying all through the night and his mind must've been playing tricks on him. But then he heard it, the ambience and the mild and distant vulcanizing. It was as if the swamp was calling out to him. Chris kept looking and listening, and the more he did, the more he wanted every nerve and sinew in his body to draw closer to the glow.

For a minute, Chris forgot all about his pains, the exhaustion; he forgot all about the events that had happened in his life. He felt light and free, like a weight had been lifted from his body. Chris was still staring when he heard Thungor's voice.

"We're almost there," he said, snapping Chris back to reality.

Everything came rushing back.

By evening, the fog had started to lose its thickness, but there was still a thin mist, and the air felt silky, which kind of felt good, just the best to cool off with after the hot and sweaty travel. They found a good spot to camp for the night.

"We can rest here and meet the others tomorrow. I'll make a fire," Thungor said.

Chris was hungry and tired from the travel. Thankfully, Thungor did not only find dry twigs but was also able to get meat. After dinner, Chris's mind wandered to the pulsating glow.

"Who are we meeting tomorrow?" Chris asked. "Is it Mom and Justin?"

"You'll see," Thungor said. "Get some rest, I'll keep watch."

Even after a night and day's travel, carrying another person, he's still not tired? Chris felt guilty for being helpless.

"You should get some rest, Thungor. I'll keep the first watch," Chris said, getting up. "Even though I don't know how to fight, I can keep alert and sense any danger coming long enough to alert you."

"We stealth warriors never get tired," Thungor replied. "We were trained to adapt to any situation, never to be seen or heard except when necessary. Whitethorn asked me to protect you, and it's my duty. This place isn't safe. It's called the Swamp of Inka. We passed the heart a long while ago. It's said that people are drawn to it in a strange way. No one has lived to tell the story—they never came back. So get some rest, we'll leave by dawn. I'll keep watch. Oh, and keep your weapons close. You never know what could happen."

Thungor's words settled Chris's guilt. He couldn't argue.

That night, Chris kept thinking about the glow and the Swamp of Inka story. He wondered what could be at the heart and what had happened to all those people who never came back. Were they dead or alive?

After a while, Chris's racing mind added to his physical exhaustion, and he drifted off to sleep.

Chris woke with a start as a menacing growl sounded from outside the tent. He heard Thungor grunt, then the *swipe* of his weapon slicing through the air.

Chris sat up, fearing that their camping spot had been ambushed. He wiped the sleep from his eyes and grabbed his bow, quiver, and knife from beside him even though he hadn't yet been taught how to use them properly against enemies.

The snarling continued from outside; Chris could make out at least three different growls, maybe more. He crept forward and crouched on all fours just before the opening of his tent.

I wonder if I can unzip this without making any noise, Chris wondered, his heart pounding. He sighed. *I have to try. I need to stop being useless.*

He reached for the zip and slowly pulled it down as Thungor continued to hack and slash at the growling creatures outside. As he brought the zip down to eye level, he peered through the opening of the tent flap. Wolves. One, two, three, four, five—a pack of huge fierce wolves.

Chris gasped but quickly smacked his hand over his mouth, hoping the wolves hadn't heard him. But it was too late.

One of the wolves broke away from the rest of the pack that was attacking Thungor and advanced toward the tent. Chris ducked below the unzipped part of the tent door and gripped the knife he'd picked from the armory. The wolf approached the door and sniffed its base, likely picking up on Chris's scent.

Chris's breathing increased as intense fear surged through his body, but he tried to be as silent as possible as he considered potential options.

The wolf suddenly barked, and Chris screamed with terror.

"Chris!" Thungor yelled, a few yards away.

Without warning, the wolf leaped into the tent and sunk its canines into Chris's left arm. A searing agony coursed through his veins and muscles, and his screech echoed throughout the entire camp. The wolf growled as it shook Chris's arm in its mouth, like an aggressive dog playing tug-of-war, and crimson blood dribbled from his limb.

"Chris! Your knife!" Thungor roared, continuing to keep the rest of the pack away from the tent.

Chris had forgotten about the knife that was in his grip; the shock and pain had completely distracted him, but he lifted his right arm and stabbed the mauling wolf in the side. The beast released its grip on Chris's left arm for a few moments and howled with pain, allowing enough time for Chris to act again.

As the wolf opened its bloody mouth for a second bite, Chris yelled and lunged his knife into the animal's neck, once, twice, three times until it whimpered and collapsed onto Chris's sleeping bag, now saturated with fresh blood.

Chris dropped the knife and grabbed his left arm as it trembled and throbbed with torturous pain. He crumbled to the floor, but he knew he had to help Thungor with the rest of the pack.

Chris groaned and dragged himself back to a sitting position. He peeped through the flap of the tent; he spotted only two wolves left, both dodging Thungor's strikes. With blurring vision and blood pouring out of his arm, Chris grabbed his bow, trembling uncontrollably. He snatched an arrow from his quiver and attached it to the bowstring, drawing it back and aiming at one of the wolves. Chris released the arrow. It sped through the air but landed with a *thud* on the ground next to the animal, attracting its attention.

The wolf left Thungor and bolted toward Chris, just as the first had.

No, not again, Chris thought, trying to ignore the agony.

As his vision distorted, Chris took another arrow from the quiver, and in one smooth motion, he hooked it onto the string, aimed haphazardly, and released the arrow.

Chris seized his knife from the floor and held it in front of him, ready to defend himself against the beast, but he looked up and noticed his arrow had impaled the wolf's head, dead center. He watched Thungor slice the last wolf's neck with his axe. Chris sunk to the ground, everything fading around him and the dream world engulfing him.

CHAPTER 13

During Chris's dream, the nurses discharged him from the hospital.

"For the meantime, you'll be placed under house arrest. This is to keep you safe while we search for the body of your father," Officer Smith said with a look of sympathy on his face.

A jolt of pain shot through Chris's body as he thought of Dad. *Is he really dead? What happened while I blacked out at the City of Gold?*

"Are you okay?" Officer Smith asked, his face painted with worry.

"I'm fine, thanks," Chris replied with a forced smile.

How would Chris be able to leave home without the ankle monitor on his leg going off? He knew the ankle monitor wasn't just to keep him safe, but to also ensure the prime suspect, the one closest to the deceased, was in place.

I need to find Dad. I have to go to Castle Forks, Chris thought while getting into Officer Smith's vehicle.

At home, Chris found the place just as they'd left it before their journey to the City of Gold. He knew he couldn't make sudden movements or actions as it could cause the police suspicion or worse, alert the invisible spies of Banlin.

Turning restlessly on his bed, unable to sleep, Chris made his way to his parents' room. The scent of mint tobacco and a trace of lavender filled his nostrils. His mom's prolonged absence was accentuated in the faint scent of lavender and wild roses, but his dad's minty tobacco scent was strong, which proved it hadn't been long since they'd left the house.

Then how could Dad have been dead since October? This is strangely weird, Chris thought.

Chris turned on the computer. There was an email from Justin sent a week ago. Chris opened it, and to his amazement, it read:

Hey, Criffer Bob,

How are you and Dad? Mom and I are doing okay over here although it rains a lot. I really want to come home, but Mom insists we must finish our work first. I was barely managing to endure the bugs, the wetness, and the constant cold and rain until I met Taala, a local from the next village. She's really tall.

Man, this girl would thrive excellently in basketball. I thought she was weird and stalky at first, but do you know she's a descendant of Dandok of the Kiern? They are called the Hairy People and are allies of the Caretakers. The Caretakers are tall angelic creatures. Awesome, right? I thought she was crazy until she showed me the red brook and a place called Machu Picchu. You need to see this, Chris, it's amazing. We received Dad's letter saying we should not come home just yet. I do hope everything is well with you and Dad. My regards to Dad.

Your handsome brother,
Justin

Still praising himself, that is so Justin. Chris smiled. But then how did he know about the Caretakers and the Kiern? Chris needed answers. This was a week ago, so he hoped they were safe.

Chris apprehensively left the house for Castle Forks, but little did he know he was being followed by Banlin's invincible spies.

After the first arrow stuck past his left ear, a near miss, Chris scanned his environment and took to his heels. He saw nothing. The situation became worse when he was blocked by Officer Smith, who was keeping watch at a hidden distance from the house. The second arrow whizzed pass and struck Officer Smith, killing him on the spot. Chris was on full alert now; someone was dead, and the arrow had been meant for him. He cut out from the path and ran into the forest, through the trees, running blindly, cuts and bruises all over... he'd even broken an arm. Suddenly he came to a slope and fell hard but landed in his dad's car, where they were found in the ditch on Route 36. Many voices muffled with his dad's.

"You've been asleep for six months," Nurse Helen's voice said. "A car accident, we don't know where your father is."

"You were in a vehicle crash on Route 36 in October, about six months ago," Officer Smith's voice followed.

"The time has come to witness the downfall of the Caretakers and their so-called legacy!" This time it was Banlin's. "You're a defenseless child, and none of your friends are in position to help. When I'm finished with them, I will find you, and I will end your generation for good." His roaring laughter echoed.

Chris! Wake up, Chris! CHRIS!

Chris opened his eyes, drenched in sweat. He stared at Thungor's blurry face. His arm stung and ached, but it had been wrapped in a soft bandage to stop the bleeding. Thungor must have done it while he was asleep.

By the time Chris could see clearly, fear was written all over Thungor's face. He must have been calling for a while.

"Are you okay? That must have been one scary nightmare for you to be screaming Banlin and Todd Cochrane in a pain-stricken way?"

Thungor gently shook Chris as though he wasn't sure he was fully awake. His gentle yet firm face reassured Chris, and Chris calmed down.

"I'm fine, it was just a dream," Chris said, trying to sound strong. But deep down, he was worried and frightened.

All the more reason to learn how to fight, to find out what happened to his dad, and to know about the well-being of his mom and Justin. *But what was that dream all about?*

CHAPTER 14

After flying for some time, Thungor and Chris began to descend through the fog line. Giant green mountain peaks were revealed and the steepest slopes Chris had ever seen. This also reminded him of the nightmare.

Each time he remembered the words of Banlin and pictured the death of his family, anger coursed through his veins like adrenaline. However, the scenery in front of him was a sight to behold.

Sitting atop the highest mountain peak of Machu Picchu was a giant fortress; it looked abandoned. Two figures were ascending up the immense staircase that served as the route to the enclave. There were ancient signs and symbols on its aging walls; the walls looked weakened, like they could give way and crumble at any time. The fortress stood majestically, way above sea level, with a peaceful and quiet ambience of flora and fauna.

After landing at the top of the staircase, Chris noticed the orb a few feet away from them. They stood alongside Thungor to wait for the approaching figures while Chris tried hard to focus and remember his dad's words. As the figures got closer, Chris could make out one male and one female; the female was taller and hairy. She seemed to fit the description from Justin's email in the dream, Chris thought—

Justin? It was Justin, his brother! His eyes widened at the realization. Justin must have spotted Chris too because their pace increased until they were practically running up the stairs.

"Chris, brother—oh it's so good to see you!" Justin exclaimed excitedly, but then a puzzled look followed. "What are you doing here? How did you get here? Where's Dad?"

Too many questions at once, but that wasn't a problem because Chris was beyond happy that Justin was safe, and if he was this calm, then his mom should be safe too.

"Todd Cochrane is alive. However, he's imprisoned at the Forks," Thungor answered for Chris. "I suppose Taala's filled you in on some details?"

"Not much, Thungor, I'm afraid. Being here has closed me up to recent information. News hardly gets through," the tall girl with the flowing hair said.

Justin gestured to the girl, who looked nothing like Whitethorn except for being really tall. "Chris, this is Taala Wolfgang, descendant of Dandok of the Kiern and one of the local guardians of this area."

She bowed her head in greeting, and Chris did the same.

"We are called the Hairy People. We are allies with a civilization of beings called the Caretakers. Among our elders is a Caretaker called Bigwig. He is a Seer. By this I mean, we knew you were coming, Chris Cochrane of the Cochrane clan. Your family has helped fight against Jerg and his Shadow Demons for many years. Thomas and Charles Cochrane are greatly respected warriors. My purpose here is to get you ready because there is someone you are going to meet soon."

"Who? Is he coming here?" Chris shouted in surprise.

Taala nodded. "We had lost all hope of saving our sacred mountain and the swamp and rebuilding Machu Picchu until Bigwig saw you. With your coming, we knew it wasn't time to lose hope just yet. So please drink from the orb of the all-knowing seeker. It will tell you all you need to know. It will guide you and show us the way to redemption."

When Taala finished, Chris was overwhelmed. Who was he going to meet?

"Have you drunk from the orb, Justin?" Chris asked.

Justin nodded. "Yeah. You might feel dizzy or sick at first, but it'll show you what I've seen."

Chris walked up to the orb and, after a moment's pause, took a drink. He felt okay at first, his thirst quenched. Then he felt dizzy.

A bright light flashed before his eyes. When it abated, he saw a war, which he somehow knew was the war between Castle Forks and the Shadow Demons in the days of the Dark Skirmishes at Windy Nip Glen. He saw his ancestors Thomas and Charles Cochrane; he saw brutal deaths, but the war against Jerg was eventually won. It was horrific. He finally understood all that Taala had been saying about showing them the way to redemption because the last thing he saw was a book. On the front of it, in blood-red letters, was *The Book of Rorik*. According to the orb, they had to find the book to defeat Jerg.

Chris! Wake up, Chris…Chris Cochrane! Taala shouted, snapping her fingers in front of his face.

Chris stared blankly. All those people…all those people had died because of Jerg and his Shadow Demons—women, children. Chris thought of Mom, Dad, and Justin. *Jerg wants to destroy our generation? No!* He pictured the dead once more and saw his family among them. This time, pain shot through Chris's body, taking hold of his brain; numbness took hold of him, and he collapsed. It felt as though he'd died a thousand deaths, that of every dead being he'd seen in his mind.

"I understand," Chris said as if he was speaking to an invisible being. Deep down, he was pained; it was like a living scar that reminded him what he'd been shown by the orb.

He looked up. "Where do we find *The Book of Rorik?*" he asked, looking at Taala.

Chris's face showed total firmness and a hidden anger. He might have been a regular California kid, but when it came to the safety of his family, he wouldn't sit still and do nothing.

"Legend says it is guarded by one of Jerg's six strongest demons at the Moad River," Taala replied. "My clan have always shared stories about it, so it must be worth investigating."

"Then we need to go there," Chris said, picturing the death of Jerg.

"Oh, it's not as easy as it sounds," Taala scoffed. "The Moad River is a windy snakelike river filled with deadly rapids. People get sick crossing the river, and some never make it. It's said that they just disappear, never to be seen again."

Chris nodded, worried that he would never live to see his mom again after embarking on such a dangerous mission. "How is Mom?" he asked. "Is she safe? Where is she?" Concern played on his creased brow.

"Mom is fine, probably lost in her usual activity. I told her I was visiting this fortress with Taala, and she approved. I'm sure she's well protected," Justin replied, much to Chris's relief.

Thungor looked around impatiently. "We can't stay here, it's too dangerous. Banlin's invisible soldiers are scattered around, and there's no telling when one could spot us and alert the others. We need to find somewhere to hide."

Thungor was right. They had much more to worry about.

"Follow me," Taala said. "That open field below the ascending steps to Machu Picchu is known as the 'Training Fields of Flat Slope Gap.' Many beings before you have mastered the art of the sword, spear, arrow, and axe weapons here." She pointed down the slope to the rocky flat ground, which was covered with standing wooden dummies. There was also a grassy clearing.

"That is where you practice your arrow shooting and spear-throwing skills." Taala gestured toward the grassy clearing. There were other cleared spaces for various weapons training, and Taala went on to explain that there was a small arena to fight for sport to earn the respect of the ancient leaders: Sun Shadow, Candar, or even Thomas Cochrane himself, who often went to watch the event. They didn't fight for money or in anger or at least not with the intention of fighting in anger, not to say that they didn't sometimes lose their temper during training or a fight.

"Every warrior that comes to train here is willed by the purpose to which they have come to train. This is also what keeps them going even in the harshest training or fight," Thungor added. "I once trained here, but that was a long time ago."

Taala led them to a cabin big enough to contain ten people. It was large and spacious with bedrooms, a kitchen, and a fireplace. Soft feathered cushions were scattered here and there for comfort. In the cabin kitchen was stored dried meat, grains, potatoes, fruits, and other edibles. There were also barrels of drinkable water.

"The elders prepared this." Taala smiled. "They knew you were coming here to start your proper training."

That night after dinner, Chris told Justin everything that had happened since they'd left, focusing on Castle Forks.

"It's so cool that you know of Castle Forks now," Justin said to Chris. "When I was a toddler, Grandpa Jim told me stories about Castle Forks. Obviously, I was too young to remember all the details, but the name stuck, also the images he put into my head of angelic creatures and hairy men."

Chris smiled at Justin but with a hint of sorrow across his face. "I wish he was still alive. We could benefit from his stories now."

But Chris couldn't avoid the elephant in the room; he had to tell Justin about the Cochrane ties with the Caretakers, Jerg, Banlin, and the Tourlt, the reason he and Chris were here together, and about the fall of Castle Forks, where its people (including their father) were all now imprisoned.

"None of that matters now since Machu Picchu is no more," Taala stated angrily, lamenting the reason for their being there and the destruction of the citadel by the Shadow Demons.

"How did it fall?" Chris asked.

"A long time ago, Machu Picchu was an ancient Caretaker stronghold that was destroyed by Jerg," she replied sadly. "It was his first victory after being exiled from the Caretakers and the realm of Castle Forks. I was born a few years later. Machu Picchu was an ancient fortress that was rich in gold. It was once called the Lost City of Gold, located in the middle of the tropical jungle, high above sea level, and protected by the Swamp of Inka. The only way to get to Machu Picchu was through the Swamp of Inka. However, to pass through the swamp, your heart must be pure and devoid of ill intentions. Those who have good intentions will arrive at the heart of the swamp, which was also a passageway to the fortress. But those with evil intention will be forever lost in its never-ending maze and fog while their body and soul become slowly absorbed by the swamp.

"The people of Machu Picchu were happy, nature was safe, and peace was guaranteed. Then came Jerg, an ambitious leader of the Shadow Demons, who has an uncontrollable lust for gold and riches for which to build his own city of gold. Jerg asked the people to join his army, and as reward, they would have riches, power, and would rule the world with him as leader. A few followed him, but the others remained adamant. With his Shadow Demons, he took control of the swamp, destroyed the fortress, captured the remaining people as prisoners, and plundered the gold.

"They took everything. Now it is said that a demon controls the swamp, and the remaining people of Machu Picchu are prisoners in the swamp, and only one with a pure heart will be able to see the heart of the swamp. They say the glow of the swamp is the glow of the souls within, and he or she will feel and hear it calling. They say that person is one who can restore balance to the ecosystem of the swamp and free the prisoners."

The Swamp of Inka, the glow, and "one with a pure heart" were all Chris could think about when Taala was finished talking. He'd definitely seen a glow; it was calling out to him. No, he was only tired from the travel. *It can't be me*, he thought. Chris couldn't fight; he could only kill bucks and does with guns. How could he be the one when he couldn't even save his own father? Chris kept thinking while he lay on the soft feathery bed that night: *Who am I?*

CHAPTER 15

As the first streaks of daylight illuminated Chris's room in the cabin, Chris peeled open his eyes and yawned. He snuggled into his duvet for a few moments longer, cherishing the comfort of the bed. Suddenly the sound of clashing metal caught his attention and snapped him properly awake.

Oh yeah, our training sessions! Chris remembered what Thungor had said the night before.

Chris rubbed his face and peered outside to see the red sun rising, filling the sky with a warm hue. He would have admired the sight, but after his alarm clock confirmed the sun's early morning call, he slumped back into the bed, groaning with sluggishness. He'd never got used to early mornings even as a schoolkid.

As the clanking of steel swords grew more intense outside, Chris dragged himself out of bed and got dressed. He trudged out of the room through the rest of the cabin and stepped outside. Thungor and Justin were engaging in a pretend sword fight, Thungor giving instructions as they slowly swiped and blocked each other's artificial attacks.

"As you know, you should always step back when your opponent attacks, but if they're particularly fast and skilled, which the Shadow Demons are, they'll try to strike you after you've moved," Thungor explained. "So you can either take a larger step back, but this could leave you unbalanced, or you can retract with a block, using the side of your weapon to defend yourself at the same time."

Justin nodded, taking in the information.

"Let's practice," Thungor said. "Ready?"

Justin readied himself, standing with his feet apart and legs bent, as Thungor slowly swung his axe. Justin stepped back and then held up his sword, attempting to block Thungor's attack.

Chris smiled from the doorway of the cabin, impressed with his brother's effort.

"Quicker, lad," Thungor advised. "Try to step back and block in the same movement rather than stepping back and *then* blocking. Your opponent could use those precious moments to get you."

Justin nodded again and prepared for another try.

Thungor repeated the same action as before, slowly bringing his axe toward Justin's face. Justin backed away, barring his strike.

"Better," Thungor said, nodding. "You're getting there, boy."

Chris held his smile and clapped with support, finally making his presence known.

"Ahh, you're awake," Thungor said. "Are you ready to start your training?"

"You'd better be, Criffer Bob," Justin said with amusement. "I need a break for a bit."

Thungor chuckled. "Go on then, get some breakfast, and we'll resume after our young archer has achieved a bull's-eye."

Justin exhaled with relief and headed toward the cabin with his sword. He patted Chris on the back as he passed and slotted his weapon into one of the racks by the door, then disappeared inside.

"Right, now it's your turn," Thungor said. He approached the rack of wooden bows that stood beside the sword rack. He grabbed Chris's bow and handed it to him with a quiver of fletched arrows.

"Now clearly you know how to hold and fire a bow," Thungor began. "We've observed your hunting skills, but we need to get you up to speed and increase your headshot ability if you're to stand any chance against Banlin, Jerg, or any of the Shadow Demons."

Chris nodded and prepared his bow.

CHRIS COCHRANE

"So first things first, I want to see how many arrows you can fire at the center of that target as fast as possible," Thungor said, pointing at the round target out in front of them. "You have fifteen arrows in that quiver, and I have a stopwatch. Ready?"

Chris chewed the inside of his cheek and shuffled his feet on the ground, his insides filling with dread.

"What is it, boy?"

Chris hesitated but finally said, "I'm just worried I won't be as good as you need me to be."

Thungor smiled and rubbed Chris's back with encouragement. "That's the whole point of these training sessions, lad. You may only get one bull's-eye and take ages firing all the arrows, but that gives us something to work with and improve upon."

Chris nodded and gave Thungor a small smile.

"Come on, you'll be fine, my lad," Thungor reassured, ruffling his hair.

Chris readied his bow again and positioned himself in line with the target, his hand all set to grab the first arrow from the quiver on his back.

Thungor held out his stopwatch and gave Chris a countdown. "Three...two...one...go!"

Chris reached back and grabbed his first arrow. He attached it to the bowstring and fired. It hit the bottom left of the target.

Damnit, Chris thought. He seized his second arrow and launched it through the air. It hit the top right of the target.

Chris huffed and snatched a third arrow from behind, fixing it to the bow and releasing it. This one missed the target. "Argh!" he grumbled, bubbling with frustration and embarrassment.

"You're doing fine, lad, keep going," Thungor said.

Chris took a fourth arrow from his quiver and hurled that one at the target—bottom left again. "Screw this!" Chris yelled. "I can't do it!" He slammed his bow onto the ground and charged back toward the cabin, clenching his fists and digging his nails into his palms.

Thungor hurried after him and took hold of his arm. "Hey, you were doing great," he said.

156

Chris scoffed. "I didn't get a single bull's-eye, and I even missed the entire target!"

"But you *could* have improved if you'd just kept going," Thungor replied. "You still had eleven arrows left."

"There's no way I would have done any better after the first four!"

"Well, let me give you a tip," Thungor said. "Don't focus too much on whether you've hit the center or not, just keep going. Pretend the target is a real enemy that you desperately need to kill."

Chris frowned sulkily. "How would that help?"

Thungor smiled. "You'd be surprised."

Chris huffed and picked up his bow from the ground. "Fine, I'll try again."

"Good lad!" Thungor said.

Chris resumed his previous position about twenty yards from the target, feet apart and knees bent, and readied his weapon again.

"Ready?" Thungor asked.

Chris nodded.

"Three...two...one...go!"

Chris grasped his first arrow and hooked it to the bowstring in one fell swoop, releasing it and letting it soar through the light morning breeze.

Thud.

Slightly off-center, but better than before.

"Don't focus on the arrow once you've released it," Thungor reminded. "Concentrate on firing the next one."

Chris bobbed his head in acknowledgment and took another arrow from the quiver.

Attach. Draw back. Fire.

Reach back. Attach. Draw back. Fire.

Chris repeated this process another twelve times until all the arrows had been launched at the target. He stretched his right arm out and tensed his muscles, a little achy from so much movement.

"Good work!" Thungor praised, and Chris grinned. "You managed to shoot all the arrows in two minutes ten seconds. Let's see how many of them hit the middle of the target."

Chris followed Thungor to the target, and they counted the arrows that stuck out from the center.

"One, two, three, *four!*" Thungor exclaimed. "That's a number to be proud of for a first attempt!"

"Thank you," Chris replied. He paused for a moment, then said, "I'm sorry for getting frustrated earlier."

Thungor chuckled. "Don't worry about it, lad. We all get that way from time to time."

Chris smiled and waited for Thungor's next instruction.

"So now you have to beat your score in under two minutes ten seconds," Thungor said. "But there's no pressure at the moment. Your arm must be sore after all."

"No, I want to try!" Chris pleaded.

Thungor beamed. "Very well. Let's get back to position."

Chris bounded back to his previous spot, and Thungor collected the arrows from the target. He followed Chris back to the start and slipped the arrows into his quiver.

"Right, are you ready?" Thungor asked, resuming his place beside Chris and resetting the stopwatch.

"Yep!"

"Good lad," Thungor said. "Three…two…one…go!"

Like before, Chris reached for the first arrow and launched it at the target.

Reach back. Attach. Draw back. Fire.

Reach back. Attach. Draw back. Fire.

A short while later, Chris had shot all fifteen arrows. "How did I do?" he asked, rubbing right arm.

Thungor smiled, and they advanced toward the target again.

"One, two, three, four, *five* bull's-eyes in…two minutes two seconds!" Thungor announced. "You beat it!"

"Yes!" Chris exclaimed, and Justin appeared at the cabin doorway, applauding Chris's progress.

"Way to go, lil' bro!" he called over.

Chris beamed. He realized he wasn't so useless after all.

CHAPTER 16

While Chris rested his firing arm, Taala taught him the best way to make different traps for catching animals or enemies.

"One of the easiest and most effective traps to make for catching prey is this simple snare trap," Taala said, leading Chris away from the cabin and a little way into the forest. "I've been scouting the area and found this rabbit trail, so we'll make our first trap here."

Chris nodded. He admired Taala's knowledge of the environment. "How many should we make along the trail?" he asked.

Taala tilted her head slightly, thinking for a moment. "I'd say maybe four or five along this one, just to increase our chances of catching something."

"Sounds good."

"Right, the first thing we need to do is cut down a thin bendy branch from one of these trees," Taala instructed, scanning around.

Chris glanced about, spotting one that could be useful. He pointed to it. "What about that one?"

"Hmm, it's a bit too thick. We need one a little thinner so we can bend it."

Chris continued to look around until he laid eyes on a slimmer branch growing from one of the thicker tree trunks. "This one?" he suggested, grabbing it and cutting it from the trunk.

Taala grinned and nodded. "Yes, that one's perfect. So now we've found that, we can get started on the first bit." She grabbed a chunky stick from the ground and held it up for Chris to see. "We need to carve a small nook into this, then hammer it into the ground."

Chris frowned. "What's the nook for?"

Taala smiled. "You'll see."

Chris watched as Taala cut a deep notch into the top side of the stick, giving it the shape of a walking stick, and hammered the other end into the ground with a camping hammer until only the part with the nook poked up from the earth. She picked up a shorter stick of the same width and created another nook.

"Does that one go into the ground as well?" Chris asked.

Taala shook her head. "No, this one's attached to the bendy branch you found over there. But first, we need to make a noose to attach to the end."

Taala rummaged through her backpack and pulled out some thin wire. She created a noose about the size of a small plate and knotted the wire to the carved end of the second stick, letting the trap dangle a little. She tied a longer piece of wire to the other end of the stick and held it up for Chris to see.

"So this end of the stick with the noose will rest under the branch in the ground, hence the nooks, waiting for an animal to trigger it, and the wire attached to the other end will fasten to the bendy branch, springing the animal up so it can't escape," Taala explained, and she fixed the lengthy piece of wire to the malleable branch.

Chris laughed with disbelief, amazed by the simple yet clever mechanism. "Where did you learn this?" he asked.

Taala beamed. "I'm a Kiern, remember? I grew up learning this stuff."

"Good point," Chris said. "Will these snare traps also work on Banlin's soldiers as well?"

Taala shook her head. "Afraid not. The most they would do to a Shadow Demon is graze the skin. For larger enemies, we'll need bear traps or something stronger. I'll show you some of those later, but for now, we need to build some more snare traps."

Chris nodded and looked at the one Taala had made. "Will those nooks hold the sticks in place then? Won't they get knocked about in the wind?"

"It's possible but not likely," Taala replied. "The bendy branch up there is pulling the second stick up against the first one, so there's not much room for movement."

"Ahh, that makes sense," Chris said. "I can't wait to show my dad how to make them. When we go hunting for the winter, we usually just rely on our rifles. We've never used traps before."

"Well, I'm glad to assist," Taala said with a smile. "Let's make some more farther up the trail."

Taala let Chris construct the next trap so he could get used to making them on his own. He located another flexible sapling and found two suitable sticks on the ground. With Taala's assistance, he used his knife to carve two nooks into each stick and used her camping hammer to bang the largest into the soil. Chris used Taala's wire to create a noose at one end of the smaller stick and tied it to the end. Finally, he fastened a longer piece of wire to the other end and reached up to secure it to the sapling, bending it over to lock the sticks in place.

"Nice job," Taala praised. "Your dad would be proud of that."

Chris beamed. His insides tingled with warmth at the mention of his dad being proud. "Will it be good enough?" he asked hesitantly.

"I don't see why not, it looks just as good as mine," Taala replied. "Come on, let's finish the rest."

Chris and Taala followed the rest of the rabbit trail and built three more snare traps along the way. Once they'd finished, Taala led Chris away from the rabbit trail and back to the cabin.

Justin and Thungor were practicing sword fighting outside, the sound of their clanking weapons filling the peaceful silence.

"Wait here, I'll go and get my sketchbook," Taala said. She eyed Justin with a smile as she headed inside.

Chris did as she instructed, watching Justin get faster and faster with his attacks and blocks. When Taala returned with an A3-sized sketch pad, she glanced Justin's way again and led Chris to the side of the cabin, where they sat down on one of the wooden benches.

"While the small snare traps we've just made won't catch Banlin's soldier's, the ones I've drawn in here might help to injure and delay them in battle," Taala said. She opened the first page of her sketchbook. "This one's called a cartridge trap."

Chris eyed the sketch. He quickly figured out how the cartridge trap would work. A sharpened stick sat upright a few inches from the ground, and a collection of twigs, leaves, and foliage covered it, making it look like a normal bit of ground.

"So an enemy would look at that and think nothing of it, step onto it, and...ouch," Chris said.

Taala nodded and smiled. "Yep. It's simple but could eliminate a lot of enemies."

She turned the page. Chris inspected the second sketch. A grenade poked up through the ground and a rectangle pack rested beside it.

"I think I know how that one would work," Chris said. "I assume that rectangle device is a switch? So when an enemy runs onto it...*boom?*"

Taala laughed. "Sort of. The rectangle pack has a hidden blowtorch inside, so when the enemy steps on it, the fire burns the grenade, filled with gunpowder, and blows it up."

Chris's mouth twitched into a grin, impressed with Taala's designs. "These are so clever! What's the next one?"

Taala turned the next page for Chris to study the third trap. Two branches stood upright in the ground, yards apart. A thin piece of wire was tied to each one, creating a trip wire but at neck height.

"Jeez, this looks lethal," Chris said. "Like something from a horror movie."

Taala snorted with amusement. "I know, and I hope you never see this one being activated, but we need to think smart to win against the enemy."

Taala showed Chris the rest of the traps she'd sketched out, and they both got started on sharpening some thick sticks to create as many cartridge traps as possible.

Chris couldn't wait to make his dad proud.

That evening, Taala took Chris back to the place they'd set the snare traps, and they found that *two* rabbits had been caught throughout the day, so they collected the animals into a bag and reset the snares.

"That's tonight's dinner sorted," Taala said.

When they returned to the cabin, Thungor prepared their meal, and they all tucked in around the table after a long day training.

"Well done, you three," Thungor said with a mouthful of food. "Chris and Justin, you're improving fast, and Taala, your traps are going to help us significantly."

Chris finished the mouthful of food he was eating. "Can I try and beat my score before bed?"

Thungor chuckled. "Oh, I don't know about that, lad. You must be knackered after today, and you'll need your strength tomorrow for another day's training."

"Pleeeease!" Chris begged. "Just one shot?"

"Go on, let him... He won't shut up otherwise," Justin joked. Taala laughed.

"Hey!" Chris protested with amusement.

"Okay, you can have another go, but we'll still need you on top form tomorrow, oy," Thungor said.

Chris saluted. "Yes, sir."

After everyone had finished, Thungor cleared the plates, and everyone gathered outside for Chris's last training session of the night. Thungor reset the stopwatch, and Chris resumed his position a short distance from the target, his bow in hand and the quiver on his back.

Justin cheered on from behind him. "You can do this, lil' bro!"

"Your time to beat is five bull's-eyes in two minutes two seconds," Thungor said. "Ready?"

Chris nodded. "Ready."

"Three...two...one...go!"

Chris snapped up his first arrow and fixed it to the string as Justin and Taala cheered him on from behind. He fixed the notch to the string and drew it back, releasing the arrow.

Reach back. Attach. Draw back. Fire.

Chris repeated this motion another fourteen times. Thungor paused the stopwatch after the fifteenth arrow had hit the middle of the target.

Chris, Justin, and Taala raced over to the target to count the number of arrows that had struck the center, and Thungor followed close behind.

"One, two, three, four, five—"

"SIX!"

Chris beamed, triumphant that he'd beaten his bull's-eye target. "But in what time?" he asked Thungor.

All three of them looked at Thungor, but his expression remained deadpan. But after a few seconds, his straight face broke into a warm smile. "One minute fifty-six seconds!" he announced.

Justin and Taala broke out into merry cheers and loud whistles, and Thungor ruffled Chris's hair. "See, I said you could do it, kid," he said.

That night, Chris went to bed with a sore arm and a heart full of pride, so much so that he couldn't wait to train again the following day. He set his alarm for 6:30 a.m. and snuggled down into his duvet, wishing his dad could have seen the improvement he'd made as a budding archer.

*****

Training with Thungor proved successful after their initial shameful and futile efforts. Thungor trained Justin and Chris in the art of sword mastery and arm-to-arm combat.

Taala showed everyone ways of making deadly traps and watched on as they developed their arrow-shooting mastery. Chris's dreams and nightmares continued more frequently, which no one knew about. Chris was also getting worried about a particular dream that frequented his night sleep. It was the dream of the pulsating glow, the soul of the swamp. It was worrisome that in each dream, the glow seemed to glow less bright.

One morning, training did not go as expected. Because of his curiosity and impatience, Justin could not master the art of waiting and listening. With a blindfold on his eyes, the task was to know when and where Thungor, who was in a state of invisibility, would strike. However, he failed woefully and kept getting beat by Thungor.

Chris could not make an active and strong trap, resulting in losing a wild boar they could have had for lunch. The thought of him failing and his dad and mom getting killed haunted him. This situation gradually caused frustration for both parties: the master and the student. By sundown, it had just gotten worse. Chris and Justin both had their weaknesses, and this was the last stage of training before their quest would begin, but it was proving difficult.

Justin angrily threw down the wooden sword and blindfold and stomped into the cabin. Thungor went to sit by the already glowing campfire Taala was making. Fortunately, Taala had caught a boar in one of her traps, and thus, they had roasted meat for dinner.

Chris was disappointed in the fact that he couldn't pass the next stage but kept on trying. Then he heard the song. It was faint at first, but soon he caught its melody. He looked to the direction of the sound to see Justin holding up his phone. It was "Immortals" by Fall Out Boy.

It was their dad's favorite song, and it soon became theirs even if they never knew the reason behind his love for the song. It was like his national anthem. Right now, it spoke about pretty much everything they were going through, so Chris assumed that Justin must have been thinking about it. It dawned on him that their dad's reason for loving this song was because of the unfathomable and mysterious history of their family with the supernatural.

He listened to the lyrics: "They say we are what we are, but we don't have to be... I'll be the watcher of the eternal flame. I'll be the guard dog of all your fever dreams. I am the sand in the bottom half of the hourglass. I try to picture me without you, but I can't..."

Right at that moment, images of his dad singing and dancing with his mom to the song flooded Chris's mind. He was so numb and lost in thought that he didn't know when the tears started to fall...

"'Cause we could be immortals, just not for long and live with me forever now, pull the blackout curtains down…'

I will save you, Dad. I will get you out of there alive, I promise, Chris thought. During this moment, Chris wasn't aware he'd made yet another trap.

As the song faded away, Chris could see and hear Justin singing in tune with the lyrics: "Sometimes the only payoff for having any faith is when it's tested again and again every day. I'm still comparing your past to my future. It might be your wound, but they're my sutures…"

Justin had the same fire in his eyes. Chris knew he was ready to master the last stage of his training. As he slept that night, Chris disappeared to another realm.

CHAPTER 17

The place Chris lay didn't feel like a bed. It was cold, and it smelled like mud and wet rots. He rolled and turned, hoping to find some warmth in the cozy duvet, but he touched what felt like water.

His eyes shot open immediately. He was wide awake. *This is not the cabin. Where am I?* he thought. The ground was wet and foggy, and there were large tightly twisted vines. The light from the sun seeped through the tiny spaces allowed by the vines and trees. It was as though the sunlight and the fog were having a battle for domination.

"Hello?" Chris called, but his voice only echoed and bounced back. "Somebody, anybody—hello?"

How did he even get here?

Just then, amid the silence was a faint echo. It sounded like a voice.

"Hello! Is somebody there? I'm kinda lost... I don't even know how I got here," Chris blabbered on and on until—

"Chris..." the voice whispered.

That voice, Chris thought. *I know that voice.*

There was the echo again, but this time it said, "Pure One."

Chris then saw a child running a little distance from where he stood. "Hey!" he called.

The child stood and turned back, about to speak, but the child giggled and dashed away. Surprised and confused, Chris followed suit, chasing after the child. It turned out to be a girl. As she ran past a large tree, she disappeared and reappeared far off atop a vine.

Fortunately, the vines were large enough to climb. Chris did, chasing after the child. As he came closer, he noticed that it wasn't a child anymore but a lady.

"Thank God, finally someone old enough to speak to. Do you know where we are?" Chris asked, looking around once more then back at her. She nodded, smiled, and gestured for him to follow her. Without saying more, she dashed away. *Oh great, more running*, Chris thought as he followed.

After a little while, she stopped in front of what seemed like a very huge tree. It was the biggest Chris had ever seen in his life. It stood tall and green.

"Help!" the lady whispered. Her voice sounded like…

"Mom?" Chris called.

The lady slowly turned. Chris came face-to-face with his mother.

"Is it really you?" Chris asked, confused. "Mom, what are you doing here? It's dangerous."

Chris walked quickly toward her to hug her, but she faded away into the huge tree. Seconds later, a very weak glow came from the tree. Chris immediately recognized it, not failing to remember the story of the Swamp of Inka. This glow…was Chris at the heart of the swamp?

The Shadow Demon, there is a Shadow Demon, but where is it?

Chris felt fear creep into his heart. Almost immediately, as though it had read his thoughts, a black shadow covered the white glow completely. It seeped out from beneath the tree and morphed into a tall beast with red eyes and fangs. It looked like a bat. It had three eyes on each side and a tail with what looked like thorns sticking out of it.

"You are too late, Pure One," it said. "The heart is dead, and the swamp is mine." It laughed a roaring laugh and beat its chest. "Salvador the Soul Eater has won. I have eaten the soul of the swamp, and your soul is next."

With that, he morphed into a huge black shadow from which cloned Shadow Demons emerged, racing toward him. Chris dodged and ducked away from the first two, surprised at how fast he was able to do that, somehow knowing they would first attack him in that way. By the time Chris stood up, he immediately felt and saw four Shadow Demons coming at him. Chris timed their coming and dodged them in such a way that they collided into each other and disappeared. More Shadow Demons died that way, and as he didn't have a sword or any weapon at all, Chris had to continue dodging for his life.

"So you are a Seer, Chris Cochrane of the Cochranes. Tasty… I am going to preserve your soul for Jerg the Almighty," the beast roared and sent more Shadow Demons toward him which Chris dodged. Finally, the beast charged at him, a malicious intent to kill in its eyes.

Chris needed to find a way to defeat this demon. *Focus, Chris, focus,* he told himself, and that was when he saw the light just behind the heart tree. Salvador had blocked him from seeing it all this while, but now that he could see it, he understood that darkness could not thrive in light. That's why the beast had come out from the root of the tree—it was hiding beneath until he was finished with the soul of the swamp.

I am going to end you, Salvador the Soul Eater, once and for all. You won't be eating any more souls, Chris thought. He made a beeline for the heart tree after dodging the demon. It must have annoyed him because he turned and ran straight for Chris. Chris dodged but wasn't quick enough for the beast's fangs tore into his back, sending jolts of pain through his entire body.

"I got you now, Seer. Under my nails are poisonous fluids, which I put into your body when I scratched you. You will feel weak very soon, Seer, and your soul won't be so pure when Jerg feeds on it."

The beast rejoiced over Chris's pain, its eyes glazed with malice. But what Salvador failed to notice was that the whole time it was speaking, Chris was moving toward the light, making sure to direct the beast's attention to him by acting scared and helpless. After a loud roar, Salvador dashed at him, a devilish smile plastered on his lips.

Chris's vision was blurry, but he used the last energy left in him to enter the light. By then, Salvador had already flown and knew there was no going back. His remains scattered in the air like ash after he was painfully burned in the light.

From his body escaped shadows that stood around Chris with glowing red eyes, coming closer and closer. Chris was already too weak and paralyzed to move or make a sound. He'd already seen himself being turned into a shadow like them when suddenly there was a glow. It was first a bright flicker which burned brighter and brighter until the whole swamp was engulfed in the bright white light. The shadows, by then almost touching him, immediately faded away to reveal actual humans, Caretakers, and Kiern. Mothers, fathers, and children were all there. The swamp changed from gloomy, dull, cold, and foggy to bright, warm, beautiful, and clear. The soft vocalizing was the last thing Chris heard before he blacked out.

CHAPTER 18

Chris, beginning to feel conscious, opened his eyes to see his brother, Thungor, and Taala staring worriedly at him. They were in the swamp. Chris was lying under a tree.

"Hey, guys. You found me." He smiled weakly.

"Yeah, you were taken through a portal in your room. I sensed your aura and smelled wet rots and smog," Justin explained. "So Thungor figured that we needed to go to the Swamp of Inka to rescue you. Luckily, it's not far from camp."

Taala nodded. "The swamp brought us here, saving us from the Shadow Demons we encountered in the forest while we searched for you. Chris, they say you are a Seer."

"Yeah, how long have you known you could sense things?" Justin added.

"Uh…for a while now," Chris replied. "I've had dreams about things, and they happened right after. I've also had lots of dreams about this swamp, and it felt like it was calling me. I didn't tell anyone because I wasn't sure about it, and I didn't want to seem weird. While coming to the Fields of Flat Slope Gap, I had a dream you sent me a letter. Is that true?"

"Yes! Yes! I did, a week before coming here," Justin answered, surprised but amused. "Cool!"

"You're not bad yourself, Justin," Thungor added. "You seem to be showing signs of becoming an all-knowing seeker. Drinking that water from the orb must have done something to you."

"That's true, I thought it was strange when you said you could hear my breath and feel my vibration back at the cabin and also how you aced Thungor's invisibility training," Taala confessed happily. "I was, however, convinced when you discovered Chris's whereabouts."

Chris tried to sit up but his back made him wince with pain.

"Are you okay, Chris?" Taala asked.

"I wasn't fast enough to dodge Salvador, and he poisoned me." Chris showed them his back. "But even though it really hurts, I don't understand why it seems to be healing on its own. Surely I should be paralyzed?"

"You were healed by the swamp," an elderly Caretaker said, gesturing toward the glow coming from the heart tree. "I am Norok, by the way."

The glow turned out to be a white female figure, beautifully draped in white flowing robes. She also had long flowing white hair and silver eyes.

"My name is Inka." She gestured to Chris. "Thank you for saving the swamp and the red brook, Pure One. We are forever indebted to you. Allow me to return the favor by helping you with whatever you need." Inka smiled gracefully. A door appeared and opened just beneath the foot of the heart tree. "This door will take you to wherever you want to go."

"We need to get to the Moad River for *The Book of Rorik*," Justin said.

"But we need weapons first," replied Chris. "When I battled Salvador, I had nothing to defend myself."

"I believe I can help with that," Inka said. "There is a blacksmith in a faraway town called Farrow. He is a great smith who has made strong and powerful weapons for different warriors. He is also the one who forged some of the weapons which are kept in the Caretaker's Hall of Protectors to this day. The portal"—she gestured toward the already opened door beneath the heart tree—"will take you there."

With that said, they stepped into the portal, and she bade them farewell.

CHAPTER 19

The little town of Farrow had a welcoming atmosphere. It turned out to be home to the dwarfs, who would often fight over little things, such as being referred to as dwarfs by their fellow dwarfs or worse, other people. The people of Farrow were skilled craftsmen and women in smithwork, handcrafting, fishing, and mining.

The cottage of Noi, the dwarf smith, stood at the edge of the town, surrounded by trees and shrubs. There was a little clearing in front of the cottage where ornamental plants grew. Beside the cottage was a garden green with shrubs, cabbages, carrots, and well-tended vegetables. At the back of Noi's cottage was his smithy, a huge wooden structure with an opening at the top for the black smoke that rose from within. All they heard was a tumultuous banging of metals, followed by a loud hissing made by hot metal coming in contact with cold water.

The group of four approached the smithy and met with a male dwarf who grumbled to himself.

"Who are you?" the angry-looking dwarf said. "What are you doing in my territory?"

Justin spoke up after stepping forward from the shocked group. "Sorry. Mr.?"

"*Noi,*" the dwarf replied, looking even grumpier.

"Mr. Noi, we, er…are sorry to have invaded your private space unannounced. We came in search of the blacksmith as we need his help," Justin said, gaining more courage as he spoke.

"He is not in business any longer. He cannot help you. Go away," Noi barked, storming to his little cottage.

"Such an annoying dwarf!" Taala huffed, and before she could say anything else—

"Who do you think you're calling annoying, *girl*?" Noi yelled, advancing toward Taala, but Thungor stood in his way.

"I once read about them," Chris said, wide-eyed. He was careful to omit the word *dwarf*. "They are magical, talented, and crafty beings, practically good with everything." This statement seemed to affect Noi. He stopped immediately.

"At least someone among you has a bit of sense," Noi said with pride and a hint of irritation in his tone. "You should watch your mouth, Kiern girl, or it's going to put you in big trouble someday," Noi warned.

"Thungor, do you still have blueberries?" Chris whispered to Thungor.

Surprised, Thungor answered, "Yes, why?'

"Give them to me. The only thing dwarfs love more than themselves is blueberries. They make it into everything they eat: blueberry pie, tart, cake, and other things."

"But you still need it to understand me. Taala and Justin already learned my tongue."

Chris sighed and put out his hands.

Without another word, Thungor emptied his berry pouch and gave the berries to Chris, who followed Noi to his cottage.

"What is it this time? I said I cannot help you," Noi shouted again but was silenced at the sight of the big juicy blueberries in Chris's opened hands. "Is that?" The grumpy expression seemed to vanish from his face.

"Blueberries," Chris answered, smiling.

"I have never seen or tasted a blueberry. I have heard stories of its taste and its value as a very special delicacy among my people. However, the last seeds and farmlands were destroyed by Jerg and his army when they came recruiting soldiers. We have been grumpy and angry ever since," Noi said.

"You can have them, all of them. Just please help us," Chris urged Noi gently.

"Can I?" Noi asked, licking his lips, his eyes dreamy.

"Yes, please do," Chris replied, holding out his hand to Noi, who picked a blueberry and slowly placed it in his mouth, closing his eyes.

Noi seemed dreamy and happy. Surprisingly, his skin color changed from dark gray to bright blue. "Yes, I will help you. Thank you for bringing blueberries into our lives again."

Chris smiled at Noi.

When they walked outside, Thungor, Taala, and Justin were beyond shocked to see the bluish happy-looking, dreamy dwarf. Another dwarf sighted Noi and scampered over to his cottage.

"People of Farrow, I give you blueberries!" Noi shouted excitedly, raising the blueberries in his hands and showing them to the overjoyed crowd. "These good strangers and the disrespectful Kiern girl have restored happiness into our lives by bringing us blueberries."

One by one, the body color of the dwarfs changed to bright blue and the grumpy looks on their faces were replaced with happy and dreamy expressions, full of hope.

On the other hand, Taala had a stupefied expression. *Disrespectful Kiern girl?* Even Thungor could not help but chuckle at the remark.

"What will happen to the berries, Noi?" Chris asked, amused.

"We will save them and plant them. Our farmlands will be revived with blueberries once again. I will get to see the ocean of blueberries my nana used to tell me about."

"I'm glad we could help you, Noi," Chris said. "Will you help us now?"

Noi nodded with eagerness. "Certainly! What is it you need?"

"We need weapons," Chris replied.

After a moment of silence, Noi sighed. "I was expecting you might say that. I'm sorry, my weapons are not for shedding blood."

"Then why do I see Jerg's insignia on your weapons?" said Thungor.

"Ohh! This one speaks! I thought you were a mute. Clever, very clever." Noi's amused expression died, and he became suddenly sad and sullen. "Many years after Jerg destroyed our blueberry farms, he did not stop there. He wanted to kill every other person that did not join his army, but my father saved us by offering his skills for our lives. This job has now been passed down to me. If I don't forge weapons for his Shadow Demons, we will be wiped out."

"My father has been captured by Jerg. If we don't do anything to rescue him, then he will die," Chris said. In his eyes, Noi could see, fear, anger, determination, and most of all, truth.

"Follow me," he said and led the group of four to a secret room.

Inside this room were weapons of many different kinds: swords, daggers, pocketknives, explosives, bows and arrows, traps, and many more.

"I do not only work with metal," he said and smiled at the astonished group of four. "I believe these can help with rescuing your father."

Taala picked out traps, explosives, a white dagger, a pocket-knife, a black bow, and a bag full of black stylishly designed arrows. Chris took a bow and a quiver full of arrows which he hung on his back, a long ninja assassin blade, double skull-blade daggers, and a pocketknife.

Justin, who was next, took a sword which Noi said was called Excalibur, followed by a Yari spear and also known as a pole arm, and finally a stainless-steel double-tang blade which he hung on his back. And Thungor, who was already armed, took a mage staff that had a magical green orb attached to it and a map.

"Good choice. The orb on the end was a gift from the elves. It has the power to kill Shadow Demons," Noi explained.

"Hopefully, it treats me well against them this time," Thungor replied.

Once everyone had selected their chosen weapons, they thanked Noi and bade the people of Farrow farewell.

CHAPTER 20

eing in the jungle once more felt uncomfortable and dangerous for the group of four, but they persevered because they had a goal in sight.

"How far is the Moad River from Farrow?" Taala asked Thungor, who set the large map on the ground to examine it.

"Miles away. It'll take a day or two depending on how fast we walk. After we get *The Book of Rorik* from the Moad River, we have to go quickly to Castle Forks because Jerg will waste no time in executing the prisoners for his entertainment."

"Wait, why can't you fly us, like before?" Chris asked.

Thungor chuckled. "I can't carry all of you. And we need to stick together."

"Then we'll just have to move quickly," Justin said.

Thungor nodded and looked at the map. "According to these directions, we can pass through Berryville to get to the Moad River. And from there, we can take a shortcut through Green Valley and Golden Valley to get back to Castle Forks." He placed the map back into his empty berry pouch.

"What will we do about you understanding my words, Chris?" Thungor asked, remembering the blueberries that used to occupy the pouch. "Taala or Justin will have to become your new interpreter. I still don't think you should have given Noi all the blueberries."

"That shouldn't be a problem. I was glad to see hope in the eyes of the dwarf people." Chris smiled.

The group traveled a few more hours until sunset and camped on a flatland surrounded by fallen rocks and trees. The moon was high and full, casting a bright glow on the hills and sending tall shadows looming out from behind the trees.

Chris dozed off and descended into another dream.

Inside his dream was a huge arena surrounded by the bones and skulls of dead people. A wall around the arena had been constructed from these bones and skulls. Justin and Chris stood above the pit of the arena on a platform; below it, the pit was covered in thick black shadow. Growls could be heard from within. Chris trembled with terror when one of the fighters (that from behind looked like their father) was brutally injured. He was also on the verge of being thrown off the platform into the black shadow where the growls were coming from. A loud roar erupted from the black shadow as a body fell from the platform, right before Chris was able to see the face and hear the sound of grinding bones. That body was none other than—

"CHRIS, WAKE UP!" Thungor shouted. He placed a peppermint leaf close to Chris's nose.

Chris woke up with a start as everyone jumped. "I need to know who fell into the pit. I need to go back!" he shouted like a madman and jumped up, rushing to grab his weapon. Justin, who understood the situation, caught hold of him and calmed him down.

After a while, Chris regained composure, and his fast breathing calmed.

"Go on, go back to sleep, you three," Thungor said. "We have a long day ahead of us tomorrow."

Chris nodded and slid back down into his sleeping bag, silently hoping to return to his dream.

The next morning, Chris was already up practicing. There were bags under his eyes from lack of sleep. He'd already packed his bag but was patient enough to wait for the rest to wake up.

By the time they were done, the group left, walking until they arrived at Berryville, a town blessed with various types of berries. These berries served different purposes. While some berries cured illness, some were used as love potions. While some—like the blueberries—enabled Chris to understand Thungor, others enhanced mood, beauty, life, and so many other special qualities. But even though there were so many kinds of berries, only one kind was allowed to each person.

As a welcoming reception on their way into town, a merchant gave them each the chance to pick a bag of their chosen berries.

"Remember, you can only choose one," the merchant warned. "If you try to smuggle more, you'll be condemned to death."

Taala began, choosing the blackberry, which she learned was responsible for giving and restoring life.

"Why don't you choose the berry for beauty, Taala?" Justin joked, turning to look at the blush that crept up Taala's cheeks. "Many girls would definitely go for that berry and might even ask for an extra pouch."

Taala playfully punched him, sending him to the ground, still laughing. "I am not like other girls. I am Taala Wolfgang, and I am content with my appearance. Besides, I thought the blackberry would come in handy someday."

"Clever thinking, Taala," Thungor commented.

"Yeah, clever thinking, Taala," Justin agreed. "You never cease to amaze me."

Justin chose strawberry, known to enhance mood, and Chris filled his berry pouch with dewberry. This berry was responsible for replenishing health and healing. He hoped he would have the chance to give them to his dad.

Finally Thungor, replenishing his blueberries once again, filled his pouch.

By the time they left Berryville, each had filled their berry pouch to the brim. They continued their journey, covering a great distance from Berryville to the Moad River.

CHAPTER 21

The Moad River was a description of chaos, confusion, danger, and death. It snaked its way around a small island which was situated in the middle. On this island was a pagoda.

Thungor handed a blueberry to Chris and waited for him to eat. "Now you can understand me again, I think we should all eat a strawberry as well. We need to keep our mood as high as possible before we go into that river."

Thungor eyed Justin who nodded and passed his berry pouch around. Chris, Taala, and Thungor each took one strawberry and ate those too.

"Right, the book should be in there," Thungor said, pointing at the pagoda. "We just need to cross the river."

Everyone scanned the riverbank.

Chris noticed a boat a little way down on their side. "Look, over there!" he said.

"Good spot, bro," Justin said. They all ran to the boat.

They climbed inside and paddled with haste. Halfway across, a dark cloud formed and covered the vicinity of the river, dropping down to envelop the boat. Inside the black cloud was like falling black ash.

"Ash rain?" Taala said, holding out her hand to catch a few drops.

"No, Taala, don't touch it!" Thungor shouted immediately. "It is not ash rain, it's the bug demon!"

Taala gasped and withdrew her hand.

"The bug demon?" Justin asked.

"It's the second strongest Shadow Demon of Jerg. It's a huge centipede that flies in the black cloud that seems to be an extension of its demonic form. It's known as 'the cloud that was left behind,'" Thungor explained. "The ashes are falling are from its body, and anyone who touches it will slowly and painfully turn to ash. Don't allow the ash to come in contact with your body."

The darkness, Chris thought, *cannot thrive in the daylight. That's why it creates this dark cloud.*

"Guys, it cannot stand the light. The demon Salvador also died as a result of being exposed to light. If we can remove the black cloud, we can kill it," Chris stated, removing his double-tang blade, ready to fight.

The others followed. Taala had her bow and arrow set, and Justin removed Excalibur, which was already flaming.

"Okay, I'll expel the light, and immediately you attack the bug demon," Thungor said, raising his mage staff, ducking quickly and striking the centipede as it glided down toward him.

It was a near miss.

The second time Thungor raised the mage staff, a bright light was emitted from it, expelling the darkness immediately and exposing the presence of a huge red-and-black centipede.

Having spotted the reason for its inability to create more black clouds, it glided down angrily toward Thungor but was shot in the eye by Taala. The huge centipede shrieked and threw spikes from its body at the boat.

Everyone ducked, but Justin was stabbed by a spike and began losing blood fast. The centipede roared and glided down again. This time, it was Chris who jumped and stabbed the centipede with his blade, following the centipede into the air.

Taala shot more arrows at the centipede while Thungor kept the mage staff high, preventing the black clouds from forming. The river began raging, threatening to overturn the boat as Chris dodged the centipede's attempt to stab him, but the centipede caught Justin instead.

Finally he worked up his way to the head of the demon and sunk his blade into its skull. They both fell into the raging river. The impact created a huge tidal wave that splashed over the riverbank and soaked everyone. The demon sunk under the water while Chris gasped for air as he flapped about in the waves. It was an intense fight.

"Chris, swim toward the pagoda!" Thungor said.

Chris nodded and managed to slowly wade through the water. Thungor also paddled the boat toward the pagoda and helped injured Justin out of the boat with Taala following.

Justin was already losing consciousness by the time he was taken into the pagoda. Chris hurriedly took a dewberry from his berry pouch and fed him gently. His stab wounds started healing, and after a few minutes, Justin regained his consciousness.

There in the middle of the pagoda sitting on a rocky stand was a box. Inside this box was *The Book of Rorik*. It was a big dark-gray book written in blood-red lettering. Taala held up the book and examined it.

"It is a diary," she exclaimed after reading the first few words. "It is said the owner of this book was Rorik Severin, the last dragon rider to ever walk the face of this earth."

"Dragon rider?"

"I never knew dragons existed, to say nothing of having riders…" Taala sounded like a child.

Going through the book, they discovered newfound knowledge they had never known before. They saw details about magical artifacts and how and where to find them. They saw magical animals and beasts that existed long before and still did.

Flipping through the book, they came across a page that was titled "The Ring of Detection, Origin and Use."

"Jerg has the ring," Chris stated, wide-eyed, looking at the group. "I heard Whitethorn mentioning it during his attack on Jerg."

"According to the book," Taala read, "it was first discovered at Triumphant Life Camp, California, in the ancient ruins of Anansi, the trickster. It was then offered as a betrothal gift to the former queen of Scotland, from whom the ring was taken after Castle Cochrane fell and she was executed."

Taala finished and looked up. There was silence for a little while; they all had thoughts going through their minds, thoughts about the killer, Jerg.

"Interesting," Justin croaked.

"There's more," Taala continued. "The Ring of Detection has two purposes. The first allows the bearer to sense the presence of approaching danger mere moments before it happens. However, it does not function as accurately as a true Seer sees. The second purpose allows its bearer to disappear and reappear elsewhere but constricted by the scope of the ring's power. This knowledge was indeed worth the journey to the Moad River." Taala smiled as she flipped to find another page that was titled "Horn of Unity."

"My mother used to tell me about this Horn of Unity. She said it was the most powerful weapon of the Kiern and one of the greatest weapons ever made. I have never come to understand the principles that revolved around the one who was worthy to be chosen by the Horn of Unity. All I knew was that it had the power to call and assemble Kiern no matter how far we were from the horn. The moment it is blown, we feel a strong urge to answer it. It's like we are drawn to it although I have never felt this urge because Sun Shadow died before I was born. Sadly, after Sun Shadow passed, the horn went missing and has not been found to this date."

Taala smiled in remembrance of her mother.

"Perhaps if my mother was alive and here, she might have an idea where the horn is, but she passed away a long time ago." Taala looked back at the book sadly and continued reading from it. Suddenly there was a change in her expression as her eyes lit up immediately.

"Wait, there's a location here. The Horn of Unity, which belonged to the Kiern, disappeared after the death of its original holder, Sun Shadow. It now sleeps in the Golden Valley, hidden from sight and waiting for the right inheritor. The Horn of Unity is in the Golden Valley," said Taala, a look of longing cast over her face.

"We head west then, taking a shortcut to Green Valley then to Golden Valley, before making our way to Castle Forks," Thungor said, looking at the map again. "Recent searches have been made to find the whereabouts of the Horn of Unity after the death of Sun Shadow. We sought for it to be added and kept safe in our Hall of Protectors, but it was never found." He folded the map.

"It's almost sunset, so let's find a place to camp so we can get some rest, and Justin can recover properly," Chris said.

The group crossed the Moad River and headed into the forest to make camp.

CHAPTER 22

"Nooooooo!" Chris cried as he awoke, also waking Thungor, Taala, and Justin.

"Chris, are you all right?" Justin mumbled, his eyes still heavy with sleep. "Is it the nightmares again? There's still some strawberries in my berry pouch."

"I saw Dad. He fell into the pit in the arena," Chris said, recalling the dream. This time, Justin immediately sat upright, followed by Thungor and Taala who opened their eyes wide. "At first, it wasn't Dad, it was Jerg. Jerg stood tall and proud, taunting me to take the kill. He told me he'd found and killed Mom and had eaten Dad's soul. He said he was going to kill you after he was done feeding on my soul. While saying this, he turned his back to me and said, 'Come.' I rushed toward him filled with anger and hate, but then something happened." Chris stopped breathing hard. "When he turned back, he was gone."

"Gone? How do you mean gone, Chris?" Justin asked impatiently, his voice rising.

The sleep had pretty much cleared from everybody's eyes.

"It wasn't Jerg anymore. The person that turned back to look at me was a human—it was Dad. He also had malicious intent in his eyes, but when he saw me, it vanished. He suddenly looked weak and sober. He dropped his weapon. But the next thing I didn't expect was him throwing himself into the pit." Chris's voice choked on the last statement, and he struggled to keep it firm. "Why would he do that? He should have just calmly walked to me. Why would he have to die? Why would he choose to die?"

The tears were flowing now, and Chris couldn't control them. His voice broke, and he could not complete the last statement or say more. He got up and walked away from the group.

"Chris?" Justin called.

"I need some time alone," Chris answered, not looking back.

All alone in the quiet forest, images of his dad falling into the pit invaded Chris's mind once more. He felt immense pain all over his body.

Please be alive, Dad. We are close, he thought.

A long while later, Chris walked back to camp and regrouped with the others.

"We were waiting for you to come back, Chris," Thungor spoke out. "From your dream, we can gather time isn't on our side anymore. We have to get to Castle Forks as soon as possible, or everyone will die in that arena. Since we've been able to rest, we'll continue the journey. Hopefully by dawn, we should be at Green Valley."

Everyone nodded in agreement. Within a short while, the group of four continued their journey to Green Valley, but when they arrived, it wasn't what they expected.

"So much for a town named *Green* Valley," Taala stated in disgust as they scanned the totally barren and desolate wasteland.

The ground was cracked and hot, and the only plants that thrived in this valley were cactuses. After walking all night and morning, the group had reduced their speed to a sluggish dragging of their feet. An oasis was sighted far off, but when they drew near, it was gone, replaced by hot and dusty sand.

Thankfully, they managed to stumble across a small settlement that had a tavern. They rushed toward it and hurried inside, their mouths as dry as the dust outside.

"Four glasses of water, please," Thungor requested at the bar.

"You'll have to wait till tomorrow, I'm afraid," the innkeeper replied. "We've got a water shortage here."

"What? Can't you even manage a cup? We will pay for it," Taala blurted out, anger and thirst evident in her already dry and throaty voice.

"No. I'm afraid this town used to be an evergreen town, as it is named. We had everything in surplus here: fresh clean water, fresh food, and fruits. Until the Shadow Demons attacked, that is. They said they would make us richer than we were and powerful if only we bowed to their master, Jerg the Almighty, but we refused. We are still suffering from our refusal today," the short chubby tavern owner with elf ears said. "Now we have allocated hours for fresh water supply and have to journey miles for fresh and good food because they control everything."

*****

By the next day, the thirst had gotten to a level that even eclipsed their hunger. When the time the allocated hour for the fresh water supply came, they drank their fill with a new appreciation for the major necessity of water. They knew they could not fight against the Shadow Demons because they were outnumbered and were not in a perfect fighting condition. Even Thungor's cracked and hoarse voice showed evidence of thirst.

When they were done drinking their fill, they bought extra to be saved and purchased edibles to be added to their supplies that would be carried along for the journey. Chris wished he could help the people of Green Valley and hoped Jerg would be defeated soon enough so that they could be free.

CHAPTER 23

The group of four approached Golden Valley at noon and decided to take a quick rest before going in search of the Horn of Unity.

"The Horn of Unity, it sleeps in a fool's gold valley and calls itself Pyrite King. Be not deceived by its riches for all that glitters is not gold. Only one who is worthy shall hear its call," Taala finished reading from the book and looked up at the listening group. "The Horn of Unity is here, I can feel it."

"Fool's gold valley?" Thungor repeated. "Could be referring to Golden Valley. From the name, it appears to have gold because it's covered by golden palms and flowers."

"Pyrite is a common mineral iron disulfide," Chris stated. "I read that when I was reading about precious stones. It's a pale brass-yellow-colored crystal." He smiled.

"*The Book of Rorik* says," mused Justin, "that the Horn of Unity calls itself Pyrite King. A king is only found among his subjects and is also protected by his subjects. By that statement, what if the horn is actually where these pyrite crystals are most plentiful or deeply hidden in their midst?"

"Good point, Justin," Taala commented. "The problem now is, where do we search in this valley full of golden flowers?" She threw up her hands in frustration.

Fool's gold valley…Pyrite King…only one who is worthy, Chris thought. "What does the book mean by 'only one who is worthy would hear its call'?" he asked.

"It could mean one with Kiern blood," Thungor said, turning to Taala. "The last bearer of the horn was Sun Shadow, your ancestor. A while ago, you said you could feel the presence of the horn here."

"Yes, yes, I did feel the presence, but now I don't know," Taala said, biting her lip with uncertainty.

Justin observed the environment for a little while before running to a nearby hill to look at the valley. After some minutes, he came running back.

"The book said, 'Only one who is worthy would hear its call.' The only option we have now is Taala, who is of Kiern blood. Also, one cannot hear a call without listening. You have to listen, Taala. Now this might sound crazy, but think about this—'It sleeps in fool's gold valley and calls itself Pyrite King.' Sleep could actually be signifying 'listening,' and as for the Pyrite King, what if there really isn't any pyrite? The color of pyrite as Chris said is pale yellow, and that is almost the color of the flowers that make up the valley. Do you know what that means?"

Justin stared at the wide-eyed group, who nodded with understanding.

"If I was a king, where would my home be?" Justin asked.

"At the center," Taala answered, smiling brightly.

The group left the covering where they stood and headed for the center of the valley. On getting there, they stood looking about. Having seen nothing, Taala was about to speak when the ground gave way, and they fell right through. Down and down they went, each trying to grab hold of something, anything at all, but to no avail. Fortunately, after the long fall, they landed in a pool of water.

The place they landed in was dark and cold although the air smelled fresh. After swimming out of the water, they squeezed out their clothes while looking around for any sign of danger.

They then began tracing their way inward through the walls, arriving at a cavern. Inside this cavern was a dull yellow glow lit up by millions of pyrite crystals. The group could see other mineral deposits such as flowstones and stalagmites, but there was still no sign of the horn.

"Pyrite," Taala exclaimed.

"I guess this is your call now, Taala," Justin said. "We've been brought into the home of pyrite and the horn sleeps in a 'fool's gold valley' and calls itself 'king.' This is where you listen and wait for its call."

Taala nodded and instantly sat down and closed her eyes.

"Anything yet?" Chris asked after a few minutes of silence.

"No, not yet," she replied and waited a while longer.

After Chris had broken Taala's concentration three times, she was beginning to feel irritated, frustrated, and angry and was about to shout at Chris when—

Taala gasped. "Wait...I feel it, I hear it." She stood up immediately and said, "I know where the Horn of Unity sleeps. This way..." She walked, picking up the pace, the group following her.

They passed through more pyrite and mineral deposits and came to a larger cavern. In the middle was a large yellow pyrite crystal that was flat at the top. There, seated majestically atop the crystal, was the shining bronze Horn of Unity.

After making their big discovery, a volley of arrows ricocheted off the walls around them.

Taala reached for the horn and grabbed it and was immediately pulled into a trance, a small gasp escaping from her lips. Just then, a black crow cawed and landed on the large crystal to stare intently at Taala.

"Everybody, GET DOWN!" Thungor shouted. He flew at Taala, bringing her to the floor as arrows flew past them, hitting the wall. "We need to get out of here now. It's the invisible soldiers of Banlin. We've been spotted."

Taala snapped out of her trance as she hit the floor, her eyes hollow and empty.

"I know the way out, this way."

Taala threw her bombs in the direction the arrows were coming from. There were explosions. Then she dashed toward a small opening at the end of the large cavern, hidden behind a crystal. As everyone entered into the opening of the tunnel, she turned and quickly touched the large crystal.

"This should buy us time to escape," she said as the crystal stopped glowing yellow and immediately turned black, the rest of the crystals in the cavern following suit.

The cavern became dark, preventing the Shadow Demons from seeing. At the same time, they were swallowed by the floor of the cavern that had become quicksand. In the tunnel, the group quickly traced their way out. They crawled in a straight file and soon after burst out into a cave. When they walked out of the cave, they discovered they weren't in Golden Valley any longer but at South Fork Mountain.

CHAPTER 24

Acalm, cool, quiet, and peaceful ambience was what welcomed the group of four to South Fork Mountain.

"Wait, how are we here?" Chris questioned. "South Fork Mountain is miles from Golden Valley!"

"Yeah, what happened? We didn't walk that far," Justin agreed, as confused as Chris.

"The tunnel acts as a portal," Thungor explained. "The Kiern built it as a way of traveling to Castle Forks quickly."

Taala nodded in agreement with a proud smile on her face.

"Wow! So we've really made it?" Chris asked joyfully, hoping to finally save his dad.

Taala breathed in awe. "Yes, and it's so beautiful!"

Chris noticed Justin gazing at Taala as if he thought she was more beautiful than the sight before them.

Justin turned to Thungor, snapping Chris and Taala from their thoughts. "So what now, Thungor? What's the plan? Chris's dreams of Dad are serious, and we shouldn't waste any more time."

"We have a plan. We've been planning an attack ever since Chris was hospitalized, but we knew we couldn't attack just yet because we needed the flaming Sword of Juniper and a Cochrane to use it. With the sword and the plan, we'll be able to banish Jerg and Banlin back to the shadows and reclaim Castle Forks. We'll attack Castle Forks in due time, but first, we need more weapons. We also need to ensure our current weapons are in good shape while we await the other invincible warriors," Thungor replied.

Justin smiled. "I think I know just the place for that. Follow me."

"What? Where?" Chris asked his brother, surprised at the statement.

"Come, you'll see" was Justin's reply as they began to slope down from the cave to enter into the forest, following Justin.

"Thungor, how did you know the invincible Shadow Demons were around?" Chris asked after he caught up to the group, breathing heavily from jogging.

"The crow," Thungor answered. "One way to detect the presence of a Tourlt, especially Jerg, would be the presence of crows in the area. Crows can sense when death's coming. The Tourlt—Jerg, Banlin, and the Shadow Demons—bring death along with them so the crows follow them to all places in large numbers. However, what I don't know is how Taala finished them all off and got us out of that cave." He turned to Taala, who was still admiring the forest. "Taala?" Thungor called, drawing her from her daydreaming. "What did you see in that cave?" he asked bluntly, drawing the attention of the others to Taala.

Taala glanced at the bag that was carrying the Horn of Unity and looked up. "Sun Shadow," she replied slowly. "I saw Sun Shadow. He spoke to me. Apparently, he hid the Horn of Unity in Golden Valley, leaving the key to finding it with Rorik, who later died, killed by the bug demon at the Moad River. He showed me the way out and how to activate the crystals that killed the invisible soldiers in the cave. Sun Shadow also told me about the Horn of Unity and how I will use it to assemble the Kiern." Taala smiled at Thungor.

A few hours later, the group approached the junction that cut toward the Cochrane house.

"Home? Justin, are you leading us home?" Chris blurted out sharply. Alert, he looked around. Thungor did the same.

"I don't think going home is a good idea. Officer Smith placed me on house arrest when I was at the hospital. I'd be declared missing by now and definitely would have boosted his suspicion on me a 100 percent."

"You don't have to worry about that, lad," Thungor said. "I left the task of clearing the suspicions to my fellow invincible warriors. Officer Smith's probably on to another case, chasing criminals by now. Your case is closed because everyone in charge of your case thinks the Cochrane family went for a vacation to Peru. There have also been sightings of Justin and your mother, which have, to a large extent, answered the questions that may arise."

"Come on, we're almost there!" Justin reminded the group of their current mission to get weapons, which also once again placed Chris in a state of confusion.

"Uh, Justin? You said you were taking us to a certain place to get and re-sharpen our weapons. I don't understand why we're at our house." He shot a puzzled and questioning look at Justin.

They had arrived at the entrance of the house. The grasses were wild and overgrown; one could probably crouch and hide in them. The rhubarb plant had also begun fruiting. Justin walked into the garage and appeared back with a key. He then led the group toward the back of the house to an old, abandoned, and rusted vehicle. Chris stood and watched, waiting to see what his brother was up to. That same moment, Justin opened the car door and turned a lock that was used to hold a plate that seemed welded to the floor of the car. He dragged it up. A trapdoor lifted, revealing an opening with steps that led underground. Chris's mouth fell open.

"That...that..." Chris stammered, pointing at the rusted car and the underground passageway. "That used to be my play car. I sat in that same place and played with the steering wheel when I was young. I always thought it was a rusted old car." Chris threw accusing eyes at Justin, who lifted his hands as though saying, "It wasn't my fault."

"Dad was teaching me blacksmithing before Grandpa Jim died. Grandpa Jim used to be a master craftsman, and he passed this art down to Dad, who tried to do the same to me, but I wasn't interested at the time. He would have taught you if not for our current situation." The statement convinced the confused Chris.

"Then how come no one told me about this?" Chris asked, throwing a devastated look at Justin.

"That's because it was just me, Dad, and Grandpa Jim that knew. Dad didn't want word to spread as it would put us in danger with the police and rogues. Mom has no idea this basement exists," Justin said, stepping into the car and descending the steps, with Thungor and Taala following.

Chris stood astonished for a little before entering the car, closing the door behind him. Once again, from outside, the car appeared to be an old, forgotten rust bucket, leaving no suspicions.

The basement was dark and silent; it smelled of metal, wood, and coal. Justin traced the wall and flipped a switch, instantly lighting up the entire basement. When the light came on, it revealed a room filled with different kinds of weapons: spears, daggers, swords, axes, traps, grenades, guns. There were other rooms and also a room that looked like a smithy. The room with the biggest space had a broad table at the center. On this table were also laid weapons of different kinds. While the group took time out in exploring the rooms, Thungor heard a movement and immediately became alert.

"Heads up, I heard something at the entrance," he cautioned. After a few moments of silence, there was yet another sound.

Faint footsteps drew closer to the large room; Thungor, Taala, Justin, and Chris stood at different positions in the room, weapons ready to attack. But almost immediately, Thungor spoke, surprising the group.

"Vannsd, brother! It's so good to see you." Thungor seemed to hug an empty space. "We've been separated for so long that I could hardly sense your presence until you got so close." Thungor joyfully hugged the air again. "These are allies, so you can make yourself visible now. It's okay." He gestured toward the group. Almost immediately, a spitting image of Thungor appeared beside him.

"This is my brother, Vannsd. He's the one that helped me protect Chris and also planted images in the head of the nurses and the officers in charge of his case."

"Hello again, Vannsd," Chris said with a smile.

"You know him?" Justin asked.

Chris nodded. "Yeah, he's the one who made our crops grow again after the flood, and he tended to everything while me and Dad were in Castle Forks for six months."

Thungor introduced his brother to the rest of the group, who also said his pleasantries which were met with a positive response from the group.

"I was also charged with protecting your grandfather. But sadly, there are some things that even the strongest man is powerless to protect." Vannsd lowered his head sadly.

"How did you meet Grandpa Jim?" Chris asked.

"On a hunting trip to South Fork Mountain, he saved me once. Ever since then, I have never left his side. After your grandfather died, I became a ranch hand and also a protector of this armory basement." He added, "With that said, there is something you all need to see." Vannsd led the group to the wall and opened a hidden door. Inside was a flaming purplish-black sword with glowing words on the blade in a language the group did not understand, but they all knew what the sword was.

"The flaming Sword..." Chris began.

Thungor completed his statement, "Of Juniper!"

"*Honor, loyalty, truth* are the words inscribed on it," Vannsd informed them. With the sword in their possession, the group felt more confident about the impending battle they were about to wage against the Tourlt. They had the Horn of Unity and now Valor, the flaming Sword of Juniper. They also had a whole lot of other weapons suitable for fighting against Shadow Demons.

"You both have to try holding the sword. Only a Cochrane can wield it. Jim Cochrane is dead, that leaves three, no...four remaining male Cochranes—Todd, Justin, Chris, and Thomas Cochrane," Thungor said, turning to the Cochrane boys. "Todd has been captured. That leaves us with you two. For this battle, one of you will have to wield the sword along with Taala, who will blow the Horn of Unity."

The Cochrane boys looked at each other.

"Wielding the sword has advantages and disadvantages," Chris started, speaking to Justin before turning back to the sword. "It gives immense strength and power but also reduces your life span."

"The sword gives great power but also does a lot of damage to the bearer's body and life." Justin closed his eyes for a moment and spoke after a few moments. "That's why I should do it."

"What? No! Do you understand what I just said? If there's anyone in our family who has to do it, it's me." Chris half-shouted his reply at Justin.

"You know it has to be me, Chris. Ever since Dad was captured, the responsibility of the household falls to me. I can't just sit still and watch my brother wield a sword that could damage his life, knowing my family is in danger of being exterminated. So for the sake of our family, I have to do this. Allow me to do this."

With that, Justin grabbed a hold of the sword and held it. The glowing purplish-black color burned brighter as a dim luminescence traced the words inscribed on the sword. An insignia of a crest appeared on the hand that held the sword, close to the palm. Justin writhed in intense pain, which forced him to his knees, groaning.

"Justin!" Chris shouted, grabbing the sword from his hand.

Chris and Justin, both with a crest freshly carved on their hands, collapsed to the floor and passed out.

CHAPTER 25

Chris could not feel his body after he saw the white flash. The last thing he remembered was seeing his brother in extreme pain, then shouting his name and grabbing a hold of the sword. Next thing, he felt the most intense pain of his life.

But after a strange numbness took over, it felt like another spirit had replaced his own. He felt its energy and power coursing through his veins. He was pumped with adrenaline, and at that moment, he felt he could take out anyone or anything. But almost suddenly as he felt this power, it slowly left his body; he felt so powerless and weak that he just wanted to die.

Suddenly everything changed, and he saw a Shadow Demon flying from Castle Forks. When he looked closely, Chris recognized the demon as Banlin. It felt like he was not really there yet but was a witness to everything that happened. While Banlin was flying hard, Chris was able to see his figure up close. When he drew nearer, Chris sighted something in his hand.

"They're Dad's!" Chris exclaimed as he recognized what he held: Dad's Rocky Balboa golden gloves and necklace. *Why does he have them?* he thought, alerted and worried.

Could it be that...no, it can't be. Chris thought hard to figure out the dream. *Dad isn't dead. He is not dead.* He kept repeating the statement like a mantra.

"Todd Cochrane is dead. In three days' time, Jerg will reveal himself after the death of all the Cochranes and also Novell, who will die by my hands," Banlin growled, chuckling devilishly as he instructed the Shadow Demons to find Chris and his friends.

"Dad is dead? Dad is dead!? *Dad?* Noooooo!" Chris shouted and woke up. He discovered his brother already awake.

"Chris! It's the dreams again, huh? Are you all right?" Justin's face showed empathy, but it slowly changed into a horrified look when his gaze fell to Chris's hand. "Chris? What's that on your hand? What did you do?" Justin exclaimed, looking at his own hand with the same sign. "You touched the sword? Why did you do that when I specifically told you not to?"

"You were in serious pain, Justin. I tried to ease it and completely forgot about touching the sword," Chris said with utmost sincerity, and that was the truth. He was so worried about Justin at that moment that he completely forgot it was the sword and that he wasn't supposed to touch it although he was still mad at Justin for forcefully rushing to wield the sword. Thungor had tried to stop him, but it was already too late.

"You're both finally awake." Thungor's voice boomed through the room as he entered, breaking the cool atmosphere that had formed in the room. "It was a difficult two days for both of you."

"Two days?" Chris voiced out. "We were out for two days?" He looked at Justin, who threw an angry glance at him.

"I think it's a little too late to get mad at each other. You both were chosen by the flaming Sword of Juniper. That's why you have the dragon crest on your hands. That aside, I have good news and bad news. Which one do you want to hear first?"

"Bad news," Justin replied quickly, just as Chris was about to say "good news."

"Some things were found in the vicinity of the house yesterday night, and we don't know who left them," Thungor said, producing the very same items of Dad's property Chris had seen in the dream.

Chris's eyes widened at the sight. He turned to gaze sharply at Justin, who was already looking at him.

"I know who left it," Chris said gravely, standing up to retrieve Dad's Rocky Balboa golden gloves and necklace. "These belong to our dad." Chris made his way to Justin. "I saw this in the dream I had before waking up. It was Banlin. In the dream, he dropped it while asking his Shadow Demons to find us. He also passed a message: 'Todd Cochrane is dead. In three days' time, Jerg will reveal himself after the death of all the Cochranes and also Novell, who will die by my hands' was what he said before I woke up."

"No...that couldn't...it's impossible...Dad couldn't..." Like Chris, Justin refused to admit that Dad was dead.

"Dad is not dead. He's lying," Chris said.

"And just how would you know that?" Justin fired the blunt question, his voice shaky.

"I know because I feel him. Something tells me he's still alive. Banlin wouldn't have come looking for us if Dad was truly dead."

"A trap..." Justin's eyes were wide open. "What if it's a trap? What if Dad escaped, and they want to use us as bait to catch him again?"

"Well said, Justin," Thungor said. "However, we can't know for sure what truly happened. We can only focus on the battle plan to attack Castle Forks. Only then can we know if Todd is truly alive."

"My father is alive," Chris blurted out angrily, still thinking about the dream.

"Calm down, Chris. No one said Dad was dead. We will take Castle Forks and rescue him," Justin said. He looked at Thungor. "Now for the good news."

Thungor chuckled. "You both can wield the flaming Sword of Juniper."

"You already said that, Thungor," Chris replied.

Thungor nodded. "And the army of invincible stealth warriors like me will arrive at sundown."

It was good news, but the bad news had already ruined Chris's mind. He could not stop thinking about Dad, Banlin, and the dream. Dad was in trouble and so was Novell.

After a few moments, Chris heard footsteps and faint voices from outside the house, and his eyes widened.

"Stay behind me," Thungor said. He edged toward the front door, his weapon in hand.

Chris and Justin followed closely behind, their knives at the ready. Thungor brought his finger to his lips to ensure the two brothers stayed silent.

"Hopefully, they're still awake," they heard a familiar voice say from the other side of the door. "Though it'd be nice if they 'ad a few more hours of ignorance."

Thungor frowned and lowered his weapon. He opened the door; Whitethorn and Si stood outside, Whitethorn with his hand raised as if he was about to knock on the door.

"Whitethorn!" Thungor said. "Si!"

"Why would it be nice if we had a few more hours of ignorance?" Justin asked. "Ignorance of what?"

Chris scanned the empty spaces either side of Whitethorn and Si. "Where's Dad?"

Whitethorn and Si remained silent as if they didn't know what to say.

"Is Dad dead?" Chris asked again. "Where is he?"

Chris's eyes welled with tears as he thought back to the dream. Taala appeared behind him and put a hand on his shoulder.

Si sighed. "We tried to bring him with us, but he was left behind in Banlin's dungeon prison."

Chris erupted into loud sobs. Taala embraced him in her long arms.

"Let me get this straight," Justin barked, stepping forward menacingly. "You lot recruited *our family* to save you all, but you LEFT HIM THERE TO DIE?"

"We...we tried, Justin—"

"YOU OBVIOUSLY DIDN'T TRY HARD ENOUGH!" Justin bellowed, and he punched the wall next to him.

"Justin!" Thungor said. "Calm down!"

"No, I WILL NOT CALM DOWN!"

"Just...just like my dream...s-said!" Chris bawled, blubbering as he spoke. "Banlin...Banlin said in my dream t-that Dad was dead and...and Novell was to be killed in three days' time!"

Justin huffed with anger and sniffled beside him. Taala squeezed Chris tighter.

"What? Three days?" Si questioned, his eyes misty, a hint of rage threatening to take over.

"I know it's hard, but we shouldn't put all our trust on that," Thungor said, eyeing Justin in particular. "If we act fast, those things might not be all true. We found the flaming Sword of Juniper and also the Horn of Unity. Taala was worthy and is now the bearer of the horn. Also Justin and Chris were chosen by the flaming Sword of Juniper."

Whitethorn and Si gasped with shock.

"You found the Horn of Unity?" Whitethorn said, wide-eyed. "The gods are on our side."

Thungor invited Whitethorn and Si into the house. A while later, they were seated in the sitting room, sharing stories of what they'd been through. Chris and Justin also told Whitethorn and Si about their powers and Chris's dreams, and they in turn told them about life as a prisoner of Jerg.

Chris couldn't bear the thought of his dad being a prisoner in that evil prison, dead or alive, so he changed the course of the conversation from stories to strategy.

"So how are we gonna get Dad back?"

CHAPTER 26

"Considering the frequent disturbing dreams that Chris has been having, we plan to attack Castle Forks in two days," Thungor lectured the group the next morning after breakfast. "It's even more honorable to have the presence of Whitethorn and Si to plan this impending battle."

While the meeting was ongoing inside, the invincible stealth warriors stood guard outside. Both parties, now a group of eight, were seated around a round table in the dining room, cups of tea in front of each.

"We'll divide our group into two and surround Castle Forks. The first group will take the front entrance and the second group will take the back. The Kiern, which Taala will summon, will remain hidden in the bushes, lying wait in an ambush. They will strike at the last minute, after both groups have fooled the Tourlt with their number. The first group will strike, pulling all the Shadow Demons to the front entrance of Castle Forks, while the second group will remain invisible, as they enter the palace stealthily, finishing off the remaining Shadow Demon guards. They will also rescue Novell and Todd."

Whitethorn nodded. "Good plan, Thungor."

"I'll be with the second group to save my father. Is there any other person that wishes to add to Thungor's plan?" Si asked, looking at the group sitting around the table.

Chris sniffled from crying and said, "W-we could make good use of traps for the first group. We discovered that a great emission of light defeats the darkness, and in our journey, we were able to get weapons, including a mage staff that Thungor picked. The staff helped us defeat the bug demon at the Moad River. I believe we could put it into good use along with Taala's traps."

The idea was extremely good. It received nods and approval from everyone, but their praise wasn't enough to stop his tears from flowing as they continued their plan.

After talking, deliberating, arguing, and agreeing, they concluded the meeting for that day. Each person was assigned tasks of their own in preparation for the battle. Chris and Justin had the task of putting the weapons in great shape in the basement. Taala taught some of the stealth warriors the art of setting dangerous traps. Si and Whitethorn had the task of overseeing the training of the warriors, plus Chris and Justin, and keeping the environment in order. Thungor also assisted, showing them how to fight with spears and throwing daggers and showing them how the mage staff worked.

Everything seemed ready and set as the day of battle arrived.

The weapons were set and ready for use, and the stealth warriors had also added new skills to their fighting inventory. That night, the group discussed battle plans once more and even a few additions were made. At dawn, they all gathered in front of the Cochrane residence as Whitethorn briefed the stealth warriors to boost their morale. Only one thing was left: to take back Castle Forks. The group was divided into two as earlier discussed. Thungor, Whitethorn, and Chris were in the first group, and Si, Justin, and Taala in the second group.

Throughout their battle at Castle Forks, both humans and Kiern were cloaked in invisibility; both Taala and Whitethorn made use of some clothing of the stealth warriors. They also took shortcuts that brought them to the castle as quickly as possible. As the first group reached the front entrance of the castle, Thungor quickly finished off the sentries guarding it.

"How are we going to enter? They took the first and second keys from Novell and Si." Thungor turned as it dawned on him in realization.

"With this," Whitethorn said and took out the third key and put it in the keyhole. The rocky wall shuddered, and a huge palace door was revealed, which opened immediately. Inside the castle was silent as the grave and dark. The first group walked in stealth mode.

"Keep your eyes sharp for any movement," Whitethorn cautioned. After walking for a little while and not meeting any Shadow Demons, it was beginning to seem strange.

"This is strange. There's nobody here," said Whitethorn, turning to the group, who let down their guard and started looking around.

"Shh! Everyone, listen…did you hear that?" Chris said.

Everyone went quiet. After what seemed like minutes of listening, they heard voices cheering for Banlin and a loud growling.

"It's comin' from the arena. The fight is about to start. Everyone, quick. To the arena!" Whitethorn dashed forward into the darkness, the group following behind him.

They surged forward with anger and speed, ready to finish off any Shadow Demons, and within a few minutes, the gate to the arena was in sight. Two guards were standing and cheering for Banlin at the gate. Whitethorn hurriedly finished both guards off and dashed into the arena followed by the rest of the group members. The two figures standing in the arena had their backs turned to them, and the group were unable to see their faces. One, however, was putting on Novell's regalia.

As soon as they entered, the gates to the arena slammed shut, alerting the group; they'd fallen into a trap. They adopted a defensive position. The people that stood facing each other inside the arena turned to face the group. They were none other than Banlin and Jerg.

Angrily, the group dashed toward the duo who flew up and out of the arena. Si immediately tried to follow, but his wings were wrapped by a thick black mass, making him unable to fly. They'd been caught; it was too late to contact the second group.

"Welcome, welcome to my castle," Jerg announced as he sat atop the canopy-covered throne. "Since my little bird told me you were coming, I have been expecting you." He grinned devilishly.

The group members inside the arena were taken aback. *Do we have an informer?* Chris thought.

As though their minds had been read, Vannsd was dragged into the arena in chains and thrown down before them. Thungor looked at his brother, surprised and ashamed.

"I'm sorry, he took my family… He said if I didn't tell him the plan and your whereabouts, he would feed them to Braagg." He was cut off by Jerg.

"Not to worry, little birds, Braagg already ate them for breakfast." He then threw down a piece of fabric, which Vannsd recognized as his wife's. He broke down in tears. "Thought you might need a little something to remember," Jerg said and laughed, his laughter echoing through the arena.

"Now for the rest of your group, who are already locked in the dungeon cell, they will join you here soon before the real fight begins."

By then, the arena was already packed with Shadow Demons, looking to watch a great fight.

"Bring in the prisoners!" Jerg commanded. A few seconds later, the arena gate was opened to let in the second group and, afterward, Novell and Todd.

"DAD!" Chris roared through floods of tears. "DAD!"

Chris opened his mouth to shout again, but Whitethorn nudged his arm and put a finger to his mouth. "I know this is hard, Chris, but if your father is strong enough to survive this, we don't want to make this situation worse. We stick to the plan and try to rescue them as swiftly as possible."

Chris nodded and wiped his eyes, his stomach twinging with guilt that he could have jeopardized the entire plan by shouting. But he couldn't help it. He didn't know what he'd do if his dad was taken from him right before his eyes.

The second group was reduced in number and some were injured, including Justin, who seemed to have cuts and bruises. Their weapons were also gone.

Both Novell and Todd looked sick, and their bodies were damaged from the beatings. They were dragged out and placed at the center of the arena where Banlin already stood. Both groups were alarmed at the sight and tried to rush forward only to be stopped by

Braagg, an enormous two-headed snake, who surged up from the pit and curled up in between Novell and the two groups, preventing them from reaching the prisoners. In front of them was Braagg and behind were Shadow Demon guards. They were outnumbered.

"Father!" Si called out in a whisper when Banlin's back was turned, and Novell moved at the sound of his son's voice.

He struggled and lifted up his head and looked back at Si.

"FATHER!" Si called again. This time his voice was shaky.

"Look at what you have turned out to be, brother." Banlin drew back Novell's attention. "I can't believe I used to be afraid of you. You were so high and mighty, so strong, but now you are nothing but a weakened old fool." Banlin laughed mockingly.

Novell struggled to his feet and staggered.

"I can still take thee Banlin. Thou are only saying this because of my current weakened state." Novell looked at his brother, a hint of sadness evident in his eyes. "Why? Why would thou betray thy own family for the Tourlt?" Novell asked, still looking at Banlin.

"I have no family. You ceased to be my family the day I left," Banlin replied angrily. "Now you are my enemy, and today, you are going to die by my hands."

Novell fell to the ground, spitting blood from his mouth.

"You cannot even properly hold your weapon. You are weak. We would have ruled Castle Forks together, side by side, brother. But look at you now…"

"It would not be right to put the lives of our people in your dark hands, Banlin. It is not too late for thee, brother. Thou haven't fully changed into a demon. Can thou not see that Jerg is trying to accomplish that by making thou kill me?"

"He didn't make me do it!" Banlin roared angrily. "You were mine for the killing. This has been my quest for ages—to avenge my banishment from Castle Forks. Do you have any idea how humiliated I felt as all those people looked at me? Now they would never dare defy Lord Banlin." He roared again, making the Shadow Demons shrink in fear.

"He is killing thee," Novell said, looking down at the pool of blood beneath him, "just like thou are killing me."

Banlin's eyes widened as mixed emotions ran through him, but almost at the same minute, they vanished.

"Everything that kills me makes me feel alive, and if killing you will kill me, then I will not waste any more time," Banlin shouted and turned his spear toward Novell who blocked it. Banlin kicked him hard in the head.

"Father! Please, GET UP."

Novell's eyes glowed white, and he immediately conjured a flaming sword and rushed at Banlin, who was taken aback but quickly regained himself.

"After our parents died, I put all my hope and trust in you, brother," Banlin started. "I dreamed about all the things I could do and be with you. I knew together we would be stronger, and we only had each other. But what I never understood was why you banished me for being who I am? I feel so right doing the wrong things, and I feel so wrong doing the right thing. How could you hate me so much, brother?"

"Then kill me but not Todd," Novell croaked. "I understand thy quarrel with me, but let this man go!"

Banlin and Jerg cackled menacingly at the same time.

"And what makes you think I would set him free?" Banlin challenged. "I want those children to suffer like I've suffered! Without their beloved father, they will be mentally weak! Weak enough for me to kill the entire Cochrane family!"

"LET MY DAD GO!" Chris bellowed through the room, rage rising above his distress. "LET HIM GO!"

"You want him? Come get him! Let the battle begin!" Jerg said. Braagg growled. "Guards! Release them! Let them fight to their deaths!"

Everyone mobilized, full of surprise that Jerg has released them that easily, but Chris paused with terror as the mighty battle broke out before him. He watched a weak Novell swing at Banlin, but his eyes panned to his dad, who dodged Braagg to get to Jerg. Todd was feeble, breathless, and covered with open oozing wounds. Todd roared like a Viking, and Jerg noticed his approach, full of anger and rage.

Tears swamped Chris's face as he watched his dad stagger toward the all-powerful Jerg with nothing but his bloody fists and a scowl. He threw a clenched fist at Jerg's head, but Jerg blocked his attack, grinning as he grabbed Todd's wrist and yanked him to the side.

Jerg unsheathed his sword and attempted to slash Chris's dad with the blade, but Todd ducked just in time. Jerg laughed and lunged forward, using his sword like a spear, trying to stab Todd. But despite his dad's weakness, Todd jumped back each time and avoided the tip of the weapon.

To Chris's surprise, Jerg threw the sword to the ground in frustration and charged at Todd with his bare hands. The force of his dive knocked Todd onto his back, and Jerg landed heavy punches into his gut, lurching him forward and making him scream in pain. Todd tried to knee and kick Jerg from underneath him, but his attempts were feeble compared to the punches to his face.

"Dad!" Chris wailed, completely frozen with fear as he watched on. "Dad!"

Jerg looked up at Chris as Todd shuffled on his back, trying to reach the sword Jerg had dropped onto the floor. Chris realized his dad's plan and decided to create as much a distraction as possible.

"Jerg!" he yelled again. "Leave my dad alone!"

Jerg growled and glowered at Chris, allowing Todd to roll over onto his stomach and get a little closer to the sword.

"Yeah, you! Come and get me instead!" Chris challenged. Within a split second, Jerg leaped up from Todd's back and marched toward Chris. "Dad!"

As Chris's every muscle twitched with horror, he fumbled for an arrow in his quiver and attached it to his bow, but before he could pull the bowstring to fire at Jerg's skull, Jerg had already lifted a second sword from his belt above Chris's head. Chris screamed and cowered, accepting his fate. Then a silver sword sliced off Jerg's head from behind; Chris watched it tumble to the ground. Todd swooped over to embrace his son.

"Dad, you're alive!" Chris said through weak whimpering.

"I'm alive, Criffer Bob," he said, quickly peeling away from their hug. "Come on, we need to help the others."

As Chris and his dad rushed to help Novell against Banlin, the black mass that held Si loosened, enabling him to fly to Novell's side. But as Si landed, Banlin's sword cut his left shoulder, causing him instant agony and suffering. Si roared with pain. Todd quickly took over, assisting Novell against Banlin with Jerg's silver sword.

But even with Todd, Novell, and Chris fighting Banlin, punching, hacking, and shooting with arrows, Banlin's attacks were faster and stronger. Banlin's sword sliced Novell's leg, making him crumple to the ground next to Si, who quickly bled out on the floor.

"Whitethorn!" Chris shouted. "Justin! Anyone!"

But everyone else was engaged in their own minibattles against various Shadow Demon guards.

Whitethorn and Thungor fought back-to-back against the guards and attempted to take them out one by one with their axes, swords, and the mage staff, but the sheer number of them made Chris question whether they could hold their own despite their abilities. The Shadow Demons roared and crowded the pair of them like birds to seed, forcing them to hack and slash as fast as they could through the fresh wounds and waning energy.

Justin and Taala used their knives and daggers to stab the two-headed snake fast and repeatedly, but by the looks of it, they spent more time sidestepping and parrying than attacking.

But Chris remembered their battle plan. He gasped and remembered the traps Taala once showed him in her sketch pad after they'd made some snares. He recalled that the snare traps would never be strong enough to catch Banlin's Shadow Demon soldiers, but the cartridge trap, the grenade trap, and the wire trap would be perfect.

As Todd continued to fight against Banlin, Chris scanned the ground and noticed several traps dotted around the floor covered with twigs and leaves.

Chris turned back to Banlin and grabbed his knife from his pocket. "Banlin!" he shouted, his voice quavering. "Come and get me!"

Banlin turned and scoffed with amusement as he looked down at Chris from his towering height. Todd slashed Jerg's sword across

Banlin's back, but he merely winced as he proceeded to march toward Chris, sneering and growling.

Chris walked backward, luring Banlin toward him, trying to remember the exact position of the cartridge traps without looking. But Banlin didn't give him the time he hoped for.

Without hesitation, Banlin advanced toward Chris with his sword drawn and swung the blade through the air, trying to slice his neck. Chris dodged the attack and veered left, leading his opponent toward the first cartridge trap on the floor. He stepped around it and prayed Banlin would step into it.

But to Chris's panic, Banlin stepped over it as if he knew it was there. His heart raced as his dad continued to wound Banlin from behind, but Todd's persistence angered Banlin like a beast repeatedly poked with a stick.

In a flash, Banlin roared and spun on his heel. He grabbed Chris's dad by the throat and lifted him from the floor, instantly blocking his airways and forcing him to wheeze for breath.

"You *dare* kill Jerg!" Banlin hissed with malice. "Prepare to die a slow and agonizing death!"

"DAD, NO!" Chris yelled.

He scanned the room for help, but everyone else was still fighting what now felt like an impossible battle despite Jerg's unexpected death. Novell and Si were unconscious on the floor, both lying in a pool of their own blood that had mixed together. Whitethorn and Thungor had been severely weakened by the Shadow Demon soldiers who appeared to be untouched. And Justin and Taala had been backed into a corner, inches from death.

Chris breathed deep and focused as much as his brain would allow, looking at the ground to avoid getting distracted by something else…when he noticed a wet trail running around the edges and through the middle of the arena. The murky blues, greens, purples, and reds shining from the liquid told him exactly what it was.

Gasoline.

Taala must have secretly trickled gasoline around the room as a last resort!

Chris was standing next to a lantern; he realized *this* was their only option. He could never live with himself if his decision caused more casualties to his family and friends than Banlin's army, but he could also never live with himself if he stood there and did nothing, allowing Banlin to take over the world.

Chris inhaled from the bottom of his lungs and released the air, trying to steady his shaky body and focus, just like his dad always told him to do. He looked back at Whitethorn and Thungor, Justin and Taala, Novell and Si, and his dad, all cornered by Banlin and his Shadow Demons.

It was now or never.

Chris grabbed an arrow from his quiver and held it in the flames of the lantern until the tip of it came alight like a matchstick. He notched it to the bowstring and aimed at a patch of gasoline on the floor.

After one last deep breath, he released the arrow. A loud *roar* filled the arena as the small flame from Chris's arrow cracked and soared, engulfing everyone and invading the dungeon with black smoke.

Chris staggered backward. His mind flashed back to the wildfire two years ago, the one he and his family had only just survived...

*****

Chris and Justin nodded and closed their eyes, but as the car rumbled forward, Chris reopened his and watched as they sped down the road. Orange flames enveloped them as the fire burned the surrounding trees and glowing cinders fell all around the car.

"Dad, will the flames get to us?" Chris panicked.

"Don't worry, son, we'll get out of this soon..."

"It's all gonna be okay," Mom said, holding their arms.

*****

His mom's comforting words rung in Chris's mind, and he abruptly snapped out of his painful flashback. "Not now!" he snapped, scolding himself for daydreaming.

From the other end of the room, Banlin dropped Todd, who plummeted to the floor with a *smack*. Then he turned to Chris, striding toward him.

"What have you done?" Banlin barked, spit flying into Chris's face as he spoke.

Chris, quavering on the spot, felt the heat of the flames surround them as they surged. Many of the Shadow Demons in battle with Whitethorn and Thungor and Justin and Taala got caught in the blaze, and others coughed and choked on the fumes, but that meant his allies must have suffered at the hands of the fire as well.

This time, Banlin seized Chris by the throat; Chris thought it was all over. Not only had he put everyone at risk, including his dad, with his stupid idea, but he'd also killed himself as well.

Chris closed his eyes, accepting his fate as he writhed and wheezed in the grip of pure evil. He heard the *whoosh* of Banlin raising his sword through the air over the crackling of the never-ending fire. But instead of feeling the searing pain of Banlin's sword slicing his flesh or impaling one of his vital organs, he dropped through the air and thumped onto the hard, hot ground. Chris gasped. His throat burned.

He looked up and saw his dad standing behind Banlin, the silver sword he'd taken from Jerg pierced through Banlin's skull. Todd retracted the blade, and Banlin collapsed to the floor. Todd kicked his dying body into the ring of flames, and they watched his skin burn and wrinkle.

"Come on, we need to save the others!" Todd rasped, his voice hoarse from being strangled. "I'll get Whitethorn and Thungor, you go help Justin and Taala."

Chris nodded and staggered over to Justin and Taala, who were surrounded by an array of dead Shadow Demons on the floor and the now headless snake, coughing and spluttering in the gray smoke.

"What...happened?" Justin croaked.

"No time, we need to go," Chris said. He extended his arm to his brother.

Chris pulled Justin up from the floor and did the same for Taala. The three of them stumbled to the middle of the arena. Justin and Taala gaped at Novell and Si slumped in their own blood.

"Are they dead?" Justin asked.

Chris shrugged. "I really don't know, but we need Dad and the others to help lift them."

At that moment, Todd returned with Whitethorn and Thungor at his side, both of them coughing and puffing for breath.

"H-help...us..." a low raspy voice pleaded from below them.

Everyone looked down and saw Si trying to move through the pain.

"We need to leave before this place collapses," Todd said. "Whitethorn, Thungor, are you strong enough to lift Novell if I carry Si?"

Whitethorn and Thungor nodded as they continued to cough and gasp, but their agony didn't stop them from lifting Novell from the ground, Whitethorn holding him under the shoulders and Thungor carrying his legs.

Todd hoisted Si up like a fireman, one arm under his knees and the other arm beneath his shoulder.

"Chris, lead the way!" Todd instructed.

Chris nodded, and they headed back the way they came. He was relieved his decision hadn't killed the ones he loved. He just hoped that Novell would make it.

CHAPTER 27

"We need to take Novell to your hospital," Si rasped desperately, turning to Todd. "We *all* need to get to a hospital."

Everyone was still coughing and wheezing, the smoke and ash irritating their lungs and airways. Chris's insides twisted with guilt at the sound of their hacking coughs and weak bodies, but he tried to remember that setting the dungeon alight had managed to save more people than he'd expected, even if Novell wouldn't make it.

"That's dangerous, he doesn't look human. It will arouse suspicions," Whitethorn answered Si.

"We do not have a choice. My father is dying, and all you have to say is he'll cause suspicion?" Anger was evident in his eyes now. Then he spotted Vannsd. "You traitor!" he screamed and rushed toward Vannsd, gripping him by the neck tightly. "It is convenient that you survived after revealing our plan and whereabouts to the enemy!"

Thungor tried desperately to remove Si's hands but to no avail. Vannsd, too, was near death; he did not resist Si's hands as he was ready to die—better that than endure the pain of losing his family.

"As you well know, Si, I can teleport between Castle Forks and Machu Picchu, so I managed to escape execution to inform Cyndee Cochrane of the situation."

Si scoffed. "How noble of you."

"Yes, well thanks to me, Cyndee Cochrane knows that her family are safe while she's stuck in Peru!"

"EVERYBODY, STOP!" Taala shouted, stopping Thungor and Si in their actions. "Can't you see that this is what Jerg and Banlin will want when they return from the dead and go back to the gold city? He doesn't—"

"Wait, what? What do you mean rise from the dead?" Chris questioned. "We killed them!"

"Yes, we did, but remember what my father told you during your first time at Castle Forks," Si said. "They can never truly die, so they will always come back, which is exactly why we need the Cochranes on our side."

Taala nodded. "Back to what I was saying. If they can kill us by making us turn on each other, that will suit them. He made Banlin kill his brother because he knew Novell had a powerful influence on the people of Castle Forks. When the leader dies, the followers scatter. Can't you see he's using a divide-and-conquer method to win this battle? And while we're here arguing and fighting, Novell is dying. Chris, Thungor, Justin, do you remember the berries we plucked at Berryville?"

Their eyes widened with joy as they turned to the group.

"We need to get back home now. Quick, Whitethorn, do you know a pass to arrive at the Cochrane residence?" Justin asked, turning to Whitethorn, who acted immediately.

Si and Todd picked up Novell and placed him in an improvised stretcher and followed the group. A short while later, they came to a dead-end. Si reached up and pushed a hidden notch in the rocky wall, which retracted to reveal an opening. From this opening, they saw the Cochrane house standing peacefully, the environment lonely and unkempt. Quickly, the group rushed out of the secret passageway to the house.

Taala and Chris bounded into the house in search of the berries. They found them in the fridge, each in a pouch.

"Check for my berries," Taala hurriedly said. Soon they found the blackberries. They rushed back out of the house and fed the unconscious Novell a blackberry.

"We picked berries at a village called Berryville. Each berry had a magic power which it embodies. My berry was the blackberry, and it is supposed to restore or replenish life. This is, however, my first time using it," Taala said to Si with hope in her eyes.

Novell coughed up blood as Si pressed a clean fabric onto the cut on his chest, but he'd lost too much blood. He gripped hard on Si's hand as he fought for his life.

"What is happening? Taala, why is he not getting better? What did you feed him? Father! Father!" Si's confusion affected and spread to everyone.

"He's too far gone, after all," Thungor realized. "I'm sorry, the berries only work up to a certain point."

Struggling to breathe and staring into Si's eyes, the light of life left Novell. Si groaned and roared a long and painful roar.

Taala was the most affected. She sat on the floor, helpless, confused, and broken. She looked at the berries in her hands and threw them away, gripping her hair. Then she got up and ran off, sobbing. Justin ran after her immediately after picking up her berries. Todd, Chris, and Thungor walked away to give Si some space alone with his dad after each resting a light hand on his shoulder one after the other. Whitethorn stayed a little longer but soon left Si crying into his father's cold hands.

At sundown, Novell's body was carried into the basement where Si froze him in an ice casket.

"What kind of relationship could they have had that a brother would kill his own brother?" Si said with a very shaky voice.

The atmosphere was heavy with gloom as they all stood and stared at Novell's body inside the ice casket. The third key was placed around his neck.

"This'll protect him from 'arm," Whitethorn said and put a reassuring hand on Si's back. "It'll provide an invisibility shield to the bearer, and with this shield, only people with good intentions can see him as he sleeps in eternal sleep."

CHAPTER 28

After a few days of recuperation, the remaining invincible stealth warriors, the Cochranes, Thungor, Taala, Whitethorn, and Si journeyed back to the castle and reclaimed it, entering through the back gate.

In the dungeons, they found a few people still imprisoned. These people were the survivors from the arena fight. After promising to come back to free them, the group continued combing through the castle, noticing the emptiness and the extent to which it had been raided by Jerg.

At the state of the castle, Whitethorn knew the demons had left. He was about to say it when a loud hissing was heard from a dark corner and a huge stinger thrust into the ground in front of Justin. Justin pounced and drew the flaming Sword of Juniper. Through the flames of the swinging sword, they could make out what looked like a huge and ugly black scorpion with a rough body.

At the sight of their enemy, the group went into defensive positions immediately, each set to strike. The scorpion hissed again and threw his stinger, but this was blocked by Thungor with the mage staff. After he blocked the scorpion's stinger, he immediately activated the luminescence by raising the staff high. The scorpion hissed as parts of its body were burned by the light emission.

That same moment, Shadow Demons who heard the commotion appeared from the shadows and began attacking the group. Each time Thungor raised the staff, many demons were burned to ashes, and as a result of that, more demons attacked Thungor to prevent him from raising the staff. The others fought off the scorpion which flung them to the wall, one by one.

The scorpion singled out Justin and made a beeline for him, hissing loudly. Justin dodged its stinger as it stabbed at the ground. Justin blocked a stamp from its leg and slashed through the stinger with the flaming sword. Immediately a new stinger grew, and this was used to hit the sword which flew from Justin's hands. Again, the scorpion struck at Justin but was blocked and fought off by Si and Whitethorn. This greatly angered the scorpion for he threw off Si and stung Whitethorn on the shoulder. Chris grabbed up the sword and sliced through the scorpion's legs, which also grew back immediately. The group noticed that the more they fought it, the angrier and bigger it got. They needed another plan.

"Wait," said Taala to the group, "I noticed a small patch on the underside of the beast—it looks like an old wound. If we stick the flaming sword in it, maybe it will die."

"It's worth a shot," Justin agreed.

The scorpion got angrier but began to reduce in size.

They had all exhausted their weapons and were in a dangerous position.

Todd was closest to the scorpion. He looked at the sword, then at the group. He knew about the sword and about the merits and demerits; he also knew what the sword did to those who wielded it. He considered their current situation and how unsafe his boys were. Without a second thought, he grabbed hold of the sword from Chris and surged toward the scorpion.

"Dad, no!" Chris yelled.

Todd shouted in both pain and courage. The scorpion threw its stinger at Todd countless times. Todd dodged it and slid under the belly of the scorpion.

The group watched as he buried the sword into the scorpion, cutting it in half from the old wound. But Todd never stood up; he was out cold, and his hair was white. There was also the dragon crest on his hand.

*****

A few days later, Todd woke up to a Castle Forks that was once again filled with people.

"Welcome back to the world of the living, Dad," Chris said and smiled. Justin did the same.

Justin shook his head. "You were out for days."

Todd winced as he sat up. "What happened?"

"We managed to defeat the Shadow Demons and free the rest of the prisoners," Chris replied.

Justin nodded. "And the ones who managed to escape Jerg's attack have come back."

"Bless them all," Todd said. "I imagine there will be a lot of mourning and healing until then."

"Yeah, including you," Chris said. "The Caretakers have said that because you wielded the sword, you have become a permanent inhabitant of Castle Forks."

Todd opened his mouth to protest, but Justin interrupted, saying, "Good news though, Mom's coming back from Peru!"

CHAPTER 29

fter the burial ceremony that allowed everyone to say goodbye to those lost, Justin and Chris stood side by side at the entrance of the castle's huge gate as it slammed shut and was replaced by the usual rock. Chris had a déjà vu of the first time he'd stood with Dad at that very spot, in front of the gate.

"So many things have happened, so many days and time have passed. It still doesn't feel real to me. It feels like a dream," Chris said.

Justin laughed in amazement. "Tell me about it. *And* we all got knighted for our bravery in the battle, how crazy is that?"

"The weirdest part for me is the facial hair," Chris said. "It's strange that wielding the sword has aged us."

"Yeah, it's sure odd hearing you with a deeper voice," Justin agreed.

"Do you think Dad will be all right being older now?"

Justin nodded and smiled. "He's got us."

Chris thought for a moment. "Could this be why Grandpa Jim died? Because he wielded the sword as an old man?"

"Yeah, Si said earlier that Grandpa Jim decided to return home after wielding the sword, and he got cancer shortly after because his body couldn't handle jumping back and forth between our world and Castle Forks, on top of wielding the sword in the first place," Justin explained.

"Oh, that makes so much sense," Chris said. "So now Dad has to take his place in the castle?"

"Exactly," Justin replied.

"So what do *we* do now?" Chris asked his brother.

"Life continues. We'll go home to welcome Mom and tell her about Dad, and then we resume school," Justin replied. "Come on, let's get there before she gets back so we can tidy!"

When they got home, the sight they met was surprising. Everything was neatly tidied.

The grass was cut short and the garden weeded. The dirt that had accumulated from months of being left unkempt was swept and cleaned. The grasses were mowed short. The house's entrance was neatly swept and mopped, and the glass windows were cleaned and polished.

On entering, they found an extremely clean house, dusted, swept, mopped, and polished, and not a speck of dust was to be seen. Everything was orderly and in place. The kitchen, which was also clean, was packed with food, and fresh meat was available in the freezer.

The boys wondered what had happened. They were also happy to find a clean house, which would save them hours of work. On the dining table was a note: "Courtesy of Castle Forks." Someone had visited the house while the Cochranes were still at the castle and had cleaned for them.

That night, Chris and Justin retired to their rooms and enjoyed peace for a few days.

*****

On a Tuesday of a cold wintry December, Mom arrived from Peru. Justin and Chris drove to the airport to pick her up in their dad's truck. They waited for a little while, holding up their Mom's name and a "Welcome" sign on a large piece of cardboard, standing among other people who were also waiting for someone.

The sun was up and high but still could not drive away the snow and the cold. Chris stood beside Justin, freezing inside his long animal-skin coat. He was grateful he'd worn thick furry boots, or he wouldn't have been able to stand. When the plane from Peru landed, the passengers began coming out in droves. There were old men and young, families, mothers and children, old and young women, and couples—then Mom, average height, light-skinned, blond hair, and blue eyes. Her long hair was packed up in a ponytail, and she wore a fitted top, jeans, and boots. Her smile was enough to lift up Chris's cold and sour mood. He had missed so much as it had been months since he'd last seen her.

Her eyes lit up at the sight of her sons. She hurried over, giving them both a bear hug at the same time. Her familiar scent of lavender and wild rose filled Chris's nostrils; Chris had missed it as much as he'd missed her.

"Justin, we have a lot of talking to do," Mom said, shooting Justin an annoyed look after she broke off the hug. "You too, Chris, you boys have a lot of explaining, and don't either of you think about lying to me." She put on her most serious look but laughed after she saw their dumbfounded reactions.

The drive home was calm and warm; Mom kept talking about the changes in the town. They stopped a few times as she greeted some old friends. After they got back, Justin shot off before she could ask questions—they'd not been able to come up with the perfect story yet. It would all sound really strange to their mom.

Their mom stood in the entrance of the house for a while and took in the environment. "I've missed this place."

Soon after she took a shower and changed into comfortable winter clothes, and the three of them sat in the living room. Justin had taken his time to brew them some hot coffee. Their mom told them about all that had happened in Peru: the school, the rains, the weather, the elders, the people, and the children. She told them what had happened after Chris went missing, and they spoke about that.

"Where's Dad?" she asked immediately, shattering whatever mental preparation they'd made toward telling her everything.

Chris looked at Justin, and he met his glance. Using their eyes, they both prompted each other to begin because they just didn't know how to start.

"Uh, Mom, about Dad…" Justin started finally to Chris's relief. "It's uh…a long story. Dad is currently at a place called Castle Forks."

Justin took his time to narrate from his point of view everything that happened, then Chris did the same.

"Why have you kept this a secret from me for so long?" their mom asked, her voice stern. "Take me to him."

"It was the only way to keep you safe, Mom," Chris replied, feeling guilty.

Justin nodded. "Yeah, the less you knew, the safer you'd be."

"I want to see him. Take me to him now!"

"We'll take you to him tomorrow, Mom. Promise," Justin said. "You should rest after your long journey."

Chris nodded. "Besides, Dad's probably sleeping. He's been sleeping a lot since the battle."

Their mom huffed. "Fine. Tomorrow then."

That night, Chris kept thinking what his mom's reaction would be when she saw Dad.

Although he had no wrinkles, Todd's face had aged and his hair had turned white, including his eyebrows. They also needed to come up with a story quickly before resuming school next week. Chris and Justin had missed out a whole lot and would have to retake their classes. Chris thought about the people of Castle Forks and about the Tourlt. The battle wasn't yet over.

The next morning, Chris got up to find breakfast had already been made. While Chris was eating with his mom, Justin came out of his room already dressed. He joined them at the table. Cyndee kept giving her sons quick glances as if to remind them of what they'd said about taking her to Castle Forks although her looks had a hint of disbelief hidden within them.

A while later, they were on the road to South Fork Mountain. Cyndee hardly ever came here because she didn't hunt, except one time when she was brought here by Todd for a picnic.

Justin stopped the car at Route 36, and they all got out. Chris led the way slowly up the mountain, and on getting close, they heard a howl. *Must be Whitethorn*, Chris thought. *He's seen us coming.*

By the time they got to the spot that revealed the gate, Chris stopped.

"So where's the castle?" Cyndee said suddenly looking around. "I can't see it. There's nothing here that resembles a castle."

Chris looked at her. She wasn't standing at the right spot to be able to see the already opened gate, so he took her hand and drew her forward to where he was. It was then she gasped and froze.

Why did she freeze? Chris thought. Then he looked up at the gate, seeing Si and Whitethorn there, looking like angelic beings. *Oh, Si!* Chris smiled and turned to his mom.

"Meet Si and Whitethorn, Mom. Si is the Caretaker of this castle, and Whitethorn is a Kiern."

Si had the third key on his neck as Novell had been returned to Castle Forks and hidden in the ice catacombs of the castle. Si stepped through the gate toward Cyndee and bowed.

"Their way of greeting," Chris said to his mom, who was still frozen stiff. For some reason, she gave Whitethorn a strange glance. "Si, this is Cyndee, my mother."

Si smiled at the words and offered blueberries.

"Oh! I completely forgot that we can't understand each other— only Justin could after drinking from the orb." Chris took the two blueberries and ate one, giving the other to his mom to eat. She took it after giving Chris a strange look and ate it.

"Si, this is Cyndee, my mother," Chris repeated.

"Welcome to Castle Forks, Cyndee Cochrane. My name is Si."

Cyndee, who was frozen at first, smiled and relaxed at Si's pleasantry. "Likewise," she replied.

Whitethorn approached Chris's mom and said, "Hello again, my ol' Kiern friend. It's a pleasure to see you again."

Chris frowned. Justin smiled, as if he knew something Chris didn't.

"You two know each other?" Chris questioned, looking between his mom and Whitethorn.

Cyndee nodded, and she and Justin burst into laughter.

"What's so funny?" Chris asked, putting his hands on his hips. "What's going on?"

"Chris, there is something I need to tell you," Cyndee said. "I meant to tell you sooner, but I haven't had the chance. And before you get mad at your brother, I told him to keep quiet so I could tell you myself."

Chris raised an eyebrow, completely confused. "What is it, Mom?"

"I am a Kiern too."

Chris gasped with surprise. "So you faked your confusion the whole way here?"

Justin sniggered. "Our mom is quite the actress."

Chris sighed and smiled. "I wish I'd known sooner."

"Yeah, there have been many times I've nearly let it slip," Justin admitted. "But you'll be pleased to know that Taala told me her people knew of our mom."

"Sorry, my loves, I just never got round to telling you, Chris," Cyndee apologized again. "But, yes, I know this place and many of the Caretakers and Kiern within. I've also heard of Taala's people as well."

"Yeah, your mother makes a smashing blueberry pie," Whitethorn said. "Please tell me you can make us some while you're 'ere?"

Cyndee smiled. "Of course. I can't wait."

Si approached Cyndee with an urgent expression. "I do not mean to interrupt, but *he* is waiting for you." Si led the way inside, followed by the Cochranes.

When the gate had shut and was once again a rocky wall, Cyndee marveled in awe at the place she recognized from before.

Soon after, they were brought to a field where some Kiern, Caretakers, and humans were busy. Cyndee looked around. Seeing the Caretakers, she looked toward Si as though making a comparison. She was, however, taken aback by the sight of the Kiern and all the more surprised by the sight of humans.

"You are not the only human here?" Cyndee asked. "Who are those people? It's been a while since I've been here." She pointed to the Kiern.

"Yes, humans also live in Castle Forks," Si answered. "And the Kiern, as you'll know."

While he spoke, they spotted a very familiar human, who was crouched down in the soil. It looked like he was planting something. Cyndee stared intently as if trying to recognize the person from the back but to no avail. Chris and Justin hadn't told her what their dad looked like but only that he'd aged.

Slowly, the person stood up and turned, hands dirty with soil.

"Todd?" Cyndee shouted, immediately recognizing his face.

Todd looked up surprised at the familiar voice, meeting eyes with Cyndee. They were both overjoyed at the sight of each other and enveloped themselves in hugs and kisses.

Chris and Justin left their dad and mom to catch up while Chris walked off with Valkyn. Justin remained with Si.

"How did the skating competitions go?" Chris asked.

Valkyn shrugged. "I didn't win anything, but competing proved that I belong with the skaters, not on the battleground."

"Ah, well done for trying though," Chris replied. "I'm sure you'll win next time with more practice."

"One can only hope, mate," Valkyn said with a smile.

After a while, Chris found Justin, and they received news that Cyndee would stay with their dad but would come back with them to pack her things and their dad's too. Then they left the castle for home, allowing Cyndee time to pack her things. Both brothers helped her fold different items of clothing, and by late evening, she was ready to go.

Justin ordered dinner: pizza and a bucket of fried chicken drumsticks. Chris took cans of soda from the fridge, and they ate. Midway through dinner, a hint of worry flashed through Cyndee's eyes as she stopped eating.

"Boys, are you both going to be all right without your dad and me?" She looked at both of them. Chris looked to Justin to do the talking.

"We'll be fine, Mom." Four words were all he said.

Justin's trying to act tough, Chris thought.

"Don't worry, Mom, we'll have Vannsd here watching over the home. Dad needs you more right now, and it wouldn't be right to leave him alone over there. Besides, you can always come see us whenever you want to. And we'll drop by too once in a while," Chris said, giving his mom a reassuring smile.

Cyndee seemed to take what they'd said with a big smile too although the worry lingered at the corner of her eyes. "Okay, so what would you do if someone tried to burgle the house and actually got inside?" Cyndee challenged.

Justin scoffed with amusement. "We've had more to deal with than just burglars, Mom!"

Cyndee sighed. "Just answer the question, Justin."

But Chris beat him to it. "We'd try to hide and call the police. We have our mobiles on us most of the time. Or we'd run out of the building to safety."

"Good," Cyndee said, satisfied with Chris's answer. "And where do you go if all the lights go out?"

"To the trip switch in the garage," Chris replied. "We had to do that after you left for Peru."

Cyndee nodded with approval and smiled. "Right, so what do you do before you go to bed?" she asked as she sipped her drink.

"Come on, Mom, we know all this," Justin complained, chewing with his mouth full. "We lock the doors, shut the windows, turn the electrics off, and brush our teeth like good little boys."

"Thank you!" Cyndee said, sighing with relief. "Just one more question."

Justin groaned, and both brothers waited for their mom's next and final question.

"How do you treat a lady you have feelings for, *Justin*?" she questioned, not taking her eyes from her eldest son.

"What? How's this related to our health and safety while in the house alone?" Justin said with a deep frown on his brow.

Cyndee smirked. "Just answer it. How do you treat a girl you like?"

Justin finished chewing and glugged some of his drink. "Um, I dunno...with respect? Why?"

Chris looked at his mom, and she winked at him; Chris knew what she was getting at even if Justin had no idea. "Taala," Chris said.

Justin choked on a mouthful of food. His eyes bulged. "What?"

"Oh, come on, bro, we've all had to put up with the way you both look at each other," Chris replied, half amused. "Even Mom's noticed, and she's only been here five minutes."

Cyndee smiled and nodded. "Yes, you both remind me of your dad and I when we were your age."

Justin laughed sarcastically. "I do *not* have feelings for Taala!"

"Oh, so you'll be mingling with all the other girls at your parties, will you?" Cyndee challenged, her face smug.

Justin froze in his seat. "Wait, how do you know about... I mean, I'm not throwing any parties. And *no*, I won't be *mingling* with other girls! What is this?"

Cyndee laughed. "It's fine if you want to throw a *small* party with a few close friends while we're away, but if you have feelings for Taala, you need to tell her."

Chris nodded in agreement. "Yeah, I've heard girls don't like playing games."

"I'm *not* playing games!" Justin defended. "How do you know what girls...fine. D'you know what, I'll ask her out just to shut you to up!"

"So you *do* like her!" Chris teased, poking him in the ribs.

"Get off!" Justin shrieked, laughing. "We're ending this conversation now!"

Cyndee smiled. "So I'll ask you again. How do you treat a lady you have feelings for?"

Justin sighed and paused for a moment before he said, "You ask her out first...and not as a last resort?"

"And?" Cyndee nudged.

Justin shrugged and looked blank.

Chris and Cyndee huffed as if it was obvious.

"You keep her close no matter what," Cyndee finished.

Justin's face turned red. He remained silent for the rest of dinner. Soon after they were done eating, everyone retired to their rooms to rest.

EPILOGUE

One year later

The boys had resumed school. Justin was preparing for graduation and for prom night, to which he'd invited Taala as his date. Chris looked forward to one more peaceful year of school before he had to start thinking about his exams.

Everyone believed they'd been on a vacation trip, and the family's frequent "vacations" became the norm. As Justin had just turned sixteen and Vannsd had agreed to continue watching over the house, Cyndee and Todd often stayed at Castle Forks, entrusting Chris and Justin to stay at the house alone under Vannsd's supervision, as well as many of the other guards of Castle Forks.

Cyndee assumed that Justin would use that time to study for his final exams, but it only gave him the opportunity to throw lots of parties at the house. Chris felt uncomfortable with Justin's raves at first, but after Chris had made a new Kiern friend, Belle, he had someone to enjoy the music with.

Images from the battle between Jerg and Banlin were still fresh but faded away gradually, yet the crest on his hand always seem to remind him. The absence of his parents most weekends also added to that reminder.

Justin tried to revive his brother's Californian attitude but to no avail; Chris wasn't ready to be revived. He found the castle more fit for his kind rather than the life as a Californian adolescent. Even at thirteen years old, he was reserved and preferred solitude to social activities, such as reading his new book, *The History of Castle Forks*, that he'd gotten from the library in the castle. He still had dreams but none that showed Castle Forks. Both boys had to readapt to living in a world without battles or swords or demons, and most of all, they had to conceal their powers.

A week before Justin's exams, Cyndee and Todd visited their sons but could not stay long because their father had to return to the sword. In spite of that, it was a worthwhile visit.

School had been difficult for Justin because of all the parties, and the exams felt impossible, but finally, it was finished.

Justin graduated, and Chris entered another year of high school. Todd could not attend the graduation ceremony, so Cyndee went on behalf of both parents. She was a proud mother of two strong, growing adolescents. A smile never left her face for the rest of that day as she took photos to show their father.

That night after Mom left through the secret pass that opened right in front of the Cochrane house, Justin threw a huge party, to which Chris decided to sit out again. He hiked up the hill and sat at his favorite place, a solitary outcrop that afforded a hidden angle looking down on the outstretched area beyond South Forks town. He saw the lights in different houses, and from afar, they seemed like stars. Chris felt peaceful and closed his eyes to settle into the feeling when—

"Hey!"

His eyes shot open as he turned to see Belle, the Kiern friend he'd made after the battle of Castle Forks.

Under the moonlight, her short shoulder-length hair danced with the wind as she brushed some over the back of her ear. She had a round face and thin lips. When she came closer to him, Chris felt his hairs standing up as he saw her long lashes accentuating her big round eyes.

"Hey, Belle," Chris said. "How did you know I'd be here?"

Belle laughed. "You're always here, especially when your brother throws another party. Plus, it's your favorite place, why wouldn't you be here?"

Chris sighed. "Touché."

Belle looked up at the clear sky and exhaled softly as she sat next to Chris on the hill. "It's a beautiful night tonight."

Chris nodded as butterflies fluttered in his stomach. "It is, but don't feel like you have to keep me company. I'll be here for a while."

Belle smiled. "Then it's a good job I brought snacks and a speaker."

Chris's new friend gestured at her satchel and began unloading chips, chocolate bars, and soda onto the grassy hill, not forgetting a small round speaker about the size of a bowl.

"We can throw our own party," she said.

Chris beamed at Belle. The pair of them sat close together and enjoyed the sweet taste of chocolate and Fanta and the dulcet tones of peaceful pop music.

After a while, Chris sensed that Belle was looking at him, so he turned to face her. "Why are you looking at me like that?" he asked, intrigued but nervous.

Belle sighed. "Something troubles you, I can feel it."

Chris upturned his mouth as he thought of what could be troubling him, but nothing immediately sprung to mind.

Admittedly, his moods and emotions were a little gloomier since the battle against Banlin and Jerg, but he just put that down to the dreaded *puberty* that he could no longer escape since turning thirteen.

"I can't think of anything," Chris replied.

Belle tilted her head and knitted her brow. "Hmm, think deeper."

Chris rummaged through his mind again, searching far and wide for something potentially haunting him. The last couple of years hadn't been easy, but Chris felt that he'd dealt with it just fine.

Suddenly, Belle delved into her satchel and pulled out a circular medium-sized candle and a pack of matches. She set the candle on the grass and struck the tip of the match across the side of the box.

Chris jumped at the sound of it, and his stomach twisted as she did so.

Belle tried again, scraping the match across the side. Chris flinched for the second time. "Are you okay?" she asked, pausing for a moment.

Chris swallowed hard and nodded. "Yeah, I'm fine."

Belle dipped her brow and tried to light the match for the third time, and this time, the end of the match glowed orange, and the flame danced in the breeze.

"Whoa, no, no!" Chris exclaimed. He leaped to his feet with a start.

But as soon as he stood, dizziness overwhelmed him, causing him to lose his balance and fall back down to the ground.

"Get that away…" Chris trailed off and descended into one of his living nightmares.

*****

After one last deep breath, he released the arrow and let the fire join with the gasoline. A loud roar filled the room as the small flame from Chris's arrow cracked and soared around the room, engulfing everyone in its way and invading the dungeon with black smoke…

Chris tried to snap out of the flashback that consumed his mind, but the terror he had experienced only descended into another.

"Oh my god, Dad, are we driving through that?" Justin yelled.

"We have to, Justin," Todd replied. "Just keep your eyes closed and try to stay as calm as you can."

Chris swallowed hard, and his breathing turned into panting. Justin rubbed his back, but Chris could tell that his brother was just as scared as him.

Todd pressed his foot on the accelerator, and the engine revved into action. The Cochranes flew past the billowing flames that swished past each window, but their surroundings just got worse.

The orange fog blocked their view of the road, and none of them could see more than a few yards in front of them.

"God, please help us," Cyndee mumbled from the front. "Todd, the car's heating up. It's gonna explode!"

"Are we gonna die?" Chris cried.

"No one's gonna die, Criffer Bob," Todd assured, maintaining his speed through the wildfire. "Look, the orange is fading out up ahead. If we can just get there and keep going…"

"Dad, what if a tree falls on us?" Justin asked, glancing out each window.

Todd upheld the pace and drove blind through the orange mist, dodging rising flames, golden embers, and falling branches.

Cyndee unbuckled her seat belt and turned around to properly embrace Chris and Justin. "It's all gonna be okay," she said, holding their arms.

His mom's words broke him from the nightmare, but he lay on the grassy hill in a pool of his own sweat, writhing and panicking. He lurched himself into a sitting position and scanned his surroundings at speed, like a petrified cat in the middle of the night.

"Put the fire out!" he shouted. "I don't want to burn!"

"Chris!" Belle said firmly, putting her hand on his back. "It's okay. There's no fire. I've put the candle out."

Belle continued to rub Chris's back as he breathed fast and deep for the next few minutes until he calmed down.

"It's okay…you're safe, Chris," Belle said. "Do you need to go home?"

Chris exhaled, deeper than he ever had before, and shook his head. "Why does this keep happening to me?" he asked, wiping the sweat from his face.

Belle sighed. "You've been through some difficult experiences… for anyone, let alone a twelve- or thirteen-year-old. Sometimes those experiences haunt us through nightmares, whether we're awake or asleep."

Chris nodded. "Do you know how to get rid of them?"

"You should tell your mom or dad first, tell them *everything* you see in your nightmares. They'll be able to help you," Belle replied. "It might also help to keep a diary of each flashback."

"What if they think I'm stupid?" Chris asked.

"They won't, not if they love you," Belle replied with a smile.

*****

Time seemed to run by quickly as prom night came and passed. Chris always ventured to his hidden spot up the hill and continued to hang out with Belle.

As the holidays began, the boys went out hunting more and sometimes dropped by to say hello to their parents, inviting Taala and Belle to go with them. There were frequent parties and more reserved solitude.

In all these periods, a certain turbulence was stirring. Dark clouds were forming, and the good forces of earth had begun awakening her protectors once more. A new age and new dawn had begun; changes had occurred, and the hearts of men had turned wicked, their lusts and greed strengthening the Tourlt, who fed on it, crouching and hiding in the shadows of their darkened hearts.

Nothing is greater than the ancient calling that echoes through the age, and nothing is stronger than destiny when she calls out to you. In the deepest darkest dome of the City of Gold, Jerg sleeps, waiting for another opportunity to strike. This time, his quest will be to bring the whole world into the dark and rule them all. Banlin roams the earth, corrupting the hearts of humans, turning them against each other as he feeds on their emotions. There is usually a calm before the storm, and maybe, just maybe, this was the calm; or was it just another chapter of their unfolding destiny?

No one knows what the future holds; the deeds of yesterday are buried in the lonesome cemetery of every mind to be dug out once in a while to mourn and to celebrate in the hours and minutes of today. The earth is green with nature, her waters fresh, and her air clean. However, in the silence of the still night, in the brightness of a rainy day, a warm day, and a cold winter, they all knew this was just the beginning, the beginning of a great war that was yet to come.

ABOUT THE AUTHOR

C hris Cochrane is the author of this book and the possessor
of an incredibly powerful imagination, which will, one
day, manage to break free from Chris's brain and go on
adventures all by itself...

Fond of nature, sports, fantasy, and sci-fi movies and TV shows,
Chris draws his writing inspiration from the world around him but
most especially from his family: wife Stephanie and their four children.

A salesman with a BS in marketing, Chris writes to entertain and
amuse and loves inventing weird and wacky words, phrases, and creatures
with which to delight his children. At his wife's suggestion, he began to
write his stories down so that other children could enjoy them too.

Like you now. Go on, what are you waiting for? Page one awaits!